"Susie Finkbeiner graces us with a quiet novel about ordinary people who use storytelling to navigate a life that has become far more complicated than they wished it was. As she peels away the layers of self-protection around her characters, revealing them to us in all of their complexity, the people we see staring back look a lot like ourselves, cloaking past hurts with present distractions and misdirections. *Stories That Bind Us* reminds us that life is messy and love hurts sometimes—but it is always worth it."

Erin Bartels, author of *We Hope for Better Things* and *The Words between Us*

"Well, Susie Finkbeiner has done it again, giving us a heart-breaking, heartwarming story so fixed in real time that reading it feels like visiting some familiar past. Her narrator is warm and genuine and brings us along at just the right pace. I'm left wishing I could spend time with the Sweet family in person, play with the boys, taste the pastries. Is there anything more wonderful than a story full of characters that take up residence in our own history? This story is a gift."

Shawn Smucker, author of the award-winning novel *Light from Distant Stars*

"There is a timelessness to the experience of reading *Stories That Bind Us*. With soft, exquisite precision, Susie Finkbeiner doesn't quite deliver a story with a discernible beginning, middle, and end. Instead, the reader enters midstream in a lifelong romance and, in a masterful interweaving of present action and flashback, feels the life of Betty Sweet lap at the edges of the page. Grieving the loss of her husband, Betty finds focus and solace in caring for her troubled sister's young son. This is especially poignant, given that she and her husband, Norm, were not able to have children during the course of their long, loving marriage. Her healing is gradual and surprising and achingly sweet. And while, yes, this is a work of historical fiction, it is an era that lives in our photo albums and home movies. In a voice that will be welcomed by fans of Anne Tyler, Finkbeiner creates compelling drama from the breath-to-breath moments of an ordinary life."

Allison Pittman, author of *The Seamstress*

"*Stories That Bind Us* is a lyrical, evocative novel about sisters, the beautiful complications of maternal love, and sacrifice. In the process of showing us how to love, Finkbeiner reminds us that we, too, are worthy to receive it."

Jolina Petersheim, bestselling author
of *How the Light Gets In*

"Rich with more texture and tenderness than the sweets from the family bakery, *Stories That Bind Us* is a novel that takes readers not only back in time, but deep into heart issues we may have forgotten but can't afford to ignore."

Cynthia Ruchti, award-winning author

Stories
That
Bind
Us

Books by Susie Finkbeiner

All Manner of Things
Stories That Bind Us

Stories That Bind Us

SUSIE FINKBEINER

Revell

a division of Baker Publishing Group
Grand Rapids, Michigan

Published by Revell
a division of Baker Publishing Group
PO Box 6287, Grand Rapids, MI 49516-6287
www.revellbooks.com

Printed in the United States of America

Library of Congress Cataloging-in-Publication Data
Names: Finkbeiner, Susie, author.
Title: Stories that bind us / Susie Finkbeiner.
Description: Grand Rapids, Michigan : Revell, a division of Baker Publishing Group, [2020]
Identifiers: LCCN 2019056085 | ISBN 9780800735708 (paperback) | ISBN 9780800738686 (hardcover)
Subjects: GSAFD: Christian fiction.
Classification: LCC PS3606.I552 S76 2020 | DDC 813/.6—dc23
LC record available at https://lccn.loc.gov/2019056085

20 21 22 23 24 25 26   7 6 5 4 3 2 1

To Jocelyn and Sonny.
Storytellers, both, and very good friends.

Be like the bird that, pausing
in her flight awhile on boughs too slight,
feels them give way beneath her,
and yet sings, knowing that she hath wings.

—Victor Hugo

CHAPTER

one

My Norman had never understood why I liked to hang laundry on the line when I had a perfectly good dryer inside. Especially considering my reluctance to create even more work for myself around the house. But on days like that morning, when the sun shone just the way a child might draw it—with beams streaking the sky and clouds full and soft as cotton balls—I simply could not resist.

Days like that made the clothes smell fresh in a way a gas dryer never could.

I pinned half a dozen of Norm's undershirts to the line along with a pair of Wranglers he liked to wear on the weekends, a soft flannel shirt he'd had since the Truman administration, and the dress socks he wore with his church shoes. His briefs I hung on the middle line so the neighbors wouldn't see them.

I certainly didn't want the entire street goggling at my husband's skivvies.

Done with that chore, I stood in the yard, laundry basket resting on my hip, and breathing in the earthy smells of late spring.

Looking around to make sure no one was watching, I put down my basket and kicked off my kitten heels so I could feel the blades of grass through my hose-covered toes. That time of day, the neighborhood was quiet. All the children were in school and the men at work. Housewives were inside mopping the floors or dusting their knickknacks like I should have been.

No one was around to see me plant myself on the soft ground, legs stretched out in front of me, my head tipped backward so the sun could warm my skin, pale from the long Michigan winter.

Shielding my eyes with one hand, I watched a bird soar far up in the sky, its dark wings spread wide at either side. Even though I knew the sun was millions and millions of miles away, from where I sat it looked as though that bird was going to fly right into the center of it.

"Now, what was that story?" I whispered to myself.

A shard of memory pierced its way into my mind. A story my mother had told my sister and me, more than thirty years before. Listing my head to one side, I tried to remember how it went. There'd been a little girl, I knew that much. A little girl who was afraid of the dark.

"She was called Lily." It was the kind of name that sounded elegant to me. A name that belonged in a story or a song. I tried with all my might to remember how it had sounded when my mother had said it.

For the life of me, I couldn't manage to bring her voice to mind. It had been so long since I'd last heard it.

What I did recall was that the story had a sad ending. At least I'd thought so when I was younger. It had made my tummy hurt and my heart feel tender for poor Lily.

I shut my eyes, letting the sun glow a pinkish-red through my lids, and tried to imagine a happily-ever-after for her.

The sound of a screen door opening and slapping shut a few houses away made me jump, causing my wandering mind to retreat back where it belonged. Namely, that wandering mind belonged inside where there were floors to be scrubbed and windows to be washed.

Getting myself off the ground, I picked up my basket, smoothing the skirt of my housedress and hoping I hadn't managed to get a grass stain on my behind.

It would have been completely normal for a younger woman to sit in the middle of her backyard, daydreaming the morning away. But a younger woman I was not, so I made my way inside.

It wasn't until I'd put the laundry basket downstairs in the basement that I remembered I'd left my shoes in the grass.

When Norman and I were first married, we had next to nothing. An apartment with very little elbow room, a rusty bicycle Norm used to make deliveries for the family bakery, and a mismatched set of dishes collected from the extras of a few church ladies. That was it. I hardly had a pot to boil water in.

Oh, but we were young and in love. We hardly realized what we lacked.

We lived in that little apartment for five years before we were able to buy a house. Of course, two of those years Norm was gone at war in Japan and I was glad I didn't have to keep up anything with a yard while he was gone.

After he came home, we bought a charming two story on Deerfield Avenue in Norm's hometown of LaFontaine, Michigan. It was a red brick house with white trim and black shutters.

The yard was a nice size with plenty of shade trees and flower beds. Norm apologized for not being able to afford something more palatial. But it was just right for me. It was a home of our own, and that was all I'd ever dared dream.

On the day we moved in, Norm had carried me over the threshold, shutting the door behind us with his foot. He didn't put me down in the living room but just kept on lugging me through to the doorway of our new-to-us bedroom.

"What are you doing?" I'd asked, giggling and blushing in a way that I hoped was becoming of a twenty-two-year-old woman. "Norman!"

"Well, sweetheart," he'd answered, "I thought it was a good time to get started on filling this house with children."

The rest of that memory was best left between my husband and me. I'd always been prone to blushing. Unfortunately, flushed cheeks on a forty-year-old woman wasn't as becoming and a signal of a different kind of change on the horizon.

As sweet as that first day in our home had been and most of the eighteen years after, there were a few bitter times.

From where I stood at my pink porcelain sink, doing up a few dishes, I could see where Norman might have built a playhouse or put up a swing set. I blinked away my imagination and drained the water from the sink before drying my hands. It was a bad habit of mine, pining away after what could never be.

"Now, Betty," I said to myself. "Carry on."

If there was one thing I'd learned, it was that God did give and take away. I didn't have to like it, I only had to accept that he knew what he was doing.

Instead of letting myself think of it too much, I made my grocery list for the week. While some women, it seemed, could work their way through the aisles of the store knowing by instinct what their pantries lacked and only getting what they needed, I tended to wander if I didn't have something to keep me on task.

My list had changed quite a bit in the twenty-three years since we'd gotten married. I no longer had to scrimp and save the way I had at the beginning. I could even splurge a little now and then.

I tried to never take it for granted.

Slipping the list into my purse, I noticed the brown paper bag on the kitchen counter. Norm had forgotten his lunch, the silly man. I grabbed it as I headed out the door.

I never did mind an excuse to stop in at the bakery and see him in the middle of the day.

LaFontaine was a Goldilocks-sized town. Not so big that someone could be completely invisible. Not so small that everyone knew the business of everybody else. It was just right. Our little community was smack-dab between Detroit and Lansing. If ever we wanted something only a bigger city could offer, it was just a forty-five minute drive in one direction or the other.

Usually, though, everything I needed was less than a mile from my front door. I could have walked to get my hair cut or have my teeth cleaned or any other number of things. Of course, I usually drove to save myself a little time.

Besides, I never felt so sophisticated as when I was behind the wheel of my coral and gray Chevy Bel Air. It had been a birthday present from my husband just a few years before. That man of mine certainly knew how to spoil me.

I was glad to find a parking spot on the street, right in front of the bakery. Sweet Family Bakery was as much home to me as the house on Deerfield Avenue.

Before I even reached the propped-open front door, I could smell the warm, inviting scent of bread baking. I tried to ignore how it made my mouth water. Being married to a baker meant that I'd never had to make my own bread or cakes. It had also caused me to be a little thicker around the waist than I needed to be.

Norman said that it was just more to love, which was kind of him, I supposed. Still, I didn't like the way I had to move to the next size up in girdle every few years. As I stepped through the door, I promised myself I wouldn't take a single goodie from the display case, no matter how delicious it smelled.

I knew I wouldn't keep that promise, but at least I made a valiant effort, even if only for a moment.

"Hey there, Betty," Stan said from behind the counter, folding the newspaper he'd been reading and tossing it next to the cash register. "Old Norm didn't say you'd be stopping in today."

I lifted the paper bag. "He forgot his lunch."

"Typical man." He shook his head.

I lowered my eyebrows and smirked at him. That brother-in-law of mine had an interesting sense of humor.

"I was out and about anyway," I said, stepping toward the display case to look at the Danishes, my resolve crumbling. "How are sales today?"

"Pretty good." He nodded at the pastries. "Raspberry. You want to try one?"

I pulled my hands up to my chest, still holding the paper bag. "Oh, I shouldn't."

"Come on. It's got fruit. That makes it healthy, doesn't it?" Stan grabbed a wax paper square and plucked a Danish from the case, passing it over to me. "It's a new recipe. Tell me what you think."

I took the goodie and held it up to my nose. "Oh, it smells wonderful."

Stan winked at me and turned when he heard Norm step beside him, then went to the back where he, no doubt, had bread dough churning in the mixer.

"Well, I thought I heard your voice," Norman said. "Hi, sweetheart."

It was in that very spot that I'd first seen him. Of course, we were both so much younger then. He was every bit as handsome as he'd been that first day. Just a little gray at his temples and some padding on his stomach too. But his smile still made my heart pitter-patter like it had years before. His hazel eyes just as bright. More green than brown.

That day, though, something wasn't quite right with him. He looked tired, a little pale.

"Are you feeling okay, honey?" I asked.

"Sure thing." He raised a fist to the middle of his chest, rubbing along his sternum. "Just a case of indigestion."

"What did you have for breakfast?" I asked.

A good wife would have been up with her husband at four in the morning when his alarm went off. I, however, was of the opinion that if the early bird wanted the worm so badly, he was free to it.

"I had some of that leftover sausage on a bun," Norm answered. "And a couple cups of coffee."

"Maybe that sausage was a little spicy." I cringed.

"Could be."

"I'm sorry."

"It's nothing to be sorry about." He came around the counter. "Besides, how can I be upset with a woman who brings me my lunch?"

I handed him the bag and accepted his kiss on my cheek.

"Thank you, sweet Betty Sweet," he whispered into my ear and put his hands on my hips. "I'm happy to show my appreciation when I get home tonight."

"Oh, you'll do up the dishes after dinner? What a treat that would be." I pulled away from him and gave him what I hoped was a flirty little wink.

"If that's what you want to call it." His grin was only half-hearted, the wrinkles at the corners of his eyes more defined than usual.

"Do you need me to get you an antacid?" I asked. "Maybe you should just come home and rest for a little bit."

"Already took one." He grimaced. "Hasn't kicked in yet, though. I'm not sick enough to leave work, hon. They need me here. I'll be all right."

"Okay. Maybe try a little baking soda in water if that doesn't work." Then I raised my voice loud enough to be heard in the back. "Have Stan send you home if you're still feeling puny."

Stan peeked around the corner. "You got it, boss."

"Well, I better get to the grocery store," I said. "Bring home a few dinner rolls if you think about it, please."

"All right," Norm said, this time kissing my lips.

I patted his chest before turning for the door, the Danish still in my hand. As I was going out, my father-in-law was coming in, leaning heavily on his cane and smirking at me in a way that made me think he was planning on a little mischief.

One of the many things I loved about Pop Sweet was that he treated everyone as if they were God's gift to him. But he reserved his teasing for those of us he called family.

"You pay for that?" he asked, nodding at the Danish.

"I've been paying for it ever since I became your daughter-in-law," I answered, raising my eyebrows and trying not to giggle at my own response.

"Oh, don't I know it." His eyes sparkled. "Best thing that ever happened was you coming along and marrying that boy of mine so he'd finally get out of my house. I could hardly afford the grocery bill while he was at home."

"Now, Pop," Norm said from behind me. "I know you cried at the wedding."

"Tears of joy!" Pop lifted his arms, wobbling just a little when the cane lifted off the ground.

"Baloney," I said. "Don't you remember what you said to me right before the wedding?"

"I'm old, Bets. I don't remember what I ate for breakfast."

"You said that I should be good to your son because he was one of your three greatest treasures." I took a good-sized bite out of the Danish. The flaky pastry full of butter and sugar nearly melted in my mouth. "And you should try one of these. They're scrumptious."

"I know." He leaned on his cane. "It's my recipe."

He patted me on the shoulder when he walked past me, his hand warm through the fabric of my dress.

I wouldn't have told him this, but I knew that the reason Norm was such a good man was because Pop had always been such a good man.

John and Lacy Sweet had raised three of the very best people I'd ever met, and I was grateful they were my family. As I walked out of the bakery, I passed a picture on the wall of the Sweets when they first opened the business. Seven-year-old Norman to the left of Pop and five-year-old Albert to his right. Mom Sweet stood beside Norman, hand on the slight bump of her belly that would eventually become round with baby Marvel.

Someone had taken an ink pen to the bottom of their picture and written "Sweet Family Bakery grand opening. February 1928."

I wondered if they had any idea that the bakery would still be open even thirty-five years later.

Looking into the photographed eyes of Mom Sweet, I saw determination enough to know that she'd entertained no doubts.

"We'll stay open until God tells us it's time to quit," she'd said to me just a few months before she passed away. "Some are meant to preach and some to build houses. We Sweets were made to bake, and that's what we intend to keep doing."

I thought that if heaven had a bakery, Mom Sweet would be there keeping the ovens going.

Goodness, I missed her something awful.

Sometimes I tried to figure out how I was so lucky to end up marrying into such an incredible family. Most of the time I realized it hadn't been luck at all.

It was nothing short of a gift.

two

*I*t wasn't yet eleven in the morning when I heard the low rumble of Norman's Impala pulling into the garage. I set my knife on the cutting board beside the onion I was chopping and opened the door to see what was the matter.

It certainly was unusual for him to be home at that hour in the middle of a workday.

He hefted himself out of his car, the collar of his shirt unbuttoned and pulled loose, his flour-covered apron still hanging from his neck but untied around his middle. Red of face and droopy of jowls, he looked horrible.

"Poor dear," I whispered, wiping my hands on the skirt of my apron and stepping aside so he could get in past me.

It wasn't often that Norm got sick, but when he did, he really got it.

He trudged into the house, sandy blond hair plastered to his forehead.

"Is it the indigestion?" I asked.

"Nah. I think I got a touch of the flu," he said, leaning against the back of a kitchen chair. "Don't get too close. It's a bad one."

"At this time of year?" I moved toward him, putting a hand on one of his. "Do you have a fever?"

"Well, I'm perspiring like a pig." He lumbered through the kitchen and to his chair in the living room, plopping down in it.

"I can see that." I took a hanky from the pocket of my apron and dabbed it along his forehead. "You're sure it's just a bug? Should I call the doctor?"

"I'm sure. Nothing to worry about." He cleared his throat.

I felt of his forehead with the soft inside of my wrist. "You don't have a fever. Are you sure it isn't something else?"

"Betty, I'll be fine. Don't worry," he said, taking my hand in his, putting it to his lips, and giving it a peck. "Your hands smell like onion."

"What a romantic you are," I said, taking my hand back and crossing my arms.

"I thought I could make it to the end of the day." He rested his head on the back of the chair. "But, thanks to you, Stan kicked me out."

"Well, I'm glad he did."

I lifted his head with one hand and pulled the apron off with the other. The smell of the bakery still clung to his clothes, mixed with his Old Spice and Brylcreem.

"I forgot your rolls." Norman lowered one side of his mouth in a half frown. "If you really need them, I can go back out."

"You aren't going anywhere," I said, shaking my head. "How about I get you a little ginger ale? And maybe a mug of beef bouillon?"

Norm nodded and then cringed as if a great pain had seized him. "You better wash that kiss off your hand. I don't want you getting this. It's awful."

"That's the least of my worries."

I went directly to the kitchen, putting water on to boil and finding a can of Vernor's in the pantry. I considered calling Doctor Lange anyway to see if he could make a house call on his way home that evening, but thought better of it.

What Norman needed was a sip or two of something to soothe his tummy and then a long rest in bed. He'd be ship-shape by the morning. He'd always healed quickly. All the Sweet men did.

I hummed "Moon River" as I moved around the kitchen, swaying my hips from side to side as I poured and stirred and reached into the cupboard for a few saltine crackers, wishing I had a voice half as smooth as Audrey Hepburn's. While I was at it, I pictured myself wearing a hanky on my head and playing a guitar on the fire escape the way she had in *Breakfast at Tiffany's*.

I shook my head, putting a small stack of the crackers on a plate for Norman. What would he have thought of me playing make-believe? And at my age. I chuckled at myself just to think of it.

By the time I carried the tray of bouillon and ginger ale into the living room, he was gone.

I found him slumped over in his chair, his right arm hanging limp over the side. The tray fell to the floor before I'd known that I dropped it. Hot broth splashed up and through my hose, and the ginger ale spilled into a puddle on the carpet.

"Norman?" I whispered, even though I knew from the deepest part of me that he couldn't hear. "Wake up, darling."

Stepping around the tray, I reached for him, trying to straighten him back up in the chair. But he was heavy, and I was weak. Try as I might, I couldn't move him more than an inch. His skin was warm to the touch, his cheek still smooth from the morning shave. But there was no life in him. No breath. No pulse.

"Oh, honey," I whimpered. "I don't know what I'm supposed to do."

I knelt on the floor, taking hold of his still dangling hand. I put my forehead on the arm of the chair.

"What am I supposed to do now?"

three

My mother died when I was teetering on the tightwire between childhood and adulthood. I'd been just twelve years old. Clara was ten. In the years after, our father moved us around from one apartment to another all over the city of Detroit. I'd overheard him once confess to his sister—Aunt Flossie—that he was trying to find a place that didn't remind him of my mother.

As it turned out, there wasn't a place in that city that didn't hold a memory of her in it for him.

So, just short of my fourteenth birthday, he got a custodial job at the William McKinley Memorial High School in LaFontaine and moved us well out of the city. It had amazed me how less than an hour's drive could take me to a place so very different than what I was used to.

Dad had found an apartment for us to rent above a bakery, and it smelled so good that it nearly made me forget the sting of leaving everything I'd ever known behind. It almost made up for the small closet that was meant to be the room my sister and I were to share.

I supposed I couldn't be too upset about it. At least it was clean and in a town that seemed friendly enough, which was a welcome change from some of the places we'd stayed.

We'd never been well off, but the years after the stock market crashed made life a bit more challenging for us, especially without a mother to make sure we girls had everything we needed. Upon our move to LaFontaine, Clara and I had four dresses between us, one of which fit me.

I never would have said anything to my father about needing something to wear when I started school. He thought Clara and I were bleeding him dry as it was, and he made sure we knew it.

As we unpacked our few things from the boxes Dad had carried up the stairs, our stomachs rumbled. It was well after three o'clock and we'd not had our lunch yet.

My father scrounged up a nickel and sent us downstairs for a loaf of bread, saying that since it was the end of the day, they might give us a deal.

"Don't forget to use your manners," he'd said. "And don't get no fancy bread. Just whatever's cheapest."

It was a fine bakery with breads of all different types in the case and yeasty rolls piled high behind the counter. I hardly let myself look at the trays of cookies. "Sweet Family Bakery" had been painted on the glass of the big window in thick, black letters.

Two boys, not much older than my sister and me, perked up when we walked in, the bell above the door jingling upon our entrance. One of them stood out front, sweeping. He was all gangly limbs and jutting collarbones. His wire-rimmed glasses were smudged, and his apron rumpled and too big for him. His eyes seemed fixed on Clara, who had of late started the process of outgrowing the cuteness of a little girl and taking on the delicate beauty of a young woman.

When she noticed him looking at her, she scowled and he went, hastily, back to his sweeping.

I'd felt sorry for that boy and the way he looked so uncomfortable in his own skin.

The boy behind the counter, on the other hand, was tall and broad shouldered and had skin with just enough tan to make him nearly golden. He smiled when I met his eyes, and I knew right away that he was something special.

When I told him that my family had just moved in upstairs, he gave me a quick look and asked what kind of bread I wanted.

"Just a normal one." I crossed one arm over my chest, hoping to hide how threadbare my dress was.

"Sure thing," he said. "But if you wanted another kind, that's all right too."

"How much does that one cost?" I asked, nodding at a brown loaf.

"It's free."

I looked at the spindly boy, whose mouth dropped open. He seemed just as surprised as I was.

"I'm sorry," I said, eyes back on the one behind the counter. "I'm afraid I don't understand."

"Rent covers one loaf of bread a week," he said.

"You're sure?" I held out the coin in the palm of my hand. "I have money. I can pay."

"Yeah, I'm sure. Our family owns this bakery and the apartment." He lowered the bread into a paper bag, so carefully I might have thought it was made of glass. "Say. What's your name?"

"Betty Johnson." I felt the blush rising in my cheeks when I looked right into his hazel eyes, wishing mine were a pretty shade of blue or green rather than just boring old brown. "And this is my sister."

"I'm Clara," she answered, her hands balled in fists on her hips and her foot tapping. "We don't need your handout."

I cleared my throat, hoping to get her attention so I could give her the you-better-knock-it-off glare, but she didn't seem to notice.

"Fair enough. But this isn't a handout. It comes with the price of rent." He nodded toward the skinny boy. "Isn't that so, Al?"

"Um," the boy said and then swallowed hard, his Adam's apple bobbing up and down his throat. "Sure it is."

"Well, there you have it on good authority." He clapped his hands together. "Next week when you come for another loaf, just ask for one of us. I'm Norm and that's my brother, Albert."

"It's nice to meet you both," I said.

Albert blinked fast and muttered out a quick greeting before going back to sweeping in earnest. I didn't think he had the heart to take another peek at Clara.

"And this is my kid sister, Marvel," Norm told us, grinning at a younger girl who had walked out from the back room, a half-eaten apple in her hand.

"Normie, is that your girlfriend?" Marvel teased. "Oh, and there's one for Albie too."

Norm smirked, and I thought I'd never seen a better-looking boy in all my life. When he handed me the bread, I nearly dropped it, my hands trembled so.

Clara stomped up the steps to our apartment, crossing her arms when she got to the landing and giving me a stink eye so severe that I worried she was thinking about slapping me across the face. It certainly wouldn't have been the first time.

"We don't beg," she whispered.

"I didn't," I said. "Besides, we paid for it."

She rolled her eyes. "You're so dumb."

"I think he's nice." I realized that I was hugging the bread to my chest and loosened my hold on it.

"You like him?" Clara asked, lips curled in a sneer. "Oh, Betty. A boy like him wouldn't ever fall for a girl like you."

It stung, and I was sure she was right. What could he ever see in me? I walked past her and pushed open the door to our apartment.

Every Monday morning for the three years my family occupied that apartment, I found a fresh loaf on the stoop outside our door.

Somehow Norm had known even then that I never would have asked for it.

Even though I knew it was of no use, I called for an ambulance to come for Norman. I couldn't think of anything else to do. Then I managed to call Marvel, who came just as fast as she could after I'd called, beating the ambulance that didn't find much reason to rush, I supposed.

Marvel let herself in like she always did, and I turned to see her but didn't get up from where I knelt at Norm's side. Even if I'd wanted to, I doubted I had the strength to move from that spot.

"Oh, Betty," she said, stopping just inside the vestibule and looking at Norm in his chair. She gasped and put both hands over her mouth, letting out a groan before crossing the room. "What . . . what happened?"

I shook my head, not knowing what to say.

Marvel lowered herself to the floor and touched the hand I wasn't holding. Her mouth turned down into a frown when she looked up into his face. She didn't speak and neither did I. The only sound was the clock ticking away the seconds and occasional sniffling from one of us.

We stayed that way until the ambulance driver knocked on the door.

"I'll let them in," Marvel said, wiping the tears from her eyes.

"I'm not ready." I shook my head. "I shouldn't have called them so soon. Can you tell them to come back later? I'm not ready."

All our years together and he was to be taken away so suddenly, without a proper good-bye? It was too much. Too fast. I wanted more time.

"Of course you aren't, honey." Marvel put a hand on my shoulder. "I'm not either."

Somehow she found the strength to make it to the door and open it to let the men in, leading them to where I held on to Norman's hand as hard as I could.

"Let's get you a cup of tea or something," Marvel said, hand pressing hard against her chest as if checking to be sure her own heart was still beating. Then she rushed toward me, grabbing my hand. "Come on, honey. We should let the men do their job."

"I don't want to leave him." I wanted to resist her, to stay with him. Still, I followed as she tugged me toward the kitchen, Norman's apron held tight to my chest. "I left him before to make some bouillon. For his stomach. He said his stomach was upset. I wasn't with him when he . . ."

I pushed my lips together as tight as I could to keep the word from exiting my mouth.

"It's all right, Betty," Marvel said.

"I should have been with him. He shouldn't have been alone."

"You couldn't have known."

"Please, I don't want to leave him." My voice sounded so small, so weak. My body offered no fight when Marvel guided me away from the living room. "I don't want him to be alone."

"You don't need to see this. It will only upset you more." Marvel gave me a weak smile. "It's better this way."

I looked over my shoulder just before stepping through the swinging door that led to the kitchen. It was the last time I'd see him in our home. That last glimpse would be part of what I remembered about him for the rest of my life.

At forty years old, I still had a lot of life left.

It certainly would be a long time to spend missing my Norman.

four

My Bible lay open where I'd left it earlier in the morning, the cracked black leather contrasting against the pink Formica tabletop. For the life of me, I couldn't remember what I'd read in it just a couple of hours earlier. I couldn't manage to make my eyes focus on the words.

Lifting my head—how heavy it seemed, how hard to move—I saw that Marvel sat across from me, the telephone receiver to her ear. She rested her forehead on her hand and spoke words I couldn't understand to whoever was on the other line. The curly cord stretched from where the telephone hung on the wall.

Done with her call, she half stood and hung up, saying something to me as she eased herself back into the pink vinyl chair. I felt like I had cotton balls in my ears, her voice sounded so muted, far away.

"Hm?" I hummed, trying to focus.

"Should we try to find out where Clara is?" she asked. "Maybe get ahold of her?"

"Who?"

"Your sister?" Marvel put her hand on mine. "Oh, honey. What a shock you've had."

"I don't know," I said, my mind catching up.

"Would you like me to try?"

"It's been so long since I've talked to her."

"But don't you think she'd want to know?" She had her finger holding a place right under Clara's name in my address book. "Do you think she's still at this number?"

"I don't know." I shook my head, which only ended up making me feel dizzy.

Had it been six years? Seven since I'd last seen my sister? I couldn't do the math just then. The fog that had encased my mind wouldn't let me. What I did know for sure was that it was long ago. Too long.

I didn't like to think of the last time I'd seen her. It was the day of our dad's funeral and we were both worn down and exhausted. I couldn't remember what had started the argument, but it hadn't taken long for it to erupt into a full-blown battle.

My sister possessed a fiery temper, the likes of which I could never match even if I'd tried my darnedest.

Needless to say, if there'd been a winner it was Clara. She out-yelled, out-stomped, and out-insulted me. When she'd run dry of accusations, she left. But not before telling me that she was through with me.

Oh, but the strings that held a family together could be flimsy.

"She wouldn't care," I said.

Marvel nodded, shutting the address book. I knew that she understood.

"Do you need anything?" she asked.

I pointed at the swinging door. "Are they still . . . ?"

"The men?" She shook her head. "No, they left a little while ago."

"I don't remember them leaving."

"How about we get a few things together for you." Marvel got up, putting out a hand for me. "Come on, Betty."

"Where am I going?" I let her pull me to standing and lead me to my bedroom.

"To my house," she answered. "You can't stay here alone. Not tonight."

"All right," I said, my own voice sounding like it had come from miles away.

"I wouldn't sleep if I knew you were here by yourself."

She packed my things, knowing as if by instinct where I kept my hairbrush and cold cream and everything else I could possibly need for a few nights away from home. I just stood in the middle of the bedroom, watching her move around me, dropping nighties and stockings and a dress or two into a suitcase.

I thought about how we'd just bought that luggage a few months before. Norman had insisted, saying that we'd need them when we went on our anniversary trip in June. Twenty-three years of marriage usually wasn't reason for a vacation, no matter how small. But we hadn't gone anywhere for our twentieth, and Norm wanted to play catch-up.

Instead, that brand-new suitcase would be used for the first time that day after . . .

Well, I didn't want to think about it.

"All set." Marvel sighed, picking up the case and nodding toward the door. "Are you ready?"

"No."

But we left the room anyway.

To get out the front door and to Marvel's car we had to walk through the living room. Everything was pushed around, out of place. The coffee table and couch had been moved against a wall and Norman's chair faced the wrong direction.

My shoulders slumped, I struggled to catch a breath.

"What is it, honey?" Marvel asked.

"It's all wrong," I said through clenched teeth.

"I know. They had to."

"Why?"

"To get him out," she answered.

"I need to straighten things up."

"It can wait. We'll fix it later." She tugged at me. "Come on. Let's get you to the car."

An overwhelming urge to scream flooded over me.

As an act of will, I kept my mouth shut.

⁓

Maybe it was a little bit of shock taking hold, but I didn't feel a thing as we drove the two miles from my house to hers. In fact, I stayed numb until I was sitting at their dining room table with Pop.

"How are you doing?" I asked Pop.

"Not good, kiddo," he answered. "Not good at all."

Then he covered his eyes with his hand and cried.

It was more than I could bear.

⁓

Marvel came down the stairs after getting her boys to sleep, her arms full of bedding. She smiled, but the bags under her eyes told me enough. It couldn't have been easy to tell Nick and Dick the news. They were only ten. Such a blow at that age.

"Are they all right?" I asked.

She shrugged. "Stan's with them."

"Poor boys."

"I'm more worried about Pop." She crossed the room and dropped the stack of sheets and blanket and pillow on the coffee table. "And you."

I inspected my fingernails, hoping she wouldn't get me crying again.

She cleared her throat and blew out a breath.

"I've told Stan a hundred times that we should have a bed in the guest room. But you know how he can be," she said, tucking a fitted sheet into the gap between the cushions and the couch. "Are you sure you'll be all right down here?"

"Of course," I said, knowing that I wouldn't sleep well wherever I ended up and wishing—really wishing—that I could have stayed at home. "Thank you."

"Just come get me if you need anything." She fluffed the pillow before leaning it against the armrest.

"I will," I said, well aware that I wouldn't disturb her. Besides, I knew where she kept everything. "What would I do without you?"

"I was just thinking the same thing about you." She kissed me on the cheek before heading for the stairs, her steps slow and weary. "Love you."

"You too."

I waited until she was out of sight and I could hear the muffled voices of her and Stan travel through the vents before I sat on the couch. My weight pulled the sheet out from where it had been tucked in. It didn't matter one way or the other.

Pulling the pillow to me and holding it tight with my arms, I buried my face into it and cried as quietly as I could manage.

My hands shook and I couldn't seem to make them stop. Wringing them didn't help and neither did holding them in tight fists at my sides.

I stood, waiting at the threshold of the church sanctuary. Someone was supposed to tell me when I should walk down the aisle, and it was not lost to me, the irony of it all. The last time I'd stood in that very spot, I'd been seventeen years old and wearing a white dress pieced together from flour sacks. Then Norm had been waiting at the front of the church for me, grinning wide.

But that day I was dressed head-to-foot in black and my eyes were fixed on the casket at the other end of the aisle that held Norm. I put my gloved hand on the doorjamb so I wouldn't keel over right there.

"Ready?" the funeral director whispered into my ear, and I nodded even if it was a lie.

I wasn't ready. How could I have been?

"I'm only forty years old," I whispered back to him, looking him in the eyes and hoping he'd understand my meaning, that I was far too young to be at my husband's funeral.

From the sympathetic upturn of his eyebrows, I thought he understood perhaps better than most people.

Of course he did.

Pop made his way to my side, offering me his arm, and I took it. Never in a hundred years could I have taken that walk by myself.

Without a word, we took the first step through the doors, the rest of our family following behind us. One step after another. Quivering organ music set the slow and solemn rhythm for our procession. I kept my face turned down, eyes fixed on the bright red carpet in front of me.

Thank goodness the church was small and there were only a dozen pews to walk past before we got to our row. The further I'd gone, the weaker I felt. Pop didn't seem much stronger.

"You made it, Bets," he said to me under his breath once we reached the front.

"So did you." I squeezed his arm before letting him help me to my seat.

Folding my hands, I placed them in my lap, praying that I could just last another hour, maybe two. Then I could go home and lock the front door and sleep for a hundred days if I wanted to.

I'd never been so tired.

Marvel drove me home in Stan's car, the music playing at a low volume. The Chiffons went on and on with their *do-lang-do-lang-do-lang*, and I tried my hardest not to hum along. I wasn't sure that it was all right to sing about handsome boys with wavy hair right after my husband's funeral.

Still, the music made me feel a little more normal, even if only by a small measure.

We pulled into my driveway, and Marvel shifted into park, letting the engine idle. Dropping her hands to her lap, she turned toward me.

"Would you like me to come in?" she asked.

I sighed and tried to think of a way to tell her I'd rather she didn't. Truth be told, I wanted to be alone. In the three days since Norm passed, I'd not been by myself unless I went to the powder room.

Even then it seemed someone waited just outside the door to make sure I hadn't fallen in.

"If it's all the same to you, I'd like to go home." Marvel reached over and squeezed my hand. "I'm tired."

"Go," I said, nodding. "Be with Stan and the boys. I'll be fine."

"You're sure?"

"Yes."

"Call if you need anything?" She released my hand.

"Thank you," I whispered.

She waited until I got my front door opened and I was inside before she pulled away and in the direction of her house. I waved and she honked the horn twice like she always did.

Another inch of normal.

I shut the door, clicking the dead bolt into place, and rested my head against the wood. Even if I had a hundred years I wouldn't be ready to see my living room for the first time since Norm's passing.

"Well, you can't stand like this forever," I muttered, forcing myself off the door and to turn around.

Standing in the vestibule, I peeked into the living room. All was back as it should be. Every chair in place and each end table where I liked them to be.

Wrapping my arms around my body against the chill that still lingered from the graveside service, I stepped forward, the floorboard underfoot making a crackling sound that was somehow comforting to me.

A potted hyacinth sat on the mantel, its purple buds filling the room with a delicate fragrance. It wasn't one from the funeral. All of those plants and arrangements had been sent home with various people from town.

No, whoever had placed the hyacinth in my living room had to have been the one to also clean and rearrange it. My money was on Albert.

Albert was nothing if not thoughtful.

I touched the flowers, letting my fingers dawdle over their smooth petals.

"Like a cluster of stars," I whispered, remembering my sister saying the very same thing so many years before.

Closing my eyes, I let memory sweep me away from the house on Deerfield Avenue and to a dingy tenement in Detroit—the first we'd moved to after Mother died. The landlord's wife had given me a transplanted hyacinth—that one a pretty white—from the makeshift flower garden she cultivated on the fire escape outside her window.

As I carried it, I breathed in the scent of the flowers, trying to think of how I could describe the way they smelled. The only word I could think of was "purple." They smelled purple to me even though they were white.

When I'd come into the apartment, Clara had wiped her face, but I could still see the swollen flesh around her pretty blue eyes and the tears clinging to her lashes.

The three of us—Dad, Clara, and I—did our very best not to cry around one another. And we most certainly didn't talk about

Mother. It might have been pride that had prevented us, or not wanting to make anyone worry. Maybe it was a little of both. But we reserved our emotions for when we were by ourselves.

"Mrs. Bunker sent this up for us," I'd said.

Clara put her hands out, and I let her take the potted flower from me. She turned it, looking at it from all different angles and sniffing at it with her eyes closed.

"What is it?" she'd asked.

"Hyacinth," I answered. "Isn't it nice?"

"Hyacinth," she echoed me, meeting my eyes. "Isn't that a pretty word?"

I'd agreed, feeling the way the word started at the back of my mouth, making its way to the tip of my teeth when my tongue touched them. Even in my squeaky twelve-year-old voice, it sounded important, special.

Breathing in the smell of the flowers, Clara closed her eyes and held the scent in her lungs as if it might be the very thing that could heal her sadness.

"They look like a cluster of stars," she'd said. "Don't you think so?"

I'd tilted my head and tried to see it.

"I wish Mama was here," Clara said, holding the pot to her chest, eyes still shut. "Don't you think she would have liked these flowers, Birdie?"

"I don't know. Maybe." I turned my back on her, not wanting her to see me crying. I cleared my throat and pushed my nails into the palms of my hands to make me straighten up. Clara didn't need me to cry. She needed me to be strong.

"Mrs. Bunker said we have to water the flowers every other day," I said. "And we should keep it near the window so it gets plenty of sunshine."

Within weeks of that morning, the hyacinth had wilted, the flower dried out. It hadn't been for a lack of care. We'd done everything we knew to do. I'd carried it to Mrs. Bunker's apartment, hoping she could save it, holding back my tears so she wouldn't know how desperate I was.

"Well, this is normal," she'd said. "The flowers can't last forever. You just wait until next spring. They'll come back."

I hadn't believed her. I thought she was trying to make me feel better the way people did when something died.

I'd mourned that plant with the ferocity of a girl losing her mother all over again.

But I'd done my grieving alone.

It was the only way I knew how.

CHAPTER

six

The night of Norm's funeral, I slept in fits and starts, my sleep shallow at best. The house seemed to make too many noises, and I found myself jolting upright out of a dream more than a couple of times. It was a cool night, and I couldn't seem to get warm no matter how many blankets I pulled on top of myself.

When I looked at Norm's old alarm clock, I saw that it was eleven o'clock. Then midnight. Then twelve forty. I rolled from one side to the other. No matter which way I lay I couldn't get comfortable. Every position hurt. The pillow was too flat. The sheets too itchy.

Finally, I shivered and rolled over just to find the other side of the bed empty where Norman should have been. I curled my spine and pulled the covers closer. It still didn't manage to warm me.

I pulled his pillow to my chest, his smell still there.

It was a horrible night, but—as much as I doubted it would—the sun rose in the morning just like it did any other day. And, just like every day, I got up with it.

A beam of light broke through a tiny separation between my curtains, resting in a line at the foot of my bed. Leaning forward, the covers still gathered on my lap, I tried to touch the light, knowing that it would only disappear in the shadow of my hand.

"It's just as well," I whispered to myself, throwing the blankets off me and swinging my legs over the side of the bed.

Sunday morning had come, and I would go to church just like I had every Sunday since I was fourteen years old. Besides, it was my week in the nursery, and I'd completely forgotten to look for a replacement.

I had been preoccupied, I supposed.

I'd never been fond of rocking babies at church, and if I were to be honest, those babies weren't too fond of me either. They'd cry themselves into a frenzy, spit up whatever I managed to feed them from their bottles, and make an unholy mess of their diapers just before their mothers were to come get them.

Because of all that, the church ladies only asked me to help out in the nursery once a year and always on Mother's Day. Years ago I was told it was so I wouldn't feel uncomfortable when the older children handed out carnations to their mothers at the end of the service.

They'd meant well, but it just added more ache to a day that had always felt like a hot poker to my heart.

I dressed and put on my face, careful to cover up the purple bags under my eyes. In my best dress, heels, and pearls I went to the kitchen to make myself a cup of coffee and poach an egg for my breakfast. But I only managed to spill the coffee grounds on the floor and overcook the egg.

"That's all right, Betty," I murmured. "Chin up."

I got the broom out to sweep up the floor. Since I had the floor swept, I decided to mop. Putting the mop and bucket back into the broom closet, I saw the vacuum and lugged that out to clean the carpets, both upstairs and down.

Then the feather duster came out, then the Windex. I polished and scrubbed and tidied and washed. As long as I worked at a chore, I could switch off my mind. I could stop thinking about the sorrow that threatened to choke me if I sat down.

I could not think of a time in my life when I'd gotten so much cleaning accomplished in one morning without my thoughts wandering to a daydream. It was more than a little bit shocking.

It wasn't until all of that was done that I checked the clock, worried that I'd worked my way into being late for church.

It was eight thirty in the morning, and I breathed a sigh of relief.

With a half an hour until Sunday school started, I'd make it in time. I'd be early, even.

I gathered all the trash into a bag and took it out the back door, the last thing to do before leaving.

Across the yard, laundry still hung on the line from the day my Norman died. Sighing, I dropped the trash into the garbage can and went directly back inside.

I simply did not have it in me to take the clothes down yet. Such a ridiculous thing, leaving them to hang there. If someone had asked me why I left them, I wouldn't have been able to put words to it. There was just a feeling around those clothes. A feeling I wasn't yet ready for.

So instead I grabbed my car keys and handbag and opened the door to the garage, taking in a good breath to bolster me to face the world.

But then I saw Norman's black Impala parked beside my Bel Air and something switched inside me like a light turning off. I sat on the concrete steps and cried, grateful that the automatic door was still closed so the neighbors wouldn't see.

The rest of my morning was spent curled up on the couch in the living room, my head on a cushion and my feet hanging off the side so my shoes wouldn't dirty the upholstery.

It hadn't occurred to me that I should kick them off.

Doing my uttermost to avoid looking at Norm's chair, I fixed my eyes on the carpet. Unfortunately, the spot I'd picked was precisely where the slightly off-color stain from the ginger ale and bouillon that I'd spilled just a few days before was. Getting down on my knees, I crawled to it, feeling of the stiff carpet with my hands, trying to think what could clean it. Worried that it was too late.

I looked up at the television. In the screen I could just barely see a reflection of myself. A small Betty Sweet kneeling on the floor, fretting over a stain. Even from a few feet away I could see that my carefully coiffed hair was flat from where I'd laid it on the cushion. I was sure that if I looked closely enough I'd find that my makeup had smudged down my face from all my sobbing.

"What a mess you are, Betty," I scolded.

Then I returned to the couch, where I lay down once again and rolled so my face pressed into the back of the cushions.

What a mess, indeed.

I woke to the sound of the doorbell. It rang once followed by a gentle rapping on the screen door. It took more than a little doing to get myself up off the couch to see who was there. Every vertebra in my spine ached when I stood, and it wouldn't have shocked me if my hips creaked with every step.

Middle-aged women were not meant to sleep on sofas.

Halfway to the door I realized that I only had one shoe on.

I tried to smooth the front of my dress, but it was of no use. The poor fabric was hopelessly crumpled. I wondered how long I'd been asleep. It couldn't have been too long, it was still light outside. When I opened the door, I squinted at the brightness of whatever time of day it was.

Funny. The sun seemed to be in the wrong part of the sky.

Albert stood on my porch, a laundry basket in his hands. When he saw the state I was in, his eyes grew large and a blush crept into his cheeks.

That poor man. He looked nearly the same as when I'd first met him more than twenty-five years before. He was still gangly and awkward. The only discernible changes in him were that his brown hair had turned salt and pepper and the frames of his glasses had gone from wire to plastic.

"Oh, hi there, Albert," I said, my voice gravelly. "Can I do something for you?"

"I suppose I should have called first." He lowered his eyes.

"I must look a fright." I touched the pearls at my neck, rolling them out of the divots they'd pressed into my flesh.

"No, not at all," he answered before clearing his throat. He lifted the basket an inch. "I thought I'd bring these to you. I took the liberty of taking them down yesterday afternoon. But there was no answer when I knocked."

"Oh," I said, confused and trying to think of how I might have missed a knock on the door the day before. And having a clear recollection of seeing the Wranglers and shirts on the line just that morning. To say I was flummoxed would have been an understatement. "You didn't have to do that."

"It was no trouble."

I pushed open the screen door, and he passed me the basket. He'd even gone to the trouble of rewashing and folding everything; I tried to find a way to tell him again that he didn't have to do that, but a lump in my throat prevented me.

"Well, I ought to . . ." Albert turned his head and nodded at the bakery delivery truck parked out in the street. "I need to get back to work."

"Work?" I said, shaking my head. "Don't tell me you're working today."

"Um, of course," he said. "Have a good morning, Betty."

"Why, Albie." I shrugged. "It's Sunday afternoon."

He met my eyes, a look of bewilderment on his face.

"Isn't it?" I asked.

"It's just after eight o'clock," he answered, looking at his wristwatch. "In the morning."

"What day is it?"

"Monday." He lowered his eyebrows. "Are you all right?"

My mouth dropped open. I'd slept nearly twenty hours. No wonder I felt so out of sorts.

"You should get on your way," I said, stepping back and pulling the screen door closed. "Thank you again. Oh, and thank you too for the hyacinth. It's lovely."

I shut the door and leaned back against it, catching a glimpse of myself in the mirror on the other side of the vestibule.

My mousy hair stuck up all over my head like I was some sort of wild woman, and mascara darkened my eyes in black smudges like I wore a raccoon mask. I even had angry-looking red lines on my left cheek from the seam of the cushion I'd slept on.

Good grief.

seven

I didn't leave my house for nearly a month after Norman died. When I needed groceries, I called the store and had them delivered to my front door, a luxury I'd never splurged on before. When I didn't come to church, the pastor and his wife stopped over, knocking on the front door.

I let them think I wasn't at home and watched out the peephole until they got back into their Ford and drove away.

Normally I would have felt guilty about doing something like that. But I just did not in those days. I simply didn't.

Marvel came over nearly every day, asking through the locked door if I'd please let her in. I'd just shout from the other side that I wasn't feeling up to company or that I'd drawn myself a bath or that I'd just put on my pajamas.

The truth was, I'd hardly changed out of my nightie since the days after the funeral. When I did, it was just to put on another one fresh from my dresser.

I collected my mail at night when the rest of the neighborhood was sleeping, opening the front door just wide enough so that I could reach my arm out toward my letter box to grab the contents and sneak my arm back in.

The only envelopes I opened were the bills, which I paid right away, hoping that Norm had left the checkbook balanced before he passed.

Knowing him, he'd kept it to the penny. Just one more thing I had to miss about him.

The telephone went unanswered. I didn't want to have to explain to whomever was calling that I was still holed up in the house, unable to leave for the time being. I was grieving and I didn't want to talk to *anyone* about it.

So, when Marvel let herself in on that Thursday morning using the for-emergencies-only key I kept hidden under a rock in the front yard, I contemplated hiding in the linen closet until she went away. I might have, had she not seen me already.

"Betty," she said, standing in my living room with hands on her hips, giving me the stern look she typically reserved for the twins and occasionally for Pop. "When was the last time you left this house?"

I didn't answer her. Merciful heavens, but had she grown up to be like her mother. Direct and bossy. Not that I would have said that out loud, of course.

"My guess is too long." She looked me up and down from head to foot. "Go get dressed and put your face on."

"Why?" Oh, how my voice sounded whiny, even to me.

"I don't know that you can set your hair fast enough." She crinkled her nose. "It's not too bad, though. We could just tie a scarf around it if we need to."

"Why?" I asked again, this time with more insistence in my voice.

"I'm taking you to lunch."

"Maybe tomorrow?"

"No. Today. Come on." She stepped toward me, her hand out. "Let's get you ready."

"But, I . . ."

She grabbed me by the arm, dragging me around my own house. "You haven't been eating, have you?"

"It's just . . . my stomach's been upset."

"I think all your dresses will be too big." She pulled me behind her into my room, pointing to the bed. "Sit. I'll find you something to wear."

"The black one is clean."

"No," she said, shaking her head. "You need something colorful to wear."

"But I'm in mourning."

"Oh, for goodness' sake, Betty."

"In the Victorian era widows were allowed to mourn for two years," I said, plopping down on the bed, slumping my shoulders. "I think I should get at least a few months."

"Well, in the Victorian era they also sent their kids to work in factories and brushed their teeth with charcoal." She pushed her lips together and raised her eyebrow at me. "Do you really think they had such great ideas?"

"I suppose not." I dropped my hands into my lap. "But who's with the boys? They're on summer break by now. Surely you can't leave them alone very long. You should go back home and make sure they're not lighting each other on fire."

"Very funny," she said. "And Pop's with them. They're fine."

I blinked slowly at her.

"They're mostly fine." She scowled at me. "Besides, Stan said we can get dessert. Goodness knows we need to get a little weight on you."

She initiated a staring contest, one that I knew for a fact I could never win.

"Fine. There's a green one," I said, resigning. "It's all the way to the right. I haven't fit into it for years."

She pushed the hangers across the rod, reaching for the jade-colored plaid dress, inspecting it before nodding her head in approval.

"Don't dillydally," she said, handing me the dress. "I'm starving."

"I wouldn't dare," I answered just before she closed the door behind her.

"And it wouldn't hurt if you gave yourself a spritz or two of perfume," she called.

I tried not to be offended.

Marvel insisted that we take a window-side booth at the Big Boy just outside of town. The jukebox was playing "Up on the Roof," and she hummed along as she looked over the menu. I knew that if I looked under the table, I'd see her toes tapping against the floor along with the easy rhythm of the song.

Oh, how she and Stan had loved going out dancing before the boys were born. The two of them certainly could cut a rug.

Marvel ordered the Reuben sandwich and I asked for the Monte Cristo. As soon as the waitress scribbled it down, I worried that I wouldn't be able to stomach any food.

Shifting in my seat, I crossed my legs at the ankles.

"I've missed you," Marvel said, taking a sip of the iced tea the waitress had brought her. "What have you been doing with yourself all this time?"

"Not much of anything," I lied.

The truth was that I had spent an obscene amount of time watching television, hoping to keep my mind occupied so that I wouldn't think too much about how sad I was. When I wasn't doing that, I busied myself composing pitch-black poetry that would have made Emily Dickinson look like a member of the Mickey Mouse Club.

But I didn't need to admit that to Marvel or anyone. Especially since I'd burned all of the awful poems in the fireplace on an unseasonably cold day the week before.

As far as I knew, that was the very thing that could have been expected of the likes of a dime-store Dickinson such as me.

"The twins made cards for you," Marvel said, rummaging in her purse.

When Marvel had been expecting her first child ten years before, no one had known that there were two in that tummy of hers. Sure, she'd been big, but we all just assumed she'd give us a healthy, fat baby. The greatest surprise of my life was when Stan telephoned to tell us there'd been a bonus boy.

I'd never known that I could love someone else's children so deep and wide. But those two yahoos had my heart.

She pulled two pieces of paper from her purse. She laid them on my place mat and patted them. The first had a rainbow spanning the front and the words "I hope you feel better soon" in red letters beneath it. Inside was written in careful, ten-year-old-boy handwriting "Love, Dick."

"Brace yourself," Marvel said of the second one. "Nick spent a long time on that one."

"Oh dear," I said, picking it up.

He must have worn the black crayon down to a nub. The gray one too. Black skies and gloomy gray clouds overshadowed jagged black grass. I was a stick figure in black with a severe red frown. Behind me was a rounded headstone with the letters "RIP" carved into it.

Over my head was a comic strip bubble in which read "I am now a widow."

"Oh my," I said, taking in the dark scene with wide eyes.

Slowly, afraid of what might be written inside, I opened the card.

I know you are sad, Aunt Betty, it read. *I am sad too. Who will take us fishing in the summer? From Nick.*

Holding the card against my chest, I thought of Christmas, when Norman had insisted on getting the twins fishing poles and lures and bait. He'd promised to take them to a pond full of rainbow trout and sunfish as soon as school let out in June.

I put the card down on top of the other, my own stick figure face frowning up at me as if she greatly disapproved of what she saw.

"I'm not the only one mourning him," I whispered.

Marvel shook her head. "No, you aren't," she said. "If you could only see everyone else, how quiet it is at the bakery. Stan says they hardly talk while they're working anymore. I found Pop crying in his apartment yesterday."

"It's too much," I said, wishing I could block out all she was saying.

"You need to know." She shook her head. "He said he was worried sick because he called and couldn't get through to you."

"I took the telephone off the hook," I admitted, cringing.

"You cannot do that." Leaning forward, she reached for my hand, and I gave it to her. "Betty, we're your family. Don't close us out."

"I'm not trying to do that," I whispered. "This is just really difficult for me."

"Honey, you may be grieving the deepest, but we're all hurting. Not only have we lost Normie, we're scared that we're losing you too."

It was the very thing my father had done after my mother died. He'd closed Clara and me out and completely ignored our grief. It wasn't right. And it was equally as wrong for me to do it to the Sweet family. To my family.

"I am so sorry," I said, whispering.

"Golly, I'm not trying to make you feel badly, you know." She put both hands on her place mat palms down. "I just don't want you to give up on living. It's okay to be brokenhearted. It isn't good to let it break your spirit, though."

"I know." I used my paper napkin to wipe under my eyes.

"When Mom died I thought I'd never recover." She rested her head on one hand. "I suppose that's as close to being depressed as I ever was. You know what Pop said?"

I shook my head.

"He said that he could find joy in losing Mom," Marvel said. "I thought he'd lost his ever-loving mind."

Her face broke into a smile, and she huffed out a little laugh.

"What did he mean?" I asked.

"He said that he'd never felt closer to God than in the days after she passed." She raised both eyebrows. "He said that having a broken heart made God draw ever nearer. His exact words."

I turned my attention out the window where a shrub had gone untrimmed and a tiny sparrow hopped from branch to branch.

"I admit that I have not felt the Lord draw near," I said, still watching the little bird and thinking of my Bible collecting dust on my kitchen table. "Maybe it's because I've ignored him."

"Well, I don't know that it's the same for everybody, honey." She reached across the table and put her fingers on my forearm. "All I know is that if Norman knew you were hiding away in that house all by yourself, giving your life up over him, well, it would kill him."

I raised both my eyebrows at her, and she slapped a hand over her mouth.

"Bad choice of words," she said through her fingers.

I could not help but chuckle at that.

Oh, how like coming back to life that felt.

The waitress delivered our meals, asking if we wanted ketchup for our french fries. Marvel did. I looked at my sandwich, hoping I'd be able to eat even half of it.

"I'm not sure that I can . . ." I started.

"It's okay if you can't." Marvel reached across the table and grabbed the salt shaker. "We'll just get a doggy bag. Nick and Dick will finish off whatever you can't."

"Thank you," I whispered, my throat clenching.

"You're welcome," she said, winking.

We ate our lunches and Marvel filled me in on the gossip I'd missed over the month I spent in hiding. She'd ordered us hot fudge sundaes and ate hers and most of mine too.

Eventually the waitress brought the check, which Marvel insisted on picking up.

By the time we slid from the booth, I felt better than I had in weeks.

At home I sat down at my kitchen table with a glass of ice water. I blew the dust off the cover of my Bible. I couldn't decide what was more shocking, that such a film of dust could have accumulated after just a month or that I'd gone so long without reading a single verse.

Either way, I decided I wouldn't allow the shame to spoil the good feelings from my lunch with Marvel.

I flipped to a page I'd kept with a clipping of Mom Sweet's obituary. I held the paper by the edges, careful not to smudge the newsprint.

Her health had failed quickly after the doctor found the cancer. Pop brought her home, setting up a bed for her in the living room so she wouldn't have to climb the stairs. It didn't take long for us to realize that even walking across the room was too much for her.

At the end, she had us all circle around her bed and asked us to sing a couple of hymns to her. We did our best, singing past the tightness in our throats. When we'd finished the last song, she smiled.

"Take care of each other," she whispered, letting her eyes meet each of ours. "Promise me that."

I pulled the twins' cards from my handbag, placing them in between the pages of my Bible along with Mom's obituary.

With a pat of the cover, I got up from the table and retrieved my handbag. Before I climbed into the car I grabbed a pair of garden clippers and a watering can.

It had occurred to me that I'd not yet been to Norm's gravesite.

It was well past time.

CHAPTER

eight

hen I pulled into the parking lot of the grocery store, I was surprised to see so many other cars. I'd have thought—hoped, even—that the drizzle would have kept all the housewives at home. How wrong I'd been.

The very last thing I wanted was to push a cart through a barrage of well-meaning condolences just so that I could get a pound of butter, a couple cans of soup, and half a dozen other necessities.

Fitting my car into an open spot, I contemplated backing out and heading for home. Sighing, I resigned myself to the fact that I would eventually have to brave the public. That morning was as good as any, I supposed. I left the engine running while I mustered up the courage to go inside.

I sat in that car for so long the windows got steamed up.

Some impulse made me take a fingertip to the glass. I made a circle with lines radiating out from it. A sunshine for a gloomy day.

Just like that, I was taken back more than thirty years. Clara and me with matching bobbed haircuts. Hers looking smarter than mine, the way her hair bounced in golden ringlets while mine laid flat. I remembered that Clara had a little knick on her earlobe where Mother had cut her by accident with the shears. Clara had never been good at sitting still during haircuts.

We kneeled at the living room window, pouting at the rain and wishing it would dry up before it was too late. Mother had promised to take us to the park if the day was nice. Offers such as that were as hard to come by as her good moods.

"We'll go," she'd said after a quarter hour of watching us sit there. "Once the sky clears up."

The way the clouds loomed, I didn't think it ever would.

"Look at you." Mother stood behind us, bent at the waist and with her hands on her knees. "A couple of gloomy Guses, huh?"

"We wanted to go to the park," Clara whined. "But the sun isn't coming out."

Mother reached over us, huffing onto the window and drawing a sunshine into the steam her breath had left.

"There." She straightened. "The sun's out. Let's have ourselves an adventure."

"But, Mama," I'd protested. "It's raining."

"Don't be silly, Betty Jane," she said, and then pointed at the glass. "It's sunny. It can't possibly rain on a day like this."

I'd scowled, but Clara's face lit up. She'd always loved when our mother's mercurial spirit ran hot.

"Let's go for a boat ride." Mother nodded toward the sofa and grabbed the broom from the corner. "All aboard."

"That's what you say for a train," Clara had said with a giggle.

"They say it for boats too," Mother said. "Now get on."

I sat cross-legged in the middle, feeling a spring push against my thigh. Clara took the very front, on her knees and leaning against the arm of the couch looking like the figurehead. Mother stood behind me on the cushion, rowing the imaginary water with the broom.

"There was once a girl who wanted to be a gondolier," Mother started. "All she ever dreamed of was propelling a long boat down the Canale Grande in Venice, singing beautiful songs for those who rode along."

I turned, facing Mother. She put a hand up to shield her eyes from the sunshine of her imagining before going back to rowing in earnest.

"The trouble was, girls weren't allowed to be gondoliers." She pulled her lips between her teeth and gave a slight shake of the head. "Her father forbade her from so much as stepping on a gondola."

The girl, as it turned out, had a rebellious streak, Mother went on. She snuck out on rainy days when her father locked himself in his study. She'd put on a striped shirt and tuck her hair into the flat-topped straw hat of a gondolier and hop into one of the many boats left along the channel.

"She was the only one brave enough to take passengers to and fro in the rain," Mother said. "She'd sing to them through the downpour. When there was no sun to be seen, she shone even brighter."

I opened my car door, putting up my umbrella before standing under the see-through plastic dome of it. Droplets misted against the canopy, making the world look like gray and white polka dots.

There was no sunshine in sight.

I hummed as I went anyway.

CHAPTER

nine

First thing on Saturday morning I took my cup of coffee to the living room to sit in my comfortable chair by the window and read the book Albert had gotten me for Christmas. It was a shame that I'd had it for half a year and hadn't yet gotten around to it.

I'd wondered if I could like a book with a cover that had little girls riding around on the back of a lion as if he was a horse. But I found that I enjoyed it very much.

So much, in fact, that I finished the whole book in a matter of hours without getting up from my chair. Not even for a second cup of coffee.

Closing the cover, I smiled down at the title. *The Lion, the Witch and the Wardrobe.* I contemplated starting over from the beginning right away, not yet ready to leave the world of Narnia.

But something caught my eye out the window, making me sit up a little straighter in my chair.

Walking down the sidewalk, shoulder to shoulder, were Nick

and Dick, pulling a wagon behind them. Identical in every way but in what color of shirt they usually wore—Nick was blue and Dick was red—they confounded most everybody who tried to tell them apart.

I, however, had little difficulty. All I had to do was look at them when they were doing something they knew they shouldn't. Dick would get shifty-eyed and Nick's mouth turned up on the left-hand side.

Fortunately for me, they were usually up to something on the naughty side. Poor Marvel.

Squinting out the window, I tried to read their expressions, but they were too far away yet. But from the careful way they navigated the wagon over a bump in the sidewalk, I knew they were up to something.

"Now, what are those two doing?" I mumbled, standing and putting the book on my chair. "And what is that on the wagon?"

I made my way to the porch just as they steered their haul up my driveway. Their bright red Radio Flyer had Marvel's lidded wicker basket in it, three decent-sized rocks placed on the top as if they wanted to keep it from opening.

I was more than a little concerned as visions of coiled snakes, ready to spring, played in my head.

"Good morning, boys," I called out to them. "Did you come to pay me a visit?"

"Hi, Aunt Betty," Nick said. "We got a present for you."

"You did?" I eyed the basket. "How come I feel a little nervous about that present?"

"It was Dick's idea." Nick nodded his head toward his twin. "But I helped."

Dick nodded. "Wanna see what it is?"

"I'm not entirely sure." I fingered the pearls around my neck. "Did your mother say it was all right?"

The twins looked at each other out of the corner of their eyes as if they wanted to get their stories straight.

"Does your mother even know you're here?"

Dick—who could never lie if his life depended on it—squirmed and let his eyes drop to his feet. Nick, on the other hand, gave me his very best Eddie Haskell grin.

Just then, from within the basket, I heard a meow and I felt my eyes grow wide.

"Oh, boys," I said. "What is in the basket?"

Another mew.

"You better get that inside." I rushed down the steps and helped them lift the basket from the wagon. "What am I going to do with you two?"

"Make us some chocolate milk?" Nick asked.

Oh. That boy.

We set the basket down on the living room floor and the boys lifted the lid slowly. All of my nerves were on edge, worried that the creature inside would pounce just as soon as it was free.

Instead, the calico cat lifted its head from where it lay curled in a ball in one corner. It meowed again, standing and sniffing the air.

"Where did you get it?" I asked, whispering so as not to alarm the cat.

"Our neighbor," Dick answered. "Do you know Mrs. Lamb?"

"I do."

"She's old," Nick said.

"Elderly," Dick corrected him.

"Boys, please don't tell me that you stole Mrs. Lamb's cat," I said, grimacing.

"We didn't, cross my heart and hope to die," Nick said. "She told Dick she needed a new home for Flannery."

"It's true," Dick said. "She said if she didn't find a place for the cat to live, she'd have to take it to the pound."

"They make glue out of cats at the pound, Aunt Betty." Nick squinted his eyes.

"Well, I don't know about that," I said. "What's the cat's name?"

"Flannery O'Calico." Dick shook his head. "Mrs. Lamb thought it was funny. I don't get it."

"It's after an author," I said. "Anyway, you took Flannery from Mrs. Lamb?"

"Uh-huh," Nick said. "Dick said you could have her."

"Well, how about that."

"So you won't be lonely anymore," Dick said.

I couldn't help but put my hand on his cheek at his sweetness. Of course, he still had something sticky on his face, presumably left over from breakfast. Syrup. I was sure that was it.

Flannery hopped out of the basket, shaking her front paw as if rejecting it completely, before looking up at me.

"Hello there," I said, feeling absolutely ridiculous for greeting a cat.

She walked near me, rubbing her face against my leg. I reached down and pet her.

"Oh, she's soft." She turned her head so I'd scratch behind her ear.

"Can you keep her?" Nick asked, putting his hands together as if begging for his life. "Please, Aunt Betty."

"But I haven't got any food for her or litter," I said. "And she'll need some shots, won't she?"

The boys both shrugged.

The cat looked up at me, as if on cue, and blinked slowly at me. I could feel the gentle vibration of her purr through her side.

"Oh, I suppose she can stay." I reached for the boys, and they came to me, letting me hug them each in one of my arms. "It's very kind of you to want me to have a companion. Thank you."

"You're welcome, Aunt Betty," the boys both said.

Just then Flannery zipped under the couch and ran right back out, batting a dust bunny with her paw and yowling her heart out.

What exactly had I gotten myself into?

I spent the afternoon and evening fretting over that cat. She'd wander the house, snooping in closets and under beds and jumping up on the kitchen counter to see what was up there. I followed her, my hands outstretched in front of me like more sane women do with toddlers rather than felines.

Every once in a while I'd pick her up and carry her downstairs to where I'd put the litter box I'd bought, showing it to her the way the man at the pet store had told me to. The very last thing I wanted was for her to forget where I'd put it and do her business elsewhere.

I wondered if I needed to put down newspapers like we'd done when we had our puppy Mitzi.

By late in the evening, I was exhausted from worrying over that cat all day. I finally gave up and let her be. When I checked the litter box one last time for the night, I noticed that she had made a deposit there after all.

When I finally settled down enough to have a piece of toast and a sunny-side-up egg for my supper, I turned the radio on in the kitchen to hear Johnny Cash singing about a burnin' ring of fire with that deeper than deep voice of his. I couldn't help but bob my head along with the horns and guitar. Sitting at the table, I dipped the corner of my toast in the bright yellow yolk and read through the LaFontaine newspaper, noting that the Five and Dime was running a sale on cosmetics and that there was a Little League baseball game the next weekend.

Down in the bottom right-hand corner of the paper, so out of the way that I nearly didn't see it, was an advertisement for Lazy Morning Bakery, announcing its grand opening in the town just half a mile outside of LaFontaine. By my count, that was one Lazy Morning in all the towns within a dozen mile radius.

I sighed, hoping Pop hadn't read the paper.

I yelped when the cat jumped up on my lap. I'd forgotten she was even there.

"Now, I shouldn't let you sit with me at the table, should I?" I asked her, rubbing between her shoulders, surprised at how unafraid I was of her. "Well, no one is around to see it, I suppose."

I put the paper away, choosing instead to eat my dinner. The song had changed, and I sang "da-do-ron-ron" between bites.

What a good day it had been.

CHAPTER
ten

From my very first day at William McKinley Memorial High School in LaFontaine until the very last, Norm walked the quarter mile with me. He'd tuck my books under his arm and grin whenever I told him he didn't have to do that, which I said every single morning.

In the afternoons he would find me, insisting on taking my books then too.

Each day it was the very same thing. There wasn't much I could depend on in those days, but I always knew that I wouldn't have to walk alone. Norman was constant, and I didn't mind that in the least.

After a while, we'd taken to walking arm-in-arm. About a year later, he'd given me a little peck on the cheek before going into the bakery to work. Then, just a week after I'd graduated from high school, we were married.

That was the story of how we fell in love. It was nothing to write a book about and wasn't the thing of a romantic film. But it was our story, and I had loved living it.

I'd loved all of it.

Slipping the buttons of my dress through their corresponding holes, I thought of how good it had felt to be at Norm's side for most of my life. It was going to take some getting used to, having him gone.

It was Sunday and I'd promised myself that I would, finally, get myself to church. I sighed, thinking of how I had to go by myself.

"Be strong and have courage," I whispered to myself.

Flannery lifted her head from where she lazed in a sun spot on my bedroom floor, blinking at me slowly.

"What? Can't an old lady talk to herself?" I crooned at the cat, bending at the knees to rub the belly she'd exposed to me.

As if I'd offended her mother and all of her better sensibilities, Flannery bolted out of the room. She certainly was an odd creature.

I'd planned to be a few minutes late to the worship service. I wanted all of the church people in their pews by the time I arrived so I could slip in undetected. And I entertained the possibility of sneaking out during the last song after the sermon so as to avoid the meet-and-greet that would inevitably ensue.

Never in my recollection had I ever been late to anything, especially not on purpose. It surprised me that I didn't feel the least bit guilty about it.

I sidled into the very last row, not wanting to flounce down the aisle to the front where my family sat. No one ever occupied that back pew, and I counted it as a mercy. I, of course, had never sat there before, so I hadn't known that it was more than a little creaky until I sat down. As soon as my bumper rested on the wood of the seat, that pew let out an unholy shriek that caught the attention of every single congregant in the LaFontaine Free Methodist Church. They turned their heads, as if on cue, and looked right at me.

So much for making a quiet entrance and exit.

"Let us . . ." Reverend Crawford began before clearing his throat. "Let us pray."

At the sound of his voice, most of the congregation turned to face front. Knowing that my cheeks were a blazing red and feeling the tears gathering in the corners of my eyes, I bowed my head and clamped my lids tight.

Good heavens. I was teetering on the verge of sobbing. Not just because of the noisy pew or unintentionally collecting the attention of the whole church. It was because I knew how tickled Norman would have been by the whole situation.

He would have loved it. Oh, how I wished he was with me.

Everything seemed more endurable with him around.

"Lord, God and Father of us all," the reverend began, his voice smooth, deep, and soft. "We offer our thanks, praise, and reverence for daily mercies . . ."

Reverend Crawford was notorious for his long prayers and—for perhaps the very first time—I was grateful for it. If nothing else, I'd have time to dab under my eyes with the hanky I'd tucked into my church gloves and compose myself.

Just as I managed to steady my breath and swallow back my emotion, I felt a warm, moist hand on my ankle.

I might have jumped and yelped if I hadn't been afraid of drawing even more attention to myself.

Opening my left eye, I looked down to see that one of my nephews had crawled under the pews and between the legs of praying church members like an Army man from where the rest of the family sat. He grinned at me with a sparkle in his eye.

"Hi, Aunt Betty," he whispered, more loudly than necessary.

I put a finger to my lips so he'd know to be quiet and then offered my hand to help him up.

From all the dust collected on the front of his white button-up shirt, I could see that no one had swept the church in a good long time.

"Now, which one are you?" I whispered even though I suspected I knew already.

"Dick," he answered.

"Are you sure?"

The boy shrugged his shoulders and grinned, giving me what I called his stinker look.

"I didn't think so," I said. "Hello, Nick."

"You got any mints?" he asked, still in that loud whisper.

Reaching into my purse, I pulled out one mint for him and one for me.

"But only if you promise to be quiet for the rest of the service," I said, whispering close to his ear.

He nodded and climbed up onto the pew, which, gratefully, didn't complain under his minimal weight. When I handed him the mint, he stuck it in his cheek and gave me his most winning smile.

It was the kind of smile that could melt my heart in ten seconds flat.

As Reverend Crawford finished his prayer and moved along into his sermon, Nick swung his legs and held his hands in his lap as if needing the reminder to keep from fidgeting too much. After a few minutes, he leaned his head against my arm. His warm, boy head was heavy, and I knew that my arm would grow tired, holding up its weight. But I didn't move. Not even an inch.

It was a rare joy, having this boy sitting still long enough for a little bit of a snuggle. I wasn't going to ruin it by calling too much attention to it.

"You're soft," he whispered, and I knew he meant it as the best kind of compliment.

A tiny edge of my grief melted away.

CHAPTER

eleven

Just days after my mother died, Dad went through all of her things. She hadn't owned much, just a few dresses and a drawer of skivvies, a handful of nearly empty paint jars, and a tiny box of jewelry too cheap to be pawned. He'd gathered it all into a pile, carrying it in his arms down to the dumpster.

I'd snuck around the apartment as soon as he stepped out the door, saving little pieces of her from dresser drawers and cupboards and closets, squirreling them away among my own things so they wouldn't be lost to me forever. None of it was of any value. Most of it was junk—a tarnished Saint George medal, a handful of mismatched buttons, a stained glove without a mate—but it had been all that was left of her.

At the time, I'd thought my dad was trying to erase her. Years later I realized that he'd just needed something to *do* about losing her, and that was the only thing he could think of.

It was a month and a day since Norm passed, and it seemed like time to let some of his things go.

I hadn't told Marvel that I'd chosen that day for the job. She would have wanted to be there to offer me her shoulder if I needed to cry or her strength if I couldn't manage to find mine.

It was work I needed to do alone, though. She wouldn't have understood if I'd said that. It probably would have ended up hurting her feelings.

I stood in the basement on Deerfield Avenue that rainy Sunday afternoon, staring down a stack of boxes lined up along the wall. I'd already emptied out Norman's dresser and most of his side of the closet, not without a good amount of tears. I'd folded his clothes, putting them in paper grocery bags for the Salvation Army to pick up the next day.

Hands on my hips, I approached those boxes that Norman had promised to unpack years before. He'd never found the time, even with my near monthly requests for him to do something—anything—with them.

Kneeling on the cold floor, I regretted ever making such a to-do about those stupid boxes. If I'd only known how little time I would have with Norm, I never would have wasted a minute of it nagging him about something so unimportant.

"Now, don't dwell on it, Betty," I whispered, rubbing my eyes. "Norman never held it against you."

I'd been with the man for the better part of my life and only known him to hold a handful of grudges, and none of them against me. He'd loved me too dearly to entertain resentment for me.

"He was a good man." I nodded and pushed back a curl that had gotten loose on my forehead.

Blowing dust off the tops of the boxes, I bolstered myself just in case spiders or mice had taken up residence inside. All I found in that first box, though, were old sales receipts from the bakery. I put it to the side in case Stan or Albert wanted to go through it. In the next were our old set of mismatched dishes we'd meant to find a new home for. Those would go with the clothes in the morning.

The third box had been sealed, the layers of tape so thick I couldn't pull it up with just my hands. In the middle drawer of Norman's desk—just an arm's length away from where I knelt—I found a razor blade and slit into the tape, careful not to cut myself in the process.

All I needed was to end up getting stitches and Marvel scolding me for doing this by myself.

Pulling up the folds of the box, I found some old bed linens and a lacy tablecloth. Pulling them out, I piled them on the floor beside me. The box had felt too heavy for just a bunch of folded-up fabric.

Meowing to let me know she was there, Flannery came up beside me, peeking into the box and making like she was going to jump inside.

"No, kitty," I said, lifting her gently and moving her to the side.

Reaching under a set of sheets, I felt something hard. A book? Pulling it out, I knew what it was as soon as it was in my hand. It had been years since I'd last seen it. In fact, I'd thought it was lost years before.

I touched the cover of it as carefully as possible, worried that it would break to pieces if I wasn't tender with it.

To anyone else it was just another old family album with black and white photographs of long-gone relatives and ancient homesteads. But it was entirely different for me.

It was my only inheritance from when my dad died. The only thing he had to will. He'd not had a business to pass down and he'd never had the privilege of owning a single acre of land. What he'd had was that album. That was it.

Inside were the photographs that told the tale of our family, as ordinary as it was.

"Is this your way of bringing Clara back to me?" I whispered, not knowing if that informal sentence even counted as a prayer. "Or is this a hint? Am I supposed to go looking for her?"

I thought, but didn't say, how unlikely that would be.

Not opening the album, I stood and—only then realizing that my foot was asleep—limped my way to the steps, leaving the linens and all on the floor beside the cardboard box.

They'd be fine until morning.

I put the album on the coffee table in the living room where I could look at it later if I wanted to.

Yawning, I thought I'd turn in early. Sorting through all of Norman's things was wearing work, both emotionally and physically. But when I looked at the clock, I saw it was just a quarter 'til eight. That seemed a ridiculous time to go to bed for the night even if I was exhausted. I decided that I'd put a little cold cream on my face and go watch some television to pass the time before it was reasonable to go to sleep.

Only after I had my face sufficiently slathered did someone knock on the door.

"Of course," I said to my reflection before trying to wipe it all off on a hand towel, hoping I hadn't missed any of it.

When I got to the front door and peeked out, I saw Albert on my porch, two glass bottles of Pepsi in his hands.

"Well, hello, Albert," I said, opening the door.

"Hi," he answered in the uncomfortable way he sometimes had. Then he wiped at a spot on his jawline. "You have a little something . . ."

"Oh, for goodness' sake." I used my thumb to rub it away, finding a good-sized glob of cream there. "Thank you."

"You're welcome." His lips twitched.

"Don't you laugh at me, Albert Sweet." I shook my head.

"I would never dream of it." He cleared his throat. "Say, Betty, I was wondering if I could ask a favor."

"It depends on what it is." I pulled the door open wider. "Why don't you come in."

He did, only to stop when he saw Flannery sitting in one of the bags full of Norman's clothes and gazing up at him.

"When did you get a cat?" he asked, handing me one of the bottles of pop. "And what's in all those bags?"

"Well, the cat arrived yesterday, actually." I looked down at her. "Our delightful nephews brought her to me as a gift."

"Oh." He went down on his haunches and rubbed his fingers and thumb together and clicked his tongue. She bounded to him, letting him scratch behind her ear. "How nice of them."

"That still remains to be seen." I chuckled. "And the bags are some of Norm's things."

"Ah." Albie didn't turn toward me. He swallowed hard. "Would you like me to help?"

"It's mostly done now," I answered, stepping into the living room. "Is there anything I can do for you?"

"It seems my television is on the fritz." He looked up at me and grimaced. "It seems such a silly problem."

"Not silly at all," I said. "Do you want to watch *Ed Sullivan* over here?"

"If it's not a problem."

"Of course not," I said. "Should I get you a glass or do you want to drink right out of the bottle?"

"I'm not particular."

I went to the kitchen and got two glasses, each with four ice cubes.

Even though he said he wasn't, I knew that he was indeed particular.

Particular. That was a good word for Albert Sweet.

Albert sat on the love seat, and I in my chair. Our glasses of Pepsi perspired on coasters and we each held a small bowl of potato chips in our laps.

That night, Mr. Sullivan was hosting several acts, but I was most interested in hearing Barbra Streisand sing. When she came on the screen, I inched to the edge of my seat, setting my chips on the end table.

Norman had bought me her record when it came out at the end of February. A late Valentine's Day gift, he'd said. He'd even pulled it out of its sleeve and put it on the turntable, placing the needle right on the very song he'd bought it for.

"Happy Days Are Here Again."

Even sitting in my chair in front of the television, listening to that young lady sing an entirely different song, I remembered the grin on Norman's face when the music began to pour out of our old record player. How he'd pushed the coffee table to the side and insisted that I dance with him.

How I'd laughed as he tried to sing along.

How he'd pulled me close to himself, wrapping his arm around my waist and leading me as we swayed to the slower version of the song.

How, even after twenty-three years of married life, he'd still managed to make my heart beat faster.

I forced myself to remember that Albert was just on the other side of the room and that it wasn't the right time to dissolve into a mess of tears. As it was, the poor man had borne witness to nearly all of my least flattering moments in the past month.

By the end of the song, though, I had tears in my eyes, as much as I had wanted to hold them back.

Albert didn't notice.

Either that or he was too much of a gentleman to mention it.

"What a voice," he'd said, clapping along with the studio audience.

It shouldn't have surprised me when he knocked a tear away from his own eye with the knuckle of his finger.

"I certainly can't imagine having such talent in anything." I drank the last of my Pepsi.

"Me either." He turned toward me and shook his head. "I don't think anyone wants to watch somebody bake bread on television."

"I'm sure you're right." I sighed. "But they might want to hear you play your cello."

"Oh, I don't think so," he said. "There are plenty of better players than me."

"Well, I've never met them." I rested my chin on my hand and smiled at him.

"You're biased." He leaned forward, his elbows on his lap, letting his hands dangle between his knees. It was a way of sitting that all Sweet men seemed to find particularly comfortable, and it was quite endearing. "You know, Norm used to brag about how good you are at writing."

"He what?" I put a hand to my chest.

"He said you kept a journal, but not as a diary." Albert gave a subtle smile. "He said you wrote poems and stories. He said they were good."

"Talk about biased."

"Do you still write?"

"Nothing I'm willing to show anyone." I shifted my eyes when he tried to meet my gaze.

"It doesn't do any good if you keep it secret."

Lucky for me, the program started back up and we both turned our attention to the television. Had I a need to remember what act came on next, I would have utterly failed. For the life of me, I couldn't pay attention.

All I could think of was how I most certainly did not want to share what I'd written. Not a word of it. Not with anyone. It wasn't out of pride or embarrassment. Those writings were the only thing I'd ever had to myself.

Keeping them secret might not have done any good for anybody else, but it did good for me.

It was purely out of selfishness, and I didn't think that was wrong at all.

Before going to bed I went to the living room to turn out the lights. Reaching for the switch on the floor lamp beside my chair, I looked down at the coffee table and saw the photo album.

I thought about bending my knees and picking it up, opening it to look through the pictures. My heart thudded at the idea of the memories inside that little book. Each snapshot held a story that bound me to something or someone I didn't allow myself to think of very often.

Knees locked and fingers pinched on the lamp's knob, I turned off the light.

twelve

J hadn't intended to park my car in front of the bakery, and I didn't mean to get out and hurry to the door. It wasn't my plan to step inside and breathe in the aroma of fresh bread. All I'd meant to do was go to the store to pick up a few things. It was Wednesday, after all. Grocery day.

Yet, there I was. Standing just inside the entrance to Sweet Family, hands hanging at my sides. I surprised myself so much, ending up there entirely by accident, that I dropped my handbag—thud—on the floor.

Old habits certainly were hard to quit.

Pop stepped out from the back, his sleeves pushed up to his elbows and tacky dough on his right hand. He seemed to have aged a decade in just a handful of weeks. I supposed that was what happened when a father lost a son.

He opened his mouth, and I half expected—or rather, hoped—that he'd say something to tease me. I wanted him to be how he usually was, clever and witty and funny. But I could tell in his eyes that it wasn't in him.

Not just yet, at least.

"Hi, Bets," he said, leaning heavily on the counter. "How are you holding up?"

It was his kindness that made my voice catch in my throat. It was how out of place I felt, standing in the bakery, knowing that Norm wasn't going to come in with a kiss for me. It was how I wondered what part I had in this family anymore aside from still bearing their name.

I half worried they'd want it back from me now that I was a widow.

But when Pop stepped out from behind the counter, hobbling over without the help of his cane, and wrapped his arms around me like the good father he was, I knew my place. It was right there with them.

***

Pop left Stan and Albert in charge and grabbed his cane, insisting that he take me to get a malt from the soda fountain a few doors down.

"But it's still morning," I said, letting him lead me by the shoulder out the bakery.

"Bets, I get up so early this is darn near evening for me." He winked and nodded for me to go out the door before him.

Sam's Sodas was the kind of place that kids would go after school for a vanilla Coke or a banana split. I usually avoided it, but Pop loved finding excuses to go. Usually he'd treat the twins, letting them pick whatever they wanted—oh, how he spoiled them.

"Hey, Pops," the man behind the counter called, tossing a hand towel over his shoulder. "How's things at the bakery?"

"Oh, you know. Just the usual," Pop answered. "We're over there just rollin' in the dough."

The man laughed and swatted a hand in the air. I smiled politely at the joke I'd heard at least a hundred times. If not from Pop, then from Norm.

"The usual?" The man raised his eyebrows.

"Yup. Two malts, please." Pop nodded at a booth. "We'll just sit over there."

"You got it."

We had the place to ourselves, which was nice. The only sound was the whirring of the blender. Just over our booth was a framed print of a girl and boy sitting at a lunch counter, both of them dressed up to the nines. The soda jerk leaned over to smell the girl's corsage, the boy looking on, proud of himself. Boy, could that Norman Rockwell ever tell a story for the eyes.

"This place always reminds me of Lacy," Pop said, staring off into space. "She loved coming here for a scoop of ice cream. I'd tease her about it, telling her how much we'd save if she just had her dish of vanilla at home. But she'd say it tasted better when somebody else served it to her."

"I have to agree with her," I said.

"Of course you would." He grinned at me.

"She was a wise woman."

The soda jerk brought our malts, and we both thanked him. Pop shut his eyes and took his first sip through the straw, a satisfied "ah" spreading his mouth into a smile.

"That's good," he said. "You want this?"

He pulled the cherry out of the whipped cream by its stem. I pushed my glass to him so he could drop it in.

"Pop, can you please tell me about when you first met Mom?" I asked, dipping my long-handled spoon into the malt.

"I guess I could."

"It would cheer me up."

"Is that so? Well, how could I say no to that?" He took another drink before starting. "LaFontaine was a bit different when I was younger. It was mostly farmland then. My folks raised milk cows and grew some soybeans. Our closest neighbor was a good mile and a half away."

"I don't know that I would have liked that," I said.

"Lots different than Detroit, huh?" He stirred his malt with his straw, mixing the whipped cream into it as he talked. "I think I was nineteen when Lacy and her family moved to town. They had a house just down the street. You know the place on Pennsylvania Avenue and Fourth?"

"The old Victorian?" I asked.

"That's the one."

"I didn't know she lived there."

"They did for a time. Her dad was a banker," he said. "Did pretty well until the thirties. That's when they lost the house. Anyway, they were the talk of the town and all I heard about was how beautiful all the girls were in that family. I decided to give them a wide berth. Rich and pretty weren't my taste back then."

"Oh, Pop."

"To be fair I hadn't met her yet." He smiled. "First time I did was when she'd come to the farm with her father on some sort of banking business. She insisted on going to the barn to see the cows, and I obliged while our dads talked about money."

"Do you remember what she was wearing?" I asked.

"Nope. She could have been in a clown costume and I wouldn't have noticed. All I saw were her sharp blue eyes." He rubbed a hand over his mouth. "I couldn't get an intelligent word out to save my life. All I could manage was a blubber and mumble here and there."

"Not you," I said, grinning.

"Well, by the end of the tour she told me she thought I was nice and that I should come to call on her sometime." He laughed. "Before she left, she told me I ought to come the next evening. Oh, but was I nervous. The next day I put on my best suit. Well, it was my only suit, if I'm telling the truth. I picked some flowers out of Mother's garden and walked the three miles to town."

"How sweet." I rested my chin in my hand.

"It might have been. But it was a hot day. Humid as all get-out. But I was too nervous to think about taking off my jacket. I was afraid I'd sweat through my dress shirt. So I walked all that way, the sun beating down on my neck and getting thirstier and thirstier with every step." He took a sip of his malt and cleared his throat. "By the time I got to her doorstep, I was feeling sick. When the maid answered my knock, I fainted dead away, falling off the porch and into a hydrangea."

I covered my mouth when I laughed. He winked at me to let me know it was funny to him too.

"Lacy came out when she heard the ruckus, asking if I was all right." His shoulders lifted in a sigh. "Still in the bush, I looked up at her and didn't know if the light feeling in my head was from the heat, the fall, or how beautiful she was."

Someone came into the soda shop and sat at the counter. Ice clattered into a glass and the man talked with the soda jerk.

"Is that when you knew you wanted to marry her?"

"Nope. I knew I wanted to hold her hand, though. And deep inside, I wanted to kiss her, although I didn't have the courage to do something like that yet," he said. "I was deeply infatuated that evening. Love came later. But when it arrived, it stuck around."

"I think that's a nice story," I said.

"Me too, kiddo." He drank from his straw. "It was our first story together. First of many."

We finished our malts, swapping stories, most that started with the words "do you remember when?" None was new to either of us, but that didn't matter. It was a comfort and a pleasure to mull over the memories.

After a little bit, we left the soda fountain. Pop walked me to my car. I stood on the other side of the open driver's side door, my fingers resting on the window frame.

"Have a good day, Bets," he said from the curb.

"You too."

Someone driving by honked their horn, and Pop lifted his hand to wave at them.

"If ever you find yourself bored silly, come on over to the bakery." He nodded. "We'll find something for you to do."

"All right," I said. "Maybe you can let me try to make bread."

"Oh, I don't know about that." He winked. "I seem to remember the last time you tried, you nearly burned down the whole town."

"It wasn't that bad." I shrugged. "I guess I could just tidy things up a bit. Maybe work the cash register every once in a while."

"That would be nice. We could use a little sunshine in that place." He half turned away from me and toward the bakery. "Welp, I'll see you around."

"Pop," I called.

He stopped and looked at me over his shoulder. "Yeah?"

"Thanks for cheering me up."

"Huh. I thought it was you cheering me up." He dipped his mouth in a thoughtful frown and raised his eyebrows. "But you're welcome, I guess."

He waved at me before going on his way.

All the while I did my grocery shopping, I thought of Pop—a younger version of the one I knew—in a bush outside the nicest house in town, well on his way to falling in love with Mom. I imagined her standing on the porch, hands on her hips and shaking her head, but growing in affection for him all the same.

So distracted was I that I didn't realize I'd bought four packages of potato chips until I got home.

What was a woman living on her own supposed to do with that many chips?

"Oh, Betty," I said to myself, not even bothering to whisper. "What a doofus you are."

I got on my step stool and stacked the bags on top of my fridge.

thirteen

I'd never been one to read the morning newspaper. In fact, I'd sometimes wondered why Norman subscribed to the *State Journal* when the *LaFontaine News* came free once a week. He'd just said that he liked reading about more than who won the church softball league or which neighbors had gotten a new roof.

As much as I thought getting the *Journal* was a waste of money, I couldn't bring myself to cancel it after Norm passed. Most mornings I'd collect it from the doorstep and promptly take it downstairs to where a good stack of papers was collecting. At the end of the summer the scout troop would hold its annual paper drive. I'd have quite a contribution for them.

That morning I'd been too preoccupied by running errands around town that I'd forgotten all about the paper until much later in the day.

"Goodness, Betty," I whispered when I stepped outside to collect the mail and saw the rolled news still on my doorstep. "You're really slipping."

When I finally retrieved it, I pulled off the thick rubber band, slipping it around my wrist, and unrolled the paper so it could lie flat on the stack with all the others.

The story that took up most of the front page caught my eye.

Printed large was the photograph of a man sitting cross-legged in the middle of a street, a crowd all around him, watching. Behind him was a car, the type of which I'd not seen before. It looked foreign, different. In fact, everything about the picture did. The shaved heads of the people in long robes, the words I couldn't read that had been painted on the building behind him, the children lined up along the street all dressed as small monks. All so very unfamiliar.

My eyes roamed the picture, unable to look away. The man was on fire, the blazes seeming to come from inside him, although I knew that couldn't have been possible.

Sitting in my chair, one leg folded up under me, I read through the article twice, trying to understand it.

It seemed the Vietnamese government had a habit of mistreating the Buddhists. Persecution, strong-arming, denying rights. The man had allowed gasoline to be poured all over him before he lit a match, engulfing himself in flame.

It was grotesque, horrifying, shocking. I had never seen anything like that in all my life and it turned my stomach sour. For the very first time I was grateful that the *State Journal* wasn't printed in color.

In all honesty, I thought about Vietnam very little. Rarely did I watch the news, and when I did, there wasn't much said about the country, let alone our involvement there. Much to my embarrassment, I wouldn't have been able to point to it on the map if my life depended on it.

The picture, though, somehow made that far-off land seem

a whole lot closer. It reminded me that even though that man had lived thousands and thousands of miles away from me, we still shared the same world.

Every feeling of the morning melted when I looked at that picture. No matter how I tried to fill my mind with other things—to find the sunshine—I couldn't extinguish the burning monk from my eyes. The afterimage of the flames rising from his body refused to leave me.

I turned on the evening news after I failed to eat a good dinner, hoping to hear more about the monk. For some reason I couldn't have explained, I found myself fascinated by the story, as well as utterly horrified.

But there was no mention of him. Instead, on the screen was a house that looked like it would belong in any neighborhood in the United States. That one, though, was in Jackson, Mississippi. And outside that house a man named Medgar Evers—a man I'd never heard of before—was murdered in his driveway with his family inside. He and his wife had three children. Two boys and a girl.

"Evers was just returning home from a NAACP meeting when he was shot in the back by a sniper hiding in the brush across the street," the reporter said. "He died at the hospital in Jackson."

The camera focused on a police officer standing by the house and pointing at what the reporter said was a bullet hole in the window.

"His wife and children were sleeping inside the house." The reporter's voice remained matter of fact, calm, even. "They were left unharmed."

I leaned forward, covering my mouth with one hand, willing myself to watch the rest of the news, hoping for a story that was at least marginally happy.

Nothing.

I got up and switched off the television, wishing I hadn't turned it on in the first place. Wishing I hadn't seen the paper that morning.

"Now that I know," I whispered to myself, "I won't be able to forget."

They were left unharmed, the reporter had said of the man's children.

I supposed the same could be said of the children in that far-away city in Vietnam who watched the man light himself on fire.

Left unharmed in respect to their arms and legs and heads. They weren't injured. Didn't catch a spark or a grazing of a bullet.

But I thought of the Evers children, maybe at that very moment getting ready for bed—the first night without their father—the shots of the sniper still booming in their ears and the cries of their father too.

Unharmed, the reporter had claimed.

Unharmed.

I wondered if I'd ever think of that word the same way again.

I couldn't sleep that night. It was no use trying. I simply couldn't drift off. Whenever I closed my eyes, I just saw the Vietnamese children in my mind, their eyes fixed on the burning man. If I tossed and turned, all I could think of was the family in Mississippi, wondering if their sleep was even more disturbed than mine.

Without a doubt it was.

After a while, I flung aside the covers, swung my feet off the side of the bed, and grabbed my robe. Flannery made a groaning sound but didn't lift her head.

"Don't get up on account of me," I said, smoothing the fur on her back with my hand.

She didn't purr. Instead she lifted a paw to cover her face.

I didn't know what came over me, but I pulled a little corner of the covers up and around her, tucking it under her warm little body. If I'd not caught myself, I might have planted a kiss on the top of her head.

Oh, would Norman have teased me for doing such a thing!

I decided to fix myself a cup of chamomile tea, hoping it would make me sleepy enough to get at least a few hours of rest. I put the kettle on to boil and took down one of my pretty pink cups from the cupboard. But when I went for a tea bag, I found that I was completely out.

Rummaging through the cupboard, I found all manner of things that were not tea. A stray birthday candle, a scrap of aluminum foil, more dust than I would ever admit to. Not so much as a single leaf of tea, let alone a full box.

I turned off the flame under the kettle just as it hinted at a whistle.

As a last-ditch effort, I got up on my tiptoes and felt of the shelf just above where I usually kept my tea canisters. It was where Norm kept his baking supplies. Flour and baking soda and other things that I never bothered with. My fingers landed on a little piece of paper.

Curious. I took it to the sink, flipping on the overhead light.

As I looked at that yellowed, aged card, my eyes grew watery. Afraid a tear might smudge the writing, I held the paper to my chest, wondering at how emotional I could get over seeing Norm's handwriting again.

Norman had given me his family's secret recipe for their popular Sweet Bread one morning as he walked me to school.

"Mom said it was all right," he'd said. "Just so long as you don't share it with anybody else."

"Thank you, but I don't know how to make bread." I'd stopped on the sidewalk to read the instructions. "I'd only ruin it."

"Nah. You'd do fine."

"Why do you have to knead it?" I pointed at one of the steps. "Can't you just stir it?"

He'd cringed and shook his head. "You have to knead it to activate the gluten."

"Oh." I started walking but then halted. "What's gluten?"

"It's what gives the bread its stretch, it's what holds it together."

"Oh," I said again, still not understanding.

"If you don't knead the bread enough, it won't rise right. It won't hold its shape," he said. "If you knead it too much, it'll be tough."

"You sure do take bread seriously."

"You got that right." He adjusted my books in his arms. "There's nothing quite so bad as bread that's not been made properly."

"I'm afraid that's the only kind I'd ever be able to make."

"I'll teach you," he said. "It isn't too hard. It's all about patience, especially at first. And it's all right if you ruin a few loaves along the way."

Over the years I'd spoiled more than my fair share of bread. After a while, I just let Norm bring it home from work.

I left the light on over the sink and the mess of odds and

ends that I'd pulled from the cupboard and went back to my room. Opening the drawer of my bedside table, I placed the recipe card in, on top of the square jewelry box where I'd put Norman's wedding ring.

Eventually I did fall asleep, and even though my dreams were unsettled, I woke the next morning feeling nearly refreshed.

As I made my coffee, I prayed that the Evers children would find comfort in good memories of their father. When I washed my breakfast dishes, I prayed for the little ones a world away in Vietnam, that they would be able to forget the monk on fire somehow, even if I suspected that was impossible.

I went through that rainy day, my heart feeling more than a little bruised.

I rubbed at my chest, willing the ache to go away.

It stayed right where it was, feeling as much like dread as loss. I couldn't seem to shake it no matter what I tried.

fourteen

I busied myself the next day by sitting in my chair and reading. If a rainy day couldn't be avoided, it was best spent with a good book. Fortunately for me, I had more than a few to choose from. I picked *A Little Princess*, a book I'd read so many times the binding was cracked and the pages soft, smelling just a little bit like a log cabin and a hint of vanilla.

Halfway through the afternoon, I opened the living room windows, letting in a cool breeze. Unfortunately, I also let in the plinking and plunking sounds of the neighbor girl practicing her piano lessons. The less-than-perfect playing of "Mary Had a Little Lamb" and "Twinkle, Twinkle Little Star" took my attention from poor Sara Crewe and the dastardly Miss Minchin.

I thought about shutting the window, but instead I leaned my head back against my chair and shut my eyes. Before I knew it, I was jolting awake, the room gone cold and the sounds of rain coming down harder on the windows. The day had gone dark and I didn't know if that was because of the storm or if it had gotten late.

Shutting the book, I sat upright, trying to gain my bearings.

The clock on the wall read seven, and I shook my head. I'd never get on a reasonable sleeping schedule again if I kept taking unintentional naps like that one.

On my feet and moving around the room to turn on lights, I noticed that a glistening of rainwater had collected on the windowsill. I pushed the window closed and headed toward the linen closet for a rag to put down on the floor under it.

"What a mess," I said.

Before I got to the closet, I heard a knock on the front door. It startled me, making me flinch and clutch at my collar. Taking a good breath, I smoothed the front of my dress and went to answer the knock.

A tall woman stood on the concrete slab, her hair pulled back loosely with frizzy curls crowning her head. Her raincoat was held tight in one hand, a small and battered suitcase in the other.

She was too thin, too angular, and I wouldn't have known her but for the eyes. Impossibly blue and clear and full of fire. That evening, though, the fire had gone down to an ember. Still, it was there.

"Clara?" I said, not even a whisper.

"Hi, Birdie." She pinched her lips together as if she wasn't sure she still had the right to call me that. "I'm sorry."

"Come in." I stepped to the side so she had room to get in out of the rain. "You'll get soaked through out there."

"I'm not alone." Her eyes darted to the side to a place on the porch I couldn't see from where I was standing.

"That's all right. Both of you come in. I'll make some coffee."

Clara released her jacket, letting it billow out around her, and extended her hand to whoever was with her. A tiny brown hand clasped her creamy-colored one.

The little boy—he couldn't have been more than six—nestled

into Clara, holding on to her for dear life and peeking out from behind her at me.

Smiling at him, I tried to mask any reaction other than pure delight in seeing him. But in my mind I had a dozen questions stirring about who—and whose—that child might be.

"Oh, hello there," I said. Then, looking at my sister, "Is he . . ."

"This is Hugo," Clara said. "My son."

Had I been wearing my pearls I may have clutched them. First at the surprise of Clara being a mother. Second at the shock that her little boy was black.

It wasn't that I was prejudiced—or at least I didn't think I was—and I knew that such things happened. I'd lived my first fourteen years in Detroit, after all. It was just that I hadn't expected to ever have a blood relative who was, well, black.

Clara watched me, and I knew she was waiting to see how I'd react to the boy. I did my best to soften my eyes, to widen my smile, and to give them both the best welcome I could muster.

"I am so glad to meet you, Hugo." I bent my knees so I'd be closer to his eye level and gave him the sweetest smile I could conjure. "Do you drink coffee?"

He shook his head and pressed his cheek into the side of her thigh, but I thought I saw just the hint of a smile.

"Honey, this is your Aunt Birdie," Clara said, then met my eyes. "Or would you prefer Betty?"

"Either is just fine." I motioned them in. "Please, come out of the rain. I'll fix something for supper."

Clara gave Hugo a little nudge toward me, but he hesitated.

"It's all right," she said. "Remember what I told you? She's nice."

He didn't let go of her hand when he walked past me and into the house.

It wasn't often that I had dinner guests and I wasn't entirely sure what to serve them. When I asked Clara what they might be hungry for, she said that Hugo wasn't picky. A peanut butter sandwich would be good enough. When I asked what she'd like, she told me that she didn't have an appetite.

My sister had never been a very good eater.

Hugo whispered a thank-you when I put a plate on the table in front of him, and Clara grinned at him.

"Would you like a glass of milk?" I asked.

"Yes please," he answered, his voice so soft I nearly didn't hear him.

While I'd grown accustomed over the years to my house being quiet when I was alone, I wasn't used to it being near silent when someone else was in it with me. Norman had filled spaces with sound—his voice, laughter, heavy footsteps. Clara and Hugo hardly made a peep, sitting at the kitchen table.

It unnerved me, making me want to fill that silence as much as I could.

"How old are you, Hugo?" I asked, pulling open the refrigerator.

When he didn't answer, I took notice of his full cheek and moving jaw. Eyes wide, he turned to Clara.

"He's five," she answered for him. "Just turned in March."

"Five is such a fun age." I, of course, didn't know what I was talking about. It had just seemed like the right thing to say. "Are you in school yet?"

He stopped just as he was about to take another bite of sandwich, closed his mouth, and shook his head.

"Not until this fall." Clara nodded at him, and he went on eating.

"Kindergarten?" I poured a tumbler all the way full with milk.

"Yes." Clara raised her eyebrows at the glass when I put it on the table.

"Is that too much?" I pulled my mouth into a cringe.

"Maybe."

"He doesn't have to drink it all," I said. "It's just Nick and Dick drink so much milk when they're over."

Sighing, I realized the twins were twice Hugo's age and size.

"It's all right," Clara said and then encouraged Hugo to take a sip.

After I put the milk away, I sat on the other side of Hugo, across from Clara. While I usually liked a good peanut butter sandwich every once in a while, the one on my plate wasn't quite appealing. I thought it was my nerves. I forced myself to take a bite anyway.

"Shouldn't Norm be home by now?" Clara asked, glancing at the clock over the stovetop.

I swallowed hard, the bread and peanut butter moving like a lump—sluggish and far too big—down my throat. Hand on my chest, I coughed until the food went down.

"Are you all right?" She leaned forward, mouth drawn in a tight line.

"Yes." My eyes watered and my throat felt tight. It wasn't entirely due to my brief episode of choking. "I'm fine."

"Let me get you a glass of water."

The hinges of the cupboard door creaked just slightly, and the faucet sputtered as she drew cold water for me. Taking a few sips, I felt instant relief.

"Thank you," I said, waiting until she was back in her seat before going on. "Norm passed away, Clara."

"When?"

"It was a month and a half ago." I drank another gulp of water. "I should have tried to find you. I just wasn't sure how."

Clara shut her eyes and bit her bottom lip. When a tear came, she swiped at it and wiped her hand on the skirt of her dress. Hugo got out of his chair and put his arms around her. She held onto him and rubbed his back, turning her head so she could kiss the top of his.

"It's all right," she whispered. "I'm fine."

When she opened her eyes, I thought I saw a familiar hurt there. In her life she'd carried that pain far too often.

"I'm so sorry, Betty."

My proper name sounded foreign in her voice.

Clara didn't offer a lick of protest when I asked if they'd like to stay over for the night. In fact, from the way her face relaxed when I offered, I thought she'd hoped I would. I put fresh linens on the beds in the small guest rooms upstairs.

Hugo would be in the room to the left and Clara to the right.

Once I finished fluffing pillows and turning down covers, I left Clara to get him in bed.

"I'll be downstairs with Aunt Betty for a little bit," Clara told him while she tucked him in. "I'll check on you before I go to bed."

"How long are we staying here?" he asked.

I stayed put on the middle stair, hoping she wouldn't know that I stood there, eavesdropping.

"We'll see."

"It's nice here," he said.

"I know it. Now, let's say your prayers."

"Can we pray for the space girl?" Sleepiness thickened his little voice, slowed it down just a tad. "Who is she?"

"Valentina?"

"What's her whole name?"

"Well, I'm not sure I'm saying it right," Clara said. "Valentina Tereshkova."

"Where's she from?" he asked.

"The Soviet Union."

"Where's that?"

"Far away," she answered.

"But not as far away as space."

"Nope." She cleared her throat. "What do you want to pray for her?"

"That she's safe."

"Well, baby, she already landed back on earth," Clara said. "Remember?"

"Do you think she liked being up in space?" Hugo asked.

"I can't be sure. What do you think?"

"If I could fly in space, I'd never want to come down."

"Is that so?"

Hugo made a humming sound. "I'd stay up there forever."

"Wouldn't you miss me?"

"You'd come with me," he answered. "I'd take care of you."

"You're kind."

A rustling of covers and the creaking of the old mattress told me that she was getting him settled in for the night.

"Go on and say your prayers," she said.

"God, thank you for making the space girl be safe," he said. "And help her not to miss the stars too much. Amen."

"Sweet dreams, baby," Clara said.

Quietly as I could, I made my way down the other half of

the steps and busied myself in the kitchen drying the dinner dishes. By the time Clara got downstairs, I had them all done and my towel hanging on the door of the oven to dry.

"I have a bottle of Dr Pepper in the fridge," I said. "Would you like to split it with me?"

"All right."

I rummaged through the drawer for the bottle opener, trying to think of something to talk to her about. Half a dozen questions occurred to me—Where have you been? Why did you come back now? How long are you going to stay?—but I didn't feel that I had the right to ask any of them.

"You're wondering about his father." She stood with her hands hanging at her sides, fingers fidgeting with the fabric of her skirt.

"Well . . ." I couldn't say I hadn't been.

"He was just another mistake I've made," she said. "But I got Hugo out of it. Sometimes good things come out of messes."

"And he's . . ."

"Negro?" she interrupted. "Yes."

"Do you ever see him?" The bottle opener in hand, I pushed the drawer closed.

"Nope. And Hugo will never know him," she answered. "I'd rather die than let him know about our son."

Clara had always had a flair for the dramatic. At the drop of a hat, she'd bemoan the state of all things. The dim lights of the tenements were making her blind, the pepper on her eggs was making her sneeze so hard she'd wind up knocking herself out, the windows leaked so much cold air she was bound to freeze into a block of ice.

The bottle of pop fizzing as I opened it, I assumed she was just being melodramatic.

But when I tried to hand her a glass of the bubbly drink, I saw in her eyes that she was dead serious. I decided it would be best not to talk about Hugo's father anymore.

"Should we go to the living room?" I asked.

We sat on either end of the couch, neither of us saying anything. After ten minutes of that, I asked if she'd like to watch something on the television.

"If you want to," she answered.

But when I got up to turn it on, she cleared her throat and said something under her breath.

"What was that?" I asked, facing her.

"I said that I'm sorry."

"Why, whatever for?"

"I never should have left," she said. "I never should have been so mean to you."

"Oh, I forgave you a long time ago." I bent at the knees, crouching beside her and taking her hand. "I have never stopped loving you."

"I almost didn't come here. I worried that you'd moved or that you wouldn't let me in." She sniffled and blinked fast. "But I didn't know where else to go."

"You will always be welcome here," I said. "You and Hugo. He's a sweetheart."

"He's better than I deserve."

"I'm sure all mothers feel that way about their children. Don't you think?"

My legs started to burn from squatting the way I was, but I feared if I tried to get up, I'd just lose my balance. I shifted so that I was kneeling.

"I lost my job," she said before biting at her bottom lip.

"What kind of job was it?"

"Waiting tables." She cleared her throat. "It was a good job. Paid well enough. But I started getting nervous about it."

"What made you nervous?" I asked.

"Everything."

I waited for her to go on, remembering how she liked to take pauses to think before speaking and how she hated to be interrupted.

"Sometimes just the idea of going to work kept me up all night. I'd think of all the things that could go wrong," she said. "That I'd spill coffee on someone or bring them the wrong meal and they'd be angry. I worried that I'd not be able to make change or that someone would rob the diner."

She shook her head and scowled.

"Silly stuff," she said.

"I don't think any of that's silly."

"Then I would get afraid for Hugo." She glanced toward the stairs. "That he'd think I didn't love him because I had to work so much or that he'd get hurt at the sitter's house. It got so that leaving in the morning made me sick."

I thought of the mornings when Clara had begged to stay home from school, crying so hard that she'd make herself throw up. Dad had called it a nervous stomach and said she'd grow out of it.

It was just another thing he'd gotten wrong.

"I don't know what to do," Clara said, her voice sounding pinched. "I can't afford a place to stay, and I have no money for food. I had to borrow a few bucks for the bus to get here."

"You can stay here as long as you need to." The words were out before I'd even given them any thought. "I have plenty of space, and it's no fun to cook for one."

"I didn't come here to beg."

"I know you didn't."

She let out a breath, and her shoulders relaxed. Deflating, it seemed, she eased into the couch cushion.

"Everything is going to be all right," I said.

Goodness. I hoped I was right.

fifteen

The last time I saw my mother was from the window of our apartment building. Dad had borrowed someone's car so he could take her back to the sanitarium. He held the door for her to get in, and she looked up at the window, pressing her hand to her lips before waving at me. I called down that I loved her but never knew if she'd heard me or not.

Months later Dad sat Clara and me down to tell us that Mother had died. He never told us how, and we hadn't asked. But he had told us that if anyone asked, we were to say that she'd died of consumption.

"No one needs to know," my dad said. "It's family business."

I had suspicions of how her life had ended, but I'd never been brave enough to say the word aloud. It was a harsh word, a hissing word. The kind that gave me nightmares when I thought about it too much.

And so, I did as Dad had asked. I didn't talk about her death around him and I didn't ask him any questions.

In bedtime whispers, though, the two of us girls would

chatter about Mother. We'd tell stories about how she'd sing us to sleep or the pictures she'd draw for us to color in. When Dad came into the room, telling us to hush up and go to sleep, we'd freeze, hoping he hadn't heard what we'd been talking about.

It was after everything was quiet and the lights were off, when the only sounds were the creaks and crackles of the building settling and Dad snoring in the other room, that Clara became afraid. She'd fidget under the covers and take an occasional gasp of air. When she thought I was sleeping, she'd cry softly to herself.

The first few times I pretended not to hear her, not to feel her trembling beside me. On the third night after Mother died, I couldn't bear to let her suffer like that.

"Are you all right?" I asked.

"No . . . no . . ." she whispered.

"What's the matter?"

"I don't know."

The streetlamp beamed in through our window with no curtain or shade to block it. The light was enough for me to see that Clara covered her face with both hands, and I didn't know if that was to keep me from seeing her or her from seeing me.

"I'm scared, Birdie," she said.

"Of what?"

"I don't know." She spread two fingers, peeking through the gap. "Will you tell me a story?"

"Will it help?"

She nodded and lowered her hands. "The one about the girl who was afraid of the dark. Do you know that one?"

I smiled. It was one of our mother's stories, one she'd told when Clara insisted on keeping the lamp on all night. Dad wouldn't allow it, not even for the few minutes it would take for her to fall asleep. The story—and the removal of the window coverings—were Mother's attempt at keeping the peace.

"Once upon a time," I said, propping myself up on my elbow, "there was a little girl who was afraid of the dark."

"Her name is Lily, remember?" Clara said.

I nodded. "Now, Lily was so afraid of the dark that she tried to figure out a way that she'd never have to be without the sunshine."

I remembered how Mother had lifted her eyebrows when telling a story, the way she leaned forward, how her voice sounded warmer than usual. How it almost sounded as if she was singing.

"She noticed the birds flying in the daytime sky. They went from one tree to another, here and there, any place they wanted," I went on. "Lily wished she could be a bird so she could fly with them. In fact, she thought, if she was a bird, she'd be able to fly all the time, following the sun to all the places it went. If she did that, she'd never have to be in the dark. Not ever."

"Do you think that's possible?" Clara asked.

"I don't know. It's just a story. It doesn't matter if it's possible." I sighed before going on. "Anyway, she closed her eyes hard, turned around four times, and said, 'I wish I could be a bird.' Then she waited."

The change in the girl wasn't instant and it wasn't easy. It took time for her nose to stretch to a pointed beak and for her hair to change to feathers. When her arms folded into wings and her body pitched forward, it hurt like nothing Lily had felt before.

"Once she was changed, she spread her wings, flapping them and jumping until she took off into the sky," I went on. "She flew toward the sun, following it eastward."

"But the sun goes west," Clara corrected.

"All right." I pulled my lips into a tight smile. "Then she followed it west."

I told about how Lily flew around and around the world, always keeping in step with the sun so she'd never see it go down.

"The first two days were the best of her life. She loved that she was never afraid, that she was never in the dark. And she saw wonderful things like the Eiffel Tower and the Grand Canyon." I sat up, tucking my feet under me. "But on the third day she got tired, her arms aching from never having a break from flying. On the fourth, she got sick of seeing the same things all over again. And on the fifth, she gave up. She knew she couldn't go any farther."

Lily found a ledge near the top of a mountain and rested there, hoping to build up her strength.

"Don't forget about the cloud," Clara said.

"I won't." I lowered my voice. "The mountain was so tall that the peak of it was inside a cloud. All Lily could see was gloomy gray. It didn't matter what time of day it was. She couldn't see her hand in front of her face."

"She didn't have hands anymore."

"Right." I cleared my throat.

"Was she afraid?" Clara asked.

"Very afraid. She cried, even," I answered. "The cloud took her tears and turned them into rain that fell on the villages below. That was how much she cried."

Lily stayed on the mountain ledge for as long as she could. But after days and days, she realized that if she stayed there, she would die. She would have to be brave and fly so she could find her way home.

"She closed her eyes tight, turned around three times, and

wished that she wasn't afraid anymore," I said. "Then she waited."

The girl-bird felt her tiny heart warm and her head clear. She felt stronger, more sure. When she opened her eyes, the cloud around the mountain was gone and she could see the sun, not too far away.

"A beam of the sun pointed right to the place where Lily's family lived," I said. "Without being afraid in the least, she spread her wings and flew back home."

Clara scowled at me, her bottom lip pushed out into a slight pout.

"That's not how the story ends," she said, voice flat. "That's not how Mama told it."

"But her ending isn't happy."

"It doesn't have to be."

She rolled over, her back to me.

I wondered what could be so wrong with a happy ending.

Just before I went to bed, I snuck up the stairs to check on Clara and Hugo. His door was ajar, and I looked in to see him, just a little lump under the covers. His breathing was just loud enough for me to hear.

Clara's door was shut, but I could see from the space around the frame that she had the light on.

CHAPTER

sixteen

Early morning sunshine filtered through my window, a welcome change from the gray skies of the days before. I rolled over to find the cat lazing in a sun spot on Norm's side.

"What are you doing in my bed?" I asked.

She lifted her head and blinked long and slow at me before tucking her nose into her crossed paws.

"Are you ready to get up? Or are you going to sleep all day, you lazy bones?" I asked, rubbing my hand along her spine. "Oh, Betty Sweet. You have really lost it. Talking to a cat."

Getting myself ready for the day, I listened for any sign of stirring upstairs but heard nothing. So I tried to be as quiet as possible when I brewed a pot of coffee and made a batch of muffins.

Half an hour later and still no stirring, I decided that they needed all the rest they could get. It didn't bother me, letting them sleep the morning away. I retrieved the morning paper from the stoop as quietly as I could, hoping not to disturb them.

Flannery, however, had another idea.

Very rarely did she venture upstairs. That morning, though,

she did, yowling at the top of her lungs, acting the part of our own rooster.

I'd never been one to rush, but that morning I did. Right up those stairs and to the landing to scoop her up, shushing her to no avail.

I caught Hugo watching me from where he still lay in his bed. He shut his eyes fast, as if he thought I'd not seen him. His little face scrunched up so tight, and I had to cover my mouth to keep from chuckling.

"Psst," I hissed into the room. "Hugo."

He opened his left eye the tiniest bit, his lid quivering.

"Are you awake?" I asked, my voice a whisper. "If you are, I have brown sugar muffins downstairs."

His left eye opened all the way.

"I might be able to find some bacon to fry up too." I stepped into the room on tiptoe, not wanting to disturb Clara in the other room. I bent at the waist once I reached his bedside, letting the cat hop out of my arms and next to him. "If you happen to be awake and hungry, that is."

He sat up, both eyes wide, and licked his lips. The cat butted her head into his shoulder, and he scowled at her.

"Oh, honey. She's not being mean. That's her way of telling you that she likes you," I said. "She certainly does have a funny way of showing it, doesn't she?"

He nodded, still frowning at the cat.

That was when I caught the whiff of something from the bedclothes.

"Are you all right, sweetie?" I asked.

He lowered his face, resting his little chin on his chest as if all of a sudden remembering that he should feel ashamed of himself.

"What is it?" I tilted my head.

"I had an accident," he whispered, drawing away from me just slightly.

"Oh, well that's all right." I stood upright. "It's easy to clean up."

"Are you mad?"

"No. Why would I be?" I smiled at him. "Let's get you cleaned up. Then we'll make that bacon."

He lowered his legs off the bed and to the floor, the old T-shirt he'd worn as pajamas hanging past his knees. In the downstairs bathroom I showed him how to draw water in the tub and where I'd put the soap that he could use.

"Make sure you get the washcloth good and sudsy, all right?" I said. "I'll find something for you to wear once you're all spick-and-span."

I helped him out of the oversized T-shirt, telling him to leave his little briefs on until I was out of the room.

That was when I saw the matching bruises on either arm. They looked like someone had grabbed hold of him so hard, too hard. The purple was faded like they'd been made a few days before. When he realized I'd noticed them, he crossed his arms, concealing the marks with his cupped hands.

"Do they hurt?" I asked, making my voice small, soft.

He shook his head. "Not anymore."

"Who did that?"

He shook his head again, a refusal to tattletale.

"You don't have to tell me." I licked my lips. "But I want you to know that you didn't deserve to be hurt. No matter what. All right?"

He blinked hard twice.

"Well, how about you get into the bath," I said. "Will you call for me if you need anything?"

"Yes, ma'am."

"Good. Just put your briefs on the floor there. I'll get them after you're done."

I closed the door behind me and waited to hear the sloshing of water before I went back upstairs to collect the bedclothes to put in the washing machine. But when I got to the top of the steps, I turned to the other bedroom, pushing the door and looking inside.

"Clara?" I said. "Are you up?"

She rolled toward me, keeping her eyes shut. "I am now."

"I have Hugo in the tub." I walked into the room and stood at the foot of the bed. "He had an accident."

Sitting up, she rubbed at her eyes with the heels of her hands. "Gosh, I'm sorry."

"It's no trouble," I said. "Truly."

"I'll clean it up." She swung her feet off the bed, her legs pale and skinny under the hem of the slip she'd worn as a nightie. "Just give me a minute."

"You don't have to do that. I'm more than happy to."

She shrugged and stood, going to the raggedy suitcase that lay open on the floor against the wall. Crouching, she riffled through the contents.

"He has some angry looking bruises on his arms," I said, fully aware of how my voice trembled.

Clara stilled her hands and let her head drop.

"I don't need to know how he got them," I went on. "But I don't want to see more like them."

"Birdie, I . . ."

"You don't have to explain yourself to me." I turned to leave the room. "I didn't say it to make you feel badly."

I was certain she felt plenty horrible about it already. I

imagined she'd already begged Hugo's forgiveness for her loss of temper. That she'd sobbed at the capacity to do harm that had burbled up inside her.

When I imagined her grief, I saw how much she'd grown to look like our mother.

"He doesn't deserve that kind of treatment," I said before looking at her over my shoulder. "We didn't either."

Those last three words out of my mouth shocked me. It was so seldom that I allowed myself to think about the days our mother had spent angry and mean. I had much rather remembered her days of whimsy and happiness. I'd even let myself think on the times when she tried to sleep away her sadness.

It was simply easier for me to tuck the memories of Mother's rage into a corner of my mind and turn my back on them. It hurt less that way.

"I hate myself for it," Clara said.

"Well, I think he still loves you," I said and stepped out in the hall, making my way to strip Hugo's bed.

It was no trouble at all.

CHAPTER

seventeen

Hugo and I sat on the front stoop, watching Marvel's station wagon inch down the street. When I'd called her after breakfast to let her know that Clara and Hugo were at my house, she'd insisted on paying a visit.

When I'd told her in a whisper that Hugo was black, she'd just lowered her own voice and told me that was all right.

"Nick and Dick would love to meet him," she'd said over the phone.

When I'd asked if she had any hand-me-downs that could fit a five-year-old, she'd yelled for the boys to go through their drawers to find anything that no longer fit. Then she'd asked if Clara could use anything. When I said she could, Marvel told me that she'd be right over.

"Forty-five minutes at the most," she'd said.

Thirty-nine minutes later, she was nearly at my house.

There was no one quite like Marvel DeYoung.

At the corner, she stopped the car, and one of the back doors burst open, letting Nick and Dick out. They ran as fast as their feet would go, trying to best each other, seeing who could reach the house first.

"What are they doing?" Hugo asked.

"Racing each other," I answered. I put a hand on Hugo's shoulder, and he didn't move away from me. "Does it look like they're having fun?"

Just then, one of the twins shoved the other off the sidewalk and into one of my neighbors' hedges.

"No," Hugo answered. "It looks like they're fighting."

"Well, sometimes I wonder if they think fighting is fun."

Hugo nodded, dubious, with his eyes wide as he watched one of the boys sprint the last few feet, jumping up and down in triumph at the end of my driveway. Hugo scooted closer to me.

"Are you feeling shy?" I asked.

He gave a tiny shrug.

"They'll be nice to you, I promise."

"Yes, ma'am," he answered.

"You cheated," the second twin said, catching up to the first.

"Nah," said the first. "Just ran faster."

"Did not." The second twin inspected a fresh scratch on his arm. Most likely from the hedge.

I cleared my throat, and they turned toward Hugo and me. "Hi, boys."

"Hey there, Aunt Betty," the one I guessed was Nick said, making his way to the porch. "Is that Hugo?"

"It is," I answered.

"Glad to meet you." He stuck out his hand to Hugo. "I'm Nick DeYoung."

"And I'm Richard," the other boy said, also offering his hand. "But my friends call me Dick."

Hugo squinted and looked at their hands as if inspecting for grime under the fingernails—which he no doubt found plenty of. Then he took both at the same time, pumping them up and down once before letting go.

"That's our mom." Dick nodded his head toward Marvel.

"Boys, come give me a hand with these, please," she called from the tail end of her car where she held a paper bag on one hip. "Hi there, Hugo."

"Hi." He lifted a hand in a wave.

Marvel made her way across the grass and to the porch. She handed a bag off to me before bending at the knee and putting another on the ground before she wrapped her arms around Hugo, pulling him close. To my surprise, he didn't flinch or pull away.

"Oh, it is so nice to meet you," she said.

"You too," Hugo said after she'd let go of him.

"Her name is Marvel," Nick said. "Like the comic books."

"That's right." Marvel smiled down at Hugo. "Do you like the Fantastic Four, Hugo?"

Hugo's eyes grew wide, and he looked at me as if he was lost.

"It's all right if you don't know them," Nick said. "We can let you read our comic books when you come to our house."

"Mom, are you Hugo's uncle?" Dick asked.

"She couldn't be his uncle," Nick said. "Uncles are men."

"Shows how much you know," Dick sneered at him, then broke into a goofy smile. "So, would you be his uncle, Mom?"

"No," Marvel said. "I'm not sure what I'd be to him."

"You said we were his cousins," Nick said.

"Then that makes Mom his uncle," Dick said.

The left side of his mouth twitched up into a smirk that he'd inherited from his father and I knew he was trying to get his mother's goat. From the exasperated sigh Marvel heaved, I could tell it was working.

"No, Dicky," Marvel said. "If anything, it makes me his aunt."

"But I'm Nick."

"You are not. Now go on in the backyard and play for a little while. We'll figure out who's who later." Marvel nodded toward the back of the house. "And don't teach Hugo any bad habits. I don't need his mother angry at me on account of you."

Nick and Dick ran to the back as if the fate of the world depended on which one of them got through the gate first. Hugo watched them go and took my hand.

"Don't you want to go play?" I asked, bending at the knees and meeting him face-to-face.

"I do," he whispered.

"Then go ahead, sweetie."

But he didn't budge.

"You'll have fun," I said. "If you need anything, I'll be inside."

"Mommy too?" he asked.

I nodded, yet still he held my hand.

"She'll be glad that you're making friends," I said. "Don't you think?"

He looked me right in the eyes as if reading something inside me before letting go and running to join the others.

Something about that made my heart ache.

We carried everything in, taking two trips each, and lined it up on the living room floor. The sounds of the boys wafted in through the open windows.

"I didn't expect you to bring so much," I said, plucking a stuffed puppy from one of the bags.

"Well, it is two boys' worth," Marvel said. "I'm glad someone can use it all. That bag's for Clara."

"She'll be glad." I lowered myself to the floor, folding my knees to one side of me. "She's taking her time this morning."

I didn't say that Clara hadn't come out of her room all morning. I'd hoped she'd get herself around when I told her Marvel and the boys were coming, but she'd told me she wasn't feeling up to it.

"What a nice surprise for you, the two of them showing up." Marvel pushed a strand of hair behind her ear. "I assume it was nice."

I nodded but didn't meet her eyes. Marvel could read me a little too well.

Marvel and I started unpacking the bags, setting everything in neatly folded piles all around us on the floor where we sat. Shirts, slacks, shorts.

"You know what I was thinking about after you called? Remember how hard it was for her when you and Normie got married?" Marvel pulled a green flannel shirt from a bag, holding it up by the shoulders before handing it to me.

"Oh, do I ever." I took the shirt, feeling of its soft fabric between my fingers. "She about barred the door so I couldn't get to the church."

"Do you think she felt like you were abandoning her?"

"Maybe."

I picked a woolly sweater from a pile, thinking Hugo wouldn't need it anytime soon, wondering if he and Clara would be long gone by then. Assuming they would be. I figured they could just take it all with them.

"Remember how he won her over again?" I asked.

Marvel shook her head.

"He had his friend Ivan take her out dancing." I smiled at the memory. "My dad never did find out about that."

"I remember now," Marvel said. "It took Albert a month to get over his hurt feelings."

"He always held a candle for her, didn't he?"

"And she hardly knew he existed." She frowned. "Poor Albie."

I pulled a bag closer to me, the one that had dresses and blouses and slacks for Clara. A pretty cream-colored skirt was folded up on top of the stack.

She'd known about Albert's affection for her. I'd made sure of that. But at my every suggestion, Clara had wrinkled her nose and told me he was "like a brother."

He would have treated her so well, though.

"Do you think Hugo will be able to use any of this?" Marvel asked, folding an empty bag.

"It's all so nice. He'll be pleased, I'm sure."

"I only brought what the boys didn't manage to tear to shreds." She rolled her eyes. "I'm surprised I found as much as I did. I'm convinced those two are part wolverine."

"It's from Stan's side." I winked at her.

"That would not surprise me at all." She handed me a bow tie with polka dots all over it.

"How sweet." I held the tie up, imagining Hugo wearing it. It would be just right for church. "He'll like that, I think."

"I'm glad someone will wear it. Nick and Dick weren't partial to it."

"I don't see why not."

Marvel shrugged, but then something caught her attention behind me. When I turned to see what it was, Clara stood in the doorway wearing the same dress she'd had on the day before. Rumpled and looking as tired as Clara did, the dress made me feel sad.

"Marvel?" she said, striding across the room.

Marvel got up just in time to greet her with a hug.

"Oh, look at how beautiful you are," she said. "And Hugo is adorable."

"Thank you."

They didn't cut the embrace short. They held on to each other a good amount of time.

It was a warmer welcome than I'd offered.

Pop and Stan came over when the bakery closed at noon with steaks from the butcher's to put on the grill. By then Clara had changed into a pair of pedal pushers and a white blouse from one of Marvel's hand-me-down bags. She had her hair rolled into a bun and put a little shadow on her eyelids.

I'd managed to get a few cups of coffee into her too. It was amazing what miracles a little joe could do for a person.

Gone was the anxious woman of the night before. So too was the sullen one of the morning. In their place was the Clara I'd always liked best. Spunky, easygoing, and radiant.

I stood at the kitchen counter, cubing boiled potatoes for a salad and looking out the window. Clara and Pop sat in a couple of lawn chairs Stan had pulled out of the shed. She leaned on the arm of the chair, listening to Pop talk and smiling wider and wider as he went.

"Albie just got here," Marvel said, coming in through the garage door with a pie balancing on her hands. "I sent him out back."

"That's fine," I said. "You can put that on the table if you want."

Out the window I saw Albert walk through the gate and close it behind him. He stopped just on the other side, all his attention on Clara.

"Did he change his clothes?" I asked in a whisper.

The collar of his shirt was too neat to have been worn in the hot bakery, his pants too clean to have been dusted with flour.

"I think so," Marvel answered, joining me at the counter.

When Clara noticed him, she smiled and I heard her greeting to him through the open window. Albert returned it but lowered his head before walking across the yard.

It was as if it was just too much, her gaze.

I decided to focus my attention on the potatoes. The last thing I needed was to cut my finger off.

CHAPTER
eighteen

*I*n the middle of the night I woke to Flannery stepping on my head so she could look out my bedroom window. I tried shooing her, but she just meowed her refusal and jumped up to balance on my headboard.

I rolled over to look at the alarm clock. The glow-in-the-dark hand pointed to half past three.

I groaned and gave a stink eye to the cat, who couldn't have cared in the least.

"This is why you got kicked out of your old house, isn't it?" I whispered at her.

Flannery flicked her tail and went on ignoring me.

I thought I should get up to go to the bathroom and get a little drink of water. When I stepped out of my bedroom door, I heard a bumping kind of sound. Drawing in a sharp breath, I stilled myself, waiting to hear another noise. When I didn't, I tiptoed into the hallway.

Just the house settling, I figured. I turned toward the bathroom before heading back to bed.

But then I heard the sound again. And again. It was coming from the basement.

My heartbeat quickened and my breathing shallowed. Before, I would have roused Norman to go check and see what it was. He'd have ventured down groggily in his undershirt and boxer shorts, tying his robe at his middle as he went. Of course, he'd find nothing and refuse my apologies for getting him up.

"My job is to make sure you're safe," he'd say, climbing back into bed and falling asleep as soon as his head touched the pillow.

Norm wasn't there and I had Clara and Hugo to look after, so I went to the kitchen and got my heaviest rolling pin, holding it cocked at the ready on my shoulder in case I needed to brain an intruder. Inching down the stairs, I felt my body go numb and noticed every sound.

Padding footsteps on the bare concrete floor. A bumping of something on metal followed by a heaving grunt.

At the bottom step, I hesitated, drawing in a good breath before stepping into the basement.

There, instead of a burglar or rat, Hugo stood in front of the washing machine, a bundle of bedclothes in his arms.

"Honey," I said, lowering the rolling pin and letting out the air I'd been holding. "What are you doing? It's the middle of the night."

"Cleaning up," he answered, trying to lift the armload to the mouth of the washer.

"Did you have another accident?" I put the roller on the bottom step and walked toward him, trying not to notice how he flinched when I drew near. I put both hands behind my back so he'd know I had no intention of grabbing or hurting him. "It's all right. Remember? It's not something to be upset about."

I reached the washer and turned on the water before measuring in the detergent. As gently as I could, I took the sheets and blanket from him, working them evenly into the drum. His arms empty, he lowered them to his sides. He'd worn an old set of the twins' pajamas. Red flannel far too warm for June, but the cowboys on horseback printed all over the material had so delighted him he'd insisted on wearing them.

"I'll need to wash those next," I said.

His eyes grew round as if he might cry.

"You can have them back tomorrow as soon as they're dry." I nodded. "I promise."

"I don't have to throw them away?"

"Of course not, honey." I ran the pad of my thumb under his eye, knocking a tear off his cheek. "Why would we throw them away?"

"Mommy says . . ."

Then he stopped and shut his mouth as if he was trying to keep something in.

"Mommy was upset when she said it?" I asked.

He nodded.

"I think sometimes adults say things they don't mean when they're upset. Don't you?"

"Yes, ma'am."

"Well, Aunt Betty says she can wash nearly anything," I said. "Besides, I think I saw a blue pair of jammies just like those when I put everything in your drawers. Isn't that something?"

He nodded.

"Let's go get you cleaned up, huh?" I put my palm on his cheek.

He walked beside me to the foot of the steps, where I leaned down to pick up the rolling pin.

"I'm sorry," he said before taking the first step.

"You didn't do it on purpose," I said. "I'm not angry."

"You won't tell Mommy, will you?"

I shook my head. "This will be our little secret."

Upstairs, cleaned up, and in the fresh blue pajamas, he helped me put clean linens on the bed. Once tucked in, he let me stay beside him until he fell back to sleep, his breath coming slower and deeper.

I stood as quietly as I could so as not to disturb him and reached for the switch on the bedside lamp. Before I turned off the light, I took one more look at his little face. His lips were parted, just slightly, and his long eyelashes curled against his cheek.

He held the silky edge of the blanket in his clenched fist just like Clara had when she was his age.

I clicked off the light, hoping they'd stick around.

By the time I made my way down the stairs, I knew that I would never fall back to sleep. So, I went to the living room, thinking about finding a book to read until Hugo got back up in the morning.

When I crouched down by the bookcase, I saw the old photo album, jutting out farther than the other spines on the shelf. Sighing, I resigned myself to looking at it. The middle of the night seemed the right time for facing memories that one would never be able to confront in the daylight.

Inside the front cover, in my mother's looping and curling script, was listed the name of each family member that she could think of. Date of birth and date of death followed their names. Behind hers—Etta Johnson—was written the day she died in Clara's uncertain and less than neat hand. February 18, 1935.

I cleared my throat and turned to the next page.

There was a photo of the four of us standing next to the steps of our apartment building. Dad had on his work clothes—a white jumpsuit that he had when he delivered milk—and stood with hands in the pockets. Clara was right in front of him, her hands clenched in fists as if ready for a fight. My hands were clasped in front of me, eyes wide as if I was afraid to blink. Both of us girls had on sad excuses for winter coats. Threadbare and thin, they did very little to keep the biting wind out.

Mother stood off to the side as if she wasn't meant to be in the picture. As if she was simply passing through, walking by a little family that she'd never seen before.

A family she wouldn't see again.

The photo had been taken the Christmas before my mother died. I only knew because it had been written on the white border of the picture.

I put my finger on the page beside the glossy photo, afraid that if I touched it, I would leave fingerprints, spoiling the picture.

Looking into the past was opening a door to recollections that were not necessarily welcome. That night I wished I could shut them out, but they filed in anyway.

One scrap of memory stood out clearer than the rest.

I was meant to be asleep. It was a school night. Clara snored, unperturbed by the sounds of my parents arguing in the next room. I, on the other hand, shook with every raised voice and jumped at each slammed door.

"Why don't you just give me a divorce?" Mother had screamed at one point. "Go marry someone better! I know that's what you want."

After a while, as usually happened, they both ran out of steam.

Dad went to bed and Mother came to our room to check on us. When she opened the door, I shut my eyes so she wouldn't know I was awake. She touched my forehead with her cold hand.

"I wish I could be the mother you need me to be," she'd whispered. "You deserve better."

By the next afternoon she was gone. My dad had taken her to the sanitarium.

I never saw her again.

Forgetting the fear of smudging the photo, I put my finger on the image of my mother.

"I didn't need a better mother," I whispered, voice cracking. "I just needed you."

With all the care in the world, I closed the album and put it back on the shelf.

nineteen

*C*lara didn't get out of bed on Sunday morning. In fact, she didn't get up until well past lunch and after I'd cleaned up the leftover roast Hugo and I had eaten after church. She hadn't stayed downstairs long before saying she was tired and needed to get more sleep.

Monday she stayed in bed until suppertime, not eating more than a few forkfuls of casserole before claiming that her stomach was upset.

Tuesday she promised to get up but never did.

On Wednesday she didn't move from under the covers, even as hot as it was.

I did my best to keep Hugo busy during the day so he wouldn't disturb her, so she could sleep off whatever ailed her.

All the while I had my suspicions. It was simply too familiar, her behavior. Her staying in bed.

When Hugo paid her visits, sitting on the edge of her mattress and talking to her, I remembered taking turns with Clara to do the same with our mother, trying to call her back to us from whatever dark place she'd retreated to.

I did my best to push away the thoughts of how it hadn't worked with Mother.

By Thursday I decided that enough was enough. I wouldn't sit by and allow her to waste away up there in my guest room. I put Hugo in front of *Captain Kangaroo* and tiptoed my way up the stairs, letting myself into Clara's room.

A more determined woman, one in command of her home, would have stormed in. She might have dragged Clara out of the bed and tossed her into the tub for a good soaking, insisting on getting her out of her dark mood.

But I was no such woman.

From the looks of Clara, that determined woman would have squashed her like a bug. She lay in the bed, greasy hair plastered against her face that seemed even paler than the day before. The purple under her eyes made her blue irises look dim.

It nearly seemed impossible, that the woman who had smiled so beautifully at Pop's stories on Saturday could appear so vacant just five days later.

I remembered what Mother had said once: "The demons drag me under fast."

I hadn't understood what she meant. How could a little girl comprehend a thing like that? But standing in the doorway, looking down at Clara, I thought I finally knew what she'd meant.

Just the idea of that made goose bumps prickle up on my arms.

"Sweetie," I said, using a soft voice just above a whisper. "How about we try to get you up and at 'em?"

She didn't roll away from me and she didn't sigh.

"I was thinking of taking Hugo somewhere today." I took a

few steps into the room and slid my hands into the pockets of my skirt. "Don't you think it would be nice for the three of us to get out of the house?"

"Did I ever tell you what Dad said?" she asked, voice crackly. "What he said to me?"

"I don't think so." I tilted my head. "What did he say?"

"He said I was just like her."

"Who?"

"Like Mama."

I took one step closer to her. "When did he say that?"

She lifted her left hand and ran it across her face, pulling the skin tight against her cheekbones.

"I don't know." She cleared her throat. "He said I was crazy just like her."

She betrayed no emotion when she spoke. Gave no clue that what he'd said had hurt her feelings. But the way her eyes searched my face, I knew that she wanted me to say something. She wanted me to say the right thing.

"You aren't crazy," I said.

It was all I could think of.

"You're a bad liar," she said.

That was when she rolled over, pulling the covers all the way up over her head. Shut out, I left the room, pulling the door closed behind me.

I called up Marvel to see what she was doing to keep her boys occupied that day, hoping she'd invite us over. She didn't disappoint.

"Join us," she said. "I've got plenty of bologna to slap on bread for lunch."

I decided that we should have a little dessert to go along with the sandwiches. When I was in need of something sweet, there was only one place to go.

Hugo held my hand as we walked from where we'd parked to the bakery, and I didn't mind in the least. The day was what Mom Sweet would have called "close," the air thick as a cloud. Even without the sun, it was hot with the promise of even more stifling temperatures in the afternoon.

I did not envy the fellas working in the bakery. It was days like that when Norm would come home at lunch to get a fresh shirt after sweating all the way through the first one.

Walking toward us on the sidewalk were a couple of ladies I recognized from around town. We were friendly enough, but I couldn't have claimed to be on a first-name basis with either of them.

I lifted my free hand in a wave that neither of them saw. Their eyes were on Hugo, as if they'd never seen such a thing as a little boy walking down the street with his aunt.

I knew, though, what it was about this particular little boy and his aunt that had so stunned them. Namely the way my skin color contrasted with his. I wanted to call out and ask if they had completely forgotten their manners, staring like that.

Instead, I put my arm around Hugo's shoulder and steered him toward the front door of Sweet Family Bakery.

"Do you like cookies?" I asked.

"Yes, ma'am," he answered.

"What kind?"

"Oatmeal raisin."

I touched my lips to remind myself not to laugh at his answer. Never in all my life had I heard of a boy liking oatmeal raisin cookies. I half wondered if Hugo wasn't really an old man trapped in a child's body.

"How about we ask Pop if he has some of those," I said, leading him through the propped open door.

As steamy as it was outside, it was downright roasting inside. Hugo, though, seemed not to notice. So taken was he by the cases full of cookies and muffins, I thought he would have stayed there all afternoon and been plenty happy.

Pop grinned at Hugo's delight and offered him whatever he'd like. "Go ahead," he said.

At the endless possibilities, Hugo seized up, unable to make a decision. Near tears, he curled his shoulders forward and blinked hard.

"Do you remember what you were going to ask for?" I said. "What kind of cookie do you like best?"

He shrugged.

"Was it oatmeal cricket cookies?" I asked.

Hugo grimaced and shook his head.

"Oh, I think I know," Pop said. "Brussel sprout chip. Am I right?"

Hugo wrinkled his nose.

"How about slug butter cookies?" I asked.

"No," Hugo said, accompanied by a giggle. "Oatmeal raisin."

"Well, why didn't you say so?" Pop winked at him. "I keep those right next to the dog food puffs."

"You're joshing me," Hugo said.

"Might be." Pop waved him behind the counter. "I'll get you a cookie. Maybe even two if Aunt Betty looks the other way."

"Don't spoil him too much," I said.

"If you don't like it, just go on back and get yourself a glass of iced tea," he said. "Al just made some fresh."

"Well, I suppose so." I sighed. "While you're at it, could you pick out a few cookies for Nick and Dick? Maybe something for Marvel and me too?"

"Sure thing."

"Hugo," I said. "I'll be right in there if you need me."

"Oh, for goodness' sake." Pop waved me off. "The boy'll be fine. Go. Go."

Stifling a protest, I did as Pop said, going around the counter and into the kitchen, breathing in the good smells of melted butter mixed with cinnamon.

"Hi, there," I said, seeing Albert at the kneading board. "What are you making back here?"

"Cinnamon rolls," he answered, grinning at me over his shoulder. "Mom's recipe."

"What's the occasion?" I poured myself a glass of tea from Mom's old pitcher and spooned in more sugar than I had any reason to.

Mom Sweet had a whole box full of special recipes that were reserved for only the very special days.

"See this box," she'd said just after I'd become Norm's wife. "These recipes are only for family. We never make them to sell."

When I'd asked her why not, she put her hand on top of the card box and lowered her voice.

"Because some things we need to keep just for ourselves." Flipping the lid, she showed me card after card. "Every one of these has a story. When I bake them, I think of memories of my children or my parents. Sometimes they make me smile and sometimes I get sad. But those memories? They're the stories that bind us. And they're meant just for special."

That recipe box of Mom's was nothing fancy, just cedarwood with a hinged top, and I suspected that Albert had no need to look at the instructions on the cards inside. Still, it sat on the kneading board, a safe distance away from the sprinkled flour and tacky dough.

"It's Stan's birthday tomorrow," Albert said, stilling his rolling pin before changing angles and pushing it again over the dough.

I set my glass on the counter. "How could I have forgotten?"

"You don't need to be hard on yourself." He shook his head. "You've had a heck of a summer already."

"Well, I know." I touched my forehead, dabbing at the beads of sweat along my hairline. "Still, I should be able to remember the good things, shouldn't I?"

"Better to be reminded today than tomorrow." He stood upright, stretching his back. "He wants to go to the drive-in to celebrate. There's some movie he's been wanting to see."

"All right." I sipped my tea.

"Uh, Clara and Hugo are invited to come too."

If I didn't know any better, I would have thought that Albert's voice cracked.

"I'll let her know," I said.

"Pop said she's having a hard time," he said, peeking at me out of the corner of his eye.

"Oh, it's nothing, really." My glass made a tapping sound when I put it on the counter. "She's just a little bit under the weather."

I bit the inside of my cheek so I wouldn't embellish on the lie. I'd had a lot of practice when I was a little girl, telling fibs to cover up for my mother's bad days. There I was, doing the same for my sister. It seemed worse, though, because it was Albert I'd lied to.

He nodded once, and I thought I read disappointment in his profile. Clara had been right. I was a lousy liar.

The back door opened, letting in a rush of humid air that cut the smell of baking with the sharpness of coming rain. Stan pulled the door shut again.

"Welp, that was an interesting meeting," he said. Then, noticing me, he smiled. "Hey, Betty. I didn't know you were going to be here."

"We just stopped by for a few minutes on the way to your house." I took another drink of tea. "Hugo's out front getting spoiled by Pop."

"It's what the old man is best at." Stan grabbed his apron and slung it around his neck. "You coming to the movie tomorrow night?"

"I hope so."

"Good deal." He tied the strings behind his back.

"What was the meeting?" I asked. "If I can be snoopy."

"It was with the man who owns Lazy Morning," Albert said, sprinkling the sugar and cinnamon mixture over the rolled-out dough. "He wants to buy us out."

"They sent me because I'm the meanest of the three of us," Stan said, crossing his arms. "I said we were doing just fine, thank you very much."

"Well, good for you." I nodded.

"I sure hope we can hold out." He loosened his arms and shoved his hands into his apron pocket. "He said they're coming to LaFontaine whether we sell or not."

Albert, never one to talk much about his feelings, just went on dropping the filling onto the dough. His shoulders slumped, and that told me everything I needed to know.

"Anyway, enough of that unpleasantness. We don't need to worry about all that." Stan swatted at the air. "You know what you're in for at my house today, don't you?"

"Oh, that question makes me a little nervous."

"Nick and Dick are digging themselves a mud pool in the backyard."

"A mud pool?"

"Yes." He gave me a crooked grin. "I know I'll regret it later, but it's keeping them busy."

"Poor Marvel," I said.

"No. Lucky Marvel," he said. "They'll be all worn out at bedtime. All she'll have to do is hose them down before supper."

I smiled at the idea of it.

"It'll be good for Hugo." He drew water from the sink, scrubbing his hands. "Let the kid get a little dirty."

"I'm not sure Hugo will want to," I said. "He's such a neat little boy."

"Betty, if ever there was a boy who needed to get a little muddy, it's him." He turned off the faucet. "I kind of wish I could be there to see it."

"I'll make sure Marvel gets a picture," I said. "I'll see you boys tomorrow."

"All right," Stan said, tossing a damp hand towel into the hamper that stood in the far corner. "Have fun."

"I'll try." I grinned. "Bye, Albie."

He told me good-bye without looking up from rolling the pastry, a pretty cinnamon line swirling in between cream-colored layers of dough. He paid the work such attention, the tip of his tongue sticking out between his lips ever so slightly.

I pictured Mom, remembering when I watched her make the cinnamon rolls the night before Christmas. She was every bit as precise as Albert, but she was as carefree as could be. She took such joy from making them.

I didn't know the story she'd assigned to that recipe. But I knew the one I had bound to those rolls. It was her, sleeves rolled up on her forearms and her hearty laugh filling the kitchen.

At the end of the rolling, Albert looked up at me and smiled.

In that look I saw a glimmer of her. Just a spark, but it was enough.

CHAPTER
twenty

Stan and Marvel DeYoung lived in the house Pop Sweet had ordered out of a Sears and Roebuck catalog when Norm was just a baby. After Mom passed away, he'd given them an interest-free loan and he'd moved into the little apartment above the bakery.

By then they'd had the twins and we knew they needed the space. There was no question, it was the right thing. Besides, it was nice to keep the house in the family.

I pulled the Bel Air into the drive behind Marvel's station wagon. Hugo was in the front seat, all the way to the edge and with his hands on the dashboard. His little fingers drummed along with the hopping rhythm of the song on the radio. It was a catchy tune, and I found myself humming along to the melody of "Walk Right In."

I suspected, though, that Hugo's tapping had less to do with the song and more with being nervous.

"What's wrong?" I asked.

He shrugged, still keeping an eye on the house.

"Are you worried about something?"

He nodded.

"Your mommy?"

"Yes."

"I tell you what." I turned in my seat so I was angled toward him. "I want you to have fun with the boys. That's your job today. All right? And it will be my job to worry about your mother today."

Eyebrows knit and lips pushed together, he turned toward me.

"We're letting her rest for another day." I put my hand on his shoulder. "I think she'd want you to play hard. She wants you to laugh a lot. Do you think you can do that?"

"Maybe I can try."

He turned back toward the house. Just seconds later, Nick and Dick came crashing through the gate from the backyard, hands and bottom half of their legs covered in mud.

"What's your job today?" I asked.

"To have fun?"

"That's right." I nodded toward the twins. "And don't be afraid to get dirty."

"Yes, ma'am," he answered before pushing the door open.

Looking at me over his shoulder, he smiled. It was a small smile, more of a grin, but it was nice to see either way.

The twins met him at the driveway and nodded toward the backyard, saying something about how they'd been waiting forever to jump in the mud with him. All three raced off, and it did my heart good to see Hugo keeping up with them. I wasn't even miffed that he'd forgotten to close the car door.

The boy needed some time to just be a boy.

Marvel's kitchen looked just the way it had when it had belonged to her mother. The cupboards were a light wood color with the white porcelain knobs Mom Sweet had loved. The counters were the light blue tile she'd always hated.

I stepped in through the kitchen door—not knocking—and put my foot on the checkerboard floor and felt nothing but happy memories.

I could almost see Norman's mother standing at the sink, her back to me and her apron tied loosely around her thick middle. When I blinked, the image passed, and Marvel came in from the hallway.

"Goodness, what a hot day. I just turned on the attic fan," she said. "Every year I ask Stanley how much it would cost to get an air-conditioner. Every year we decide it's too expensive. But on days like this, I wonder if it might be worth it."

"Oh, just wait a few months." I dropped my purse onto the counter. "We'll be freezing again."

"Isn't that the truth." She dabbed a white hanky against her forehead. "I saw Hugo out back. I warned the boys to be on their best behavior."

"I just hope he can let himself have fun." I set the cookies down and pulled at the folds in the bag. I took out two, making sure neither had raisins, and handed one to Marvel.

"Just what I need," she said, taking a bite. "At the rate I'm going, I won't fit in my swimsuit."

"I'm just impressed that you still have one." I broke my cookie in half. "I don't think I've worn one since Norman and I got married."

"Oh, honey, you need to get out more." Marvel winked at me. "We'll go to the lake this summer with the boys."

"That would be fun."

"Do you think Hugo and Clara will still be around in a few weeks?" She licked a crumb off the pad of her thumb. "We could go over to Grand Haven or Holland once the lake warms up a little. Just a day trip."

"Well, I'm not sure," I said. "We'll have to see what happens."

Out the window I saw Hugo standing on the dry edge of a puddle that took up nearly a quarter of the backyard. Nick and Dick were both sitting in it, already completely filthy. From the looks of it, they were trying to convince Hugo to join them.

"I can't believe you let the boys make a mud pit," I said, turning toward her.

"I can't either." She opened the refrigerator and pulled out a pitcher of lemonade. "You want some?"

"Yes, please." I grabbed two glasses out of the strainer, catching another glimpse at the boys through the window over the sink.

It didn't take nearly as much begging as I would have thought before Hugo pinched his nose and jumped right in the middle of the puddle, sending the dirty water in splashes all over the twins. Nick and Dick put their arms up, cheering for him.

I couldn't help but hoot with laughter. What a delight to see him do a thing like that.

When the water settled, I saw Hugo covered in mud and wearing the biggest smile I'd seen on him yet.

It was such a departure from the boy with worried eyebrows and pinched-together lips.

"Would you look at that," Marvel said, standing close beside me and resting the pitcher on the counter. "I knew he had it in him."

She filled our glasses and smiled.

We sat at the table, each of us enjoying just one more cookie. Marvel squinted her eyes and put a finger to the tip of her chin.

"I lied to Albie today," I said.

"Don't beat yourself up too much about it," Marvel said. "I lied to him yesterday."

"You did?"

"Well, I don't feel good about it." She slouched in her chair. "I guess he bought some new cologne at the Five and Dime. He wanted to know if it smelled good."

"And?"

"Oh, Betty. It didn't." A laugh broke through and she shook her head. "It was—oh—it was strong. But I didn't want to hurt his feelings."

"He bought cologne? And wore it?"

Marvel nodded. "I think it has something to do with you-know-who."

"Clara?" I sighed. "That poor man."

"Now, spill it." Marvel leaned forward. "What did you lie to him about?"

"I told him that Clara was under the weather," I said. "But I think it's worse than that."

"Oh." Her smile dropped and she moved back in her chair. "What's wrong?"

I took a sip of my lemonade, glancing out the window again to see what the boys were up to. All I could see was mud and all I could hear were loud voices from out back.

I put my glass on the table. "I don't know exactly. She's scared and sad and refuses to get out of bed."

"Do you think that's why she came home?"

I shrugged, no answer to her question. But the last word stuck in my mind. Home. Clara had come home. It was where she belonged.

"I've told you about my mother," I said. "Haven't I?"

Marvel nodded.

"Clara's a bit like her."

From outside I heard a long laugh and a sploosh. When I looked up, I saw splashes of muddy water splattering into the air.

"I worry most about him." I nodded toward the backyard. "It's hardest on him and I'm at a loss as to how I can help."

"You know what I was just thinking about the other day?" she asked. "When Dick was so sick with the measles and pneumonia. Do you remember that?"

"How could I forget?" I shook my head. "It was terrifying."

"We had more than a few close calls, didn't we?" She pushed out a puff of air.

The poor thing had been in the hospital for so long and he was so very miserable. I'd come sit with him late at night so Marvel could sleep, even if it was just in a cushion-less armchair in the corner of the hospital room.

"What made it even worse was how frightened Nick was," she said. "Gosh, it made me mad that they wouldn't let him visit Dick. All it did was make his imagination run wild and give him awful dreams about his brother dying."

"Those were difficult days. I remember."

"And what did you do?" She crossed her arms and grinned at me. "You came over every night before bedtime to tell Nick stories. And then you'd come to the hospital and tell the same ones to Dick."

"Well, Nick said it would make him feel better if I did that."

"It did, honey." Marvel reached for me, cupping her hand around my bent elbow. "Maybe Hugo needs a couple of Aunt Betty's bedtime stories."

"I don't know," I said. "It's been so long."

She shook her head. "Not that long."

I nodded and caught a tear on the back of my hand. "I don't know why I'm crying."

"Because you love him."

"I wish he had it easier," I said, sniffling. "I wish Clara had it easier. Her life has been so difficult."

"I know, Betty. I know." She leaned forward in her chair. "She'll get there eventually. Don't you think so?"

"Oh, I hope so."

"Now, how about we make a few sandwiches for the mud monsters?" she said. "I'll bet they're working up quite the appetite."

"I'm sure they are."

I took my empty glass to the sink and watched the boys while I waited for her to get all the fixings out of the fridge. I could only tell which one was Hugo because he was quite a bit smaller than the twins.

He took a great glob of gunk and smashed it right on top of his own head. I covered my mouth, catching a laugh that felt so good when it came out.

It little mattered to me how long it would take to spray the mud off of his skin or scrub it out of his curls. What mattered—truly mattered—was watching him being a little boy.

I just wished that Clara could have seen him too.

twenty-one

$\mathcal{I}$ had a little notebook that held all the stories that I'd told Nick and Dick over the years. They weren't *Grimms' Fairy Tales* or anything deserving a proper binding, but they were good enough.

Hugo was already in his bed, an old teddy bear from the twins safe in the crook of his elbow.

"What's that?" he asked, squinting at the notebook.

"Well, it has some stories that I've made up," I answered.

"You make up stories?" His face opened up in awe.

"I try." I sat on the end of his bed, not taking offense when he pulled his feet up toward himself. The boy liked his space. I didn't need to let it hurt my feelings. "Would you like me to tell you one?"

He nodded and drew his knees up to his chin, wrapping his arms around his legs.

"There once was a boy named Hugo," I started, looking up from the book to see his expression.

Where I'd hoped to see delight, I instead noticed indifference.

"What's wrong?" I asked.

"No. Not Hugo," he said, his lip curled.

"Oh, I thought you'd want a story about you."

"I already know all my stories." He pushed his lips to one side. "Can he have a different name?"

"Sure. How about Jimmy?"

He nodded and moved just a tiny bit closer to me. I reached forward and patted the arm that he had slung around his bear's neck. Hugo had on his red flannel cowboy pajamas even though it had been in the upper eighties that day. It little mattered to him how hot it had been. He loved those jammies.

"Jimmy lived in a big city with loud cars and trucks always driving up and down the streets and noisy people shouting wherever he went."

"Why were they shouting?"

"Well, that was the only way anyone could be heard. That's how loud it was," I said. "All throughout the day he'd look up to see the sky, but there was too much smog making dirty gray clouds above his head. At night he couldn't see the stars because of the too-bright lights that dimmed them."

"Were there any birds?"

"If there were, Jimmy never heard them over the shouting people and honking horns," I answered. "One day, while Jimmy looked out his window, he saw a balloon floating through the air."

"What color was it?" Hugo asked in his tiny voice. "Was it yellow?"

"It was," I answered. "How did you know that?"

"Just did."

"Well, you're very smart." I winked at him and was so glad to see his gentle smile. "The boy jumped from rooftop to rooftop, swinging from laundry lines when the buildings were too far apart, climbing up fire escapes, all so he could chase that balloon."

"Why did he want to chase it?"

"Because it called to him. Above the traffic and noise of people yelling out their windows, the balloon called to him. Somehow it even knew his name."

"Jimmy," he said, drawing it out like a beckoning.

"By the end of the day, Jimmy reached the very last building of the city. The telephone lines ended and so did the paved roads. The things of the city were replaced by trees and grass and fields of flowers."

The boy, I went on to say, stepped in the grass, pleased by its softness. He took in air not thickened by the exhaust of cars. He closed his eyes to hear the peeping tweets of birds that flew just over his head.

"And that was when he first felt afraid," I said.

"What was he scared of?" Hugo asked. "Does this story get scary? I don't like those kinds."

"Don't worry. I don't tell ghost stories," I said. "Poor Jimmy was afraid of all of it. The sky was too blue and the grass too cool under his feet. The air was so clean it made his body feel too alive. The birds were so beautiful that he was sure his heart would break."

"Why's he afraid of that?"

"Because he was just sure it would never last."

"He didn't have to go back, did he?" Hugo said. "Aunt Betty, don't make him go back."

"Hold on, sweetie. The story isn't over yet." I cleared my

throat. "The boy thought that if he ran into the fields, if he could get far enough away from the city, he'd be able to escape. He'd finally be free."

So, the boy ran until he came to a river. The balloon bobbed in the sky, leading him along the bank until it stopped.

"That yellow balloon floated in the air right in front of a castle," I said.

"Was it a real castle?" Hugo asked. "Where a king lived?"

"That was just what Jimmy wondered." I nodded. "You sure are smart, you know. Jimmy looked up at that castle. It was made of stone and yellow plaster and had spires that pointed up to the sky."

Hugo made a perfect circle with his lips.

"An old woman lived in that castle," I went on. "She was the queen of all the land."

"A good queen or a bad one?" He leaned forward, shifting his weight so he was on the side of his hip. I could almost feel the warmth of him so close to me.

"A good one this time." I touched his nose. "And she gave him a bowl of tomato soup that tasted better than anything he'd ever eaten. She followed it with a piece of cake so soft and with frosting so sweet he thought maybe he'd made it all the way to heaven."

I told Hugo about how the woman let the boy sleep in a warm bed with clean covers and a feather pillow that eased him into only good dreams of beautiful days.

"Jimmy stayed there for months, climbing the big oak around back of the castle and catching fireflies at night. Sometimes he even went fishing for pike and catfish. He ate sweet peas right out of the garden and picked juicy raspberries that the woman made into pies every afternoon."

"I like raspberries," Hugo said.

"Me too." I couldn't help but smile at that boy. "The queen enjoyed having Jimmy around so much, she asked if he'd like to be a son to her."

"He'd be a prince?"

"If he wanted to be."

"But something bad has to happen, remember?" Hugo asked. "Mommy says if it doesn't, it's not a good story."

"Thank you for reminding me," I said. "One morning when the boy woke up, he saw that the leaves turned from dazzling green to blazing reds and oranges. The air had a bit of a nip to it. Some of the birds left. Then, a few days later, the leaves all dropped to the ground, and the trees were naked."

At that, Hugo let out a little giggle.

"The boy thought the trees had all died."

"But they didn't. It was just fall."

"Well, you know that, and I know that. But poor Jimmy sure didn't. What a shock he had that morning." I lowered my voice. "He went to the oak, the one who had become such a good friend to him. He put his hands on the trunk, trying to feel life in it, but all he could feel was the rough bark as he worked his fingers into the furrows and ridges. He climbed up in the branches, inspecting where the leaves had once been, wondering what could have happened."

"Poor Jimmy."

"Yes. Poor Jimmy indeed." I shook my head. "The days became shorter, and he feared the sun was going away forever. The clouds became a gloomy gray and the air was colder than it had been."

"Did he have a coat?"

"I'm sure he did."

"What happened to the balloon?"

"Why, it went away when the weather turned. One day it was there, the next it was gone."

"That's too bad," Hugo said.

"Through it all, the old queen didn't seem alarmed. She went out and raked the crisped leaves and brought out extra blankets from the linen closet. She chopped wood into logs for the fire and preserved what she'd harvested from the garden. All the while, Jimmy mourned the beautifully bright days he'd come to love."

"Why didn't she tell him it was just fall?"

"Because . . ." I started, hoping to come up with something good enough.

"She thought he already knew?"

"Exactly that." I sighed. "Poor Jimmy's fears that the good couldn't last seemed to be coming true."

I told about how the boy wasn't quick to rise in the mornings and he was sluggish during the day. When it came time for sleep, he burrowed deep beneath the pile of blankets the woman had put on his bed. He looked to the sky and despaired of ever seeing a bright color again.

"The old woman noticed the change in him," I continued. "She came to him with a cup of tea . . ."

"Hot cocoa," Hugo corrected.

"All right, hot cocoa," I said, trying not to laugh. "With whipped cream?"

"Marshmallows."

"Ah yes. Of course. And she asked him to tell her what was the matter."

"She was nice about it?"

"Why wouldn't she be? There's no use being mean to someone

who's upset," I said. "And he told her how sad and frightened he was. He asked if it was his fault that everything was dying."

"She didn't laugh at him," Hugo said.

"She did not. It's rude to laugh when someone's upset, don't you think?"

He nodded.

"But she did put her soft arms around him and let him cry for the oak tree and the leaves, for the drooping flowers and empty garden. She listened to him speak of missing the birds and the sunshine."

"She said it was okay to be sad."

"Yes, because it is. And then she kissed his forehead and told him she had good news," I said.

The old woman spoke softly, gently. She told the boy that if he could wait a handful of months more, they'd all return. The trees would flower with new leaves and the ground would soften again, ready for fresh seeds. Day would last longer than night again and the birds would come back home with new songs to sing.

"She told him that the cold and dark was only for a little while. She warned him about the snow that was soon coming," I said. "But she also told him about building snowmen and making snow angels."

"And catching snowflakes in his mouth?"

"Of course. That too." I rubbed my thumb on the back of his hand. "The old woman told Jimmy about a new time that would come and that he would love the spring more because of the winter. He learned to find beauty in the frost that spread over the glass window in his room. She taught him how to skate on the frozen river and to build the perfect snow fort. After their days playing outside, he enjoyed coming in to a steaming cup of hot cocoa."

"And a sweater she made him?" Hugo asked.

"Oh, that was the best of all," I said. "Then one day he found that the snow was melting, that the sun peeked out more often, that the air smelled new again. Another day he heard the honking return of geese and noticed bits of yellow on the fingertips of branches."

The boy climbed up the tree, I went on to say, inching himself to the very end of a strong branch, daring to touch the small twigs shooting out of it. It was there he saw the flower of gold that soon would burst into leaf.

"And, far off in the sky, he saw the yellow balloon, bobbing up and down on the breeze," I said. "This time not calling him. This time, reminding him that he was right where he belonged."

"The end?" Hugo asked.

"Yes. The end."

"It was a good story." He rested his head against my shoulder, and I tried not to move.

"I'm glad you liked it," I said.

"Can you tell me another tomorrow?"

"I'll see if I can come up with something good." I patted his cheek before standing. "Now, get settled in."

"Can you tuck me in?" he asked, moving toward the head of his bed and hunkering down on his pillow.

"Of course I can." I clicked my tongue to call Flannery and let her jump up past me to get to Hugo's side before I pulled the sheet up to cover him just at the waist.

"I like being here with you," he said. "Can I stay here forever?"

"Well, I like having you here too." I straightened the covers at the foot of the bed. "You and your mommy can stay as long as you'd like."

"Do you promise?"

I nodded, the warmth in my chest having nothing to do with the hot evening.

"Good night," I whispered.

"Aunt Betty?"

"Yes?"

"Are castles real?" he asked. "Or are they just in stories?"

"They're real."

"Have you ever seen one?"

"Hm." I touched a finger to the end of my chin. "As a matter of fact, yes."

"You have?"

I bent at the waist to be closer to him. "Would you like to see it tomorrow?"

He nodded and he reached his arms up, pulling me down into a hug.

It very nearly took my breath away.

CHAPTER
twenty-two

When I was a young wife, I kept a journal hidden in my bedside table. Every morning after Norm went off to work, I'd scribble down a thought or two in it. Sometimes I even dared write a poem. They'd been silly little verses about being in love, nothing worth sharing at all.

It wasn't until after our second anniversary that Norman found it, riffling in my drawer for spare change to pay a bill that had come due. He'd brought it to me, his face beaming.

I had been utterly and completely mortified.

"You didn't read it," I'd asked. "Did you?"

"You like to write," he'd said by way of answering.

"That's private, Norman." I'd gone on tiptoe to pluck it from his hand. "I'm so embarrassed."

"Don't be." He let me have it. "I like what you wrote about me."

"Don't tease me, Norman John."

"I'm not." He'd put his arm around me. "You shouldn't hide it away like that, you know. I bet you could write a whole book."

"That's silly."

"No, I mean it."

And he had.

Not two weeks later he borrowed his father's old pickup and took me for a ride to see something special, refusing to tell me what it was until we got there. When we'd rounded a corner and I'd seen the yellow castle up ahead of us, I asked him what in the world he wanted to show me that for.

"Haven't you ever heard of James Curwood?" he asked, pulling the truck up along the side of the road.

"The author?" I'd asked.

"Yup." He got out of his side and hustled his way around the front of the truck to get my door for me. "He's a third or fourth cousin of mine."

"Really?" My mouth dropped open.

"Well, twice removed or through an uncle." He shrugged. "Something like that."

"How about that." I joined him on the curb, where we looked at the castle. "Anyway, what's this?"

"It was where he wrote his books." He extended his arm to me. "Someday I'll make you a place where you can write."

"Oh, Norm."

"It might not be as fancy as this." He nodded at the castle. "But it will be just for you."

I never wrote a whole book, and Norm didn't make me a place to write. It hadn't mattered. They'd just been dreams that ended up forgotten in the everyday happenings of life.

Hugo and I leaned over a map of Michigan that I'd spread out on the dining room table, me on my feet, him kneeling on a chair beside me. I traced the triple red line that was a highway that connected to the double blue that would lead us to Owosso.

"We just go north here," I whispered. "And that should lead us right to the spot."

"Is it far?" he asked.

"Not too far."

"Will we be gone long?" He rested his elbows on the table.

"Oh, I don't know." I peeked at him, hoping he wouldn't lose his nerve to leave the house.

"Can Mommy go with us?"

"We can ask if she'd like to."

Before I could stop him, Hugo had sprinted up the stairs and let himself into Clara's room. I followed behind him, taking the steps slowly, not wanting to interrupt him.

By the time I reached the door, he was already begging her to get up, jabbering on about going on an adventure.

"Can you just let me be?" she said, her voice flat and hollow. "Can't you see I'm not feeling good?"

"But, Mommy, I want you to come."

"Hugo, get off my bed."

"Please." His little voice was full of desperation. "Don't stay in bed anymore. Don't be sad."

"I said get off."

It was when I heard the thud that I rushed into the room.

Hugo was on the floor, looking up at Clara with eyes wide, unbelieving. She looked at him from where she sat up on the bed, the very same expression on her face.

I knelt on the floor next to him, touching his face with my hands, asking if he was all right.

"I'm okay," he said, taking his eyes off Clara. "It didn't hurt."

"Oh, baby," Clara said, moving to get up off the bed. "I didn't mean to . . ."

"It didn't hurt, Mommy," he said. "It was an accident."

The tears in her eyes disgusted me, and I had to look away from her.

"I'm taking Hugo on a little day trip," I said. "We'll be back later."

"Birdie, I didn't mean to."

I didn't respond to her and regretted it as soon as I stepped out the door.

The wind tried its very hardest to pull my umbrella inside out as Hugo and I stood on the white walkway leading up to Curwood Castle. It wasn't raining terribly hard, but it had come down all morning, and the humidity made me feel damp through my dress, slip, and unmentionables.

But the gray and gloom just made the yellow of the castle even more brilliant. The Shiawassee River—usually so calm in that spot—caught the raindrops in a song of plinking and fizzing sounds. I breathed in the summer smells of water and trees and wildflowers added to the hard-to-identify crispness of rain.

Hugo pressed against my side.

"What do you think?" I asked.

"Is it real?"

"Of course it is."

"Does Jimmy live there?"

"Well, no. But a man named James built it a long time ago."

Spires and turrets and stately curved windows. I wondered at the imagination of a man who would dream up such a thing to sit on land in understated Owosso. What had the neighbors thought when a thing like that was going up down the street?

"Would you like to go inside?" I asked.

"Can we?"

I answered by putting my hand on his shoulder and leading him up the path.

We didn't stay inside Curwood Castle too long. The caretaker seemed especially vigilant, following us from place to place, clearing his throat every few minutes as if he wanted us to move along.

What I at first took as scrutiny for our dripping umbrella and squeaking shoes later occurred to me as trying to figure us out. The man made little effort to hide his looks between Hugo and me. After a little while I started to get the feeling that the man didn't think we went together. We didn't match. Me with my light skin and Hugo with his dark.

My temptation was to leave right away to not make the man uncomfortable.

But when, at each new corner or photograph or bookcase, Hugo stopped and asked me to read the plaques or to notice something he found wonderful, I decided the man's discomfort wasn't my concern.

I decided that the man would just have to buck up and deal with it.

Hugo kept his hands clasped behind his back as if needing the reminder not to touch anything. He never raised his voice above a whisper, and I had to stay very close so I could hear him say, "That's like the fireplace where Jimmy warmed up after playing outside," or "That's like the chair the queen sat in when she told him stories, isn't it?"

At the very last, I lifted Hugo, holding him just high enough to look out one of the narrow, arched windows that overlooked the river. The man once again cleared his throat. When I turned my attention to him, I saw he was checking his watch.

"We are so enjoying our time," I said. "Thank you for being patient with us."

If he didn't catch the sarcasm in my voice, he truly was not as smart as he thought he was.

By the way he turned and let us be, I figured maybe he had caught it after all.

When we walked back out into the rain, I crouched down so the umbrella would cover the both of us. Hugo drew close to me, his shoulder pushing into my hip, and I dared to put my arm around him.

"I wish Mommy could've come," he said.

"I know. Me too." I sighed. "I should have brought a camera with me. I would have taken a picture of you in front of the castle so she could see it."

"Don't worry." He turned his face toward me. "I'll make a picture."

"I would love that."

Somewhere, not too far off, I heard the squeaky cheeping of a goldfinch, and I turned to see a dash of bright yellow in the boughs of a pine.

That tiny bird sang despite the rain.

Oh, what a beautiful song it was.

twenty-three

Mom Sweet had always been of the opinion that celebrating birthdays was every bit of an occasion as Thanksgiving, Christmas, or Easter. She'd plan the day to suit the birthday boy or girl with streamers and special meals and heartfelt gifts. The presents were never anything extraordinary, but they were well thought out.

And she'd sing "Happy Birthday" at the very top of her lungs, not caring that she couldn't carry a tune to save her life.

Oh, how I missed her.

Ever since Stan became a part of our family, his birthdays meant cinnamon rolls for supper and taking in a movie. That year his birthday fell on a Friday, just right for a family trip to the drive-in.

He insisted on all of us riding together in the station wagon. It was a tight fit—the three boys in the way back and Pop and Albie on either side of me in the middle—but we liked each other well enough and didn't mind too terribly.

I thought it was a good thing that Clara had decided to stay home. It would have been hard to decide which twin to strap on the roof.

"I heard sometimes people hide in the trunk so they don't have to pay," Nick said from the back as soon as Stan pulled into the line for the tickets. "They get six people in free that way."

"We could get under this blanket," Dick said. "Then you wouldn't have to pay for us kids."

"Son, that's stealing," Stan said.

"Yeah, Dick," Nick said. "Dad's right."

"Golly," Marvel said. "A man turns thirty-six and starts sounding like Ward Cleaver."

"Well, and Nick is doing his Eddie Haskell act." Stan winked at her.

"Who are all these people they're talking about?" Pop asked me.

"From a show on television," I said. "Haven't you ever seen *Leave It to Beaver*?"

"Beaver? Is it a show about a beaver?"

"No. It's about a family. The boy's name is Beaver."

"What kind of name is that for a child?" Pop shook his head.

"Well, that's not his real name," I said. "His name's Tom or Tim . . ."

"Theodore, I think," Marvel said, turning halfway in her seat.

"They just call him Beaver. As a nickname," I said.

"Is something wrong with his teeth?" Pop asked. "Or does he chew on wood?"

"Oh, I don't know."

Pop had a glint in his eye, the one that was always just in the corner when he was up to no good.

"You," I said, batting at his arm. "All right, you stinker."

The rain from earlier in the day had dried up but left mud

puddles in the tire tracks and ruts of the dirt at the drive-in theater. The rest of the ground looked absolutely gushy.

"Don't you boys splash in those puddles," Marvel called back, giving Nick and Dick a severe look. "Do you hear me?"

"Aw, Mom," Dick said, putting his head between Albert's and mine. "What if we take off our shoes?"

"Yeah. We're just wearing shorts," Nick added. "We promise we won't get too dirty."

"Don't make promises you can't keep." Marvel turned back around in her seat.

Stan found a spot as close to the middle of the lot as he could, claiming it was good we'd gotten there so early. Marvel sent the boys to the playground, making them promise to stay with Hugo the whole time.

"When it starts to get dark, come back to the car, all right?" she said. "We'll have hot dogs and popcorn if you can behave yourselves. And stay together!"

"Come on, Hugo," Dick said, cocking his head to the side to show which way they'd go.

Hugo hesitated, waiting for me to nod that it was okay. Then he ran along between the twins, all three of them hopping over puddles.

"You know they're going to get muddy, don't you?" Stan said. "They're boys."

"Oh, I know." Marvel sighed.

"How about I get us something cold to drink." Stan pulled the latch of his door. "Coke all right for everyone?"

"I'll go," Pop said. "I wanna see what they've got."

"Do you think they'd make me a cherry Coke?" Marvel asked.

"Don't know," Stan answered. "Why don't you come along

and ask for yourself. I'll even let you hold my hand if you're nice to me."

Marvel giggled and got out of her seat.

They all shut their respective doors and I slid out of the middle and pivoted, resting my arm on the back of the seat.

"How are things, Albie?" I asked.

"All right." He turned his upper half so he could face my way. "Hugo seems to be enjoying the twins."

"He sure does. They're good for him."

Albert nodded. "Didn't Clara want to come?"

"Oh, not tonight." I crossed my ankles, finding it hard to sit like a lady in the position. "I think she wanted the house to herself."

"Is it something I did?" he asked after a pause.

"Albie, it has nothing to do with you," I said. "She's just having a hard time right now. She'll bounce back."

A car carrying at least a dozen teenagers drove past, the radio turned up so loud I could hear every word of the song that was playing. It was Elvis belting out "Return to Sender" in his crooning, trembling voice.

"Do you like Elvis?" I asked, hoping to steer the conversation away from my sister.

"I guess I've never listened to him very much."

"Norm thought he was something else," I said. "He insisted we watch whenever he was on TV."

"We always had different taste in music." Albert grinned. "I can't tell you how many times we argued over it."

"Do you remember when he bought that plaid jacket?" I shook my head. "It was after the first time Elvis was on *Ed Sullivan*."

"He did look smart in it, even if I never would have told him so."

"He did."

It had been cream colored with black and gray plaid and fit him to a tee. When he put it on for me, he grabbed the collar, tugging at it just like Elvis had on the show. Then he swayed in front of me singing "Love Me Tender" and I felt light-headed, trying not to swoon like the girls in the audience.

Norm couldn't croon, and only about half of the notes were on pitch. But the way his eyes stayed locked on mine made him every bit as dreamy as Elvis. Quite a bit more, if I were to be honest.

I regretted that I didn't have a single photo of Norm wearing that jacket. It certainly had been a good fit for him before he outgrew it and gave it away.

As a matter of fact, I didn't have nearly enough pictures of him. Of course, I had the ones Marvel had managed to take over the years and a few from other people. But I had missed so many great opportunities because I'd never thought I needed a camera of my own.

"I need to buy a camera," I said, not realizing it was out loud until Albert perked up.

"I'm sorry, what did you say?" he asked.

"That I need a camera so I can get some pictures of Hugo." I sat up straight. "And Nick and Dick. And the rest of the family."

"All right." Albert's voice betrayed his confusion at my sudden divergence of conversation.

I'd never been a woman of great resolve and determination. I'd usually left that for people like Norman or Marvel.

I couldn't help but smile. It felt good to make a decision.

As soon as it was full dark, a trumpet sound came through the speakers we had hanging in the windows of the car with a slight crackle that almost sounded like fire. The screen turned dark with three slashes of light.

"What's this?" one of the twins asked, hanging over the driver's side of the car from where he and the other two boys sat on the roof.

"It's a newsreel," Marvel said before shushing him.

"Yeah, quiet, son," Stan said. "Your mother doesn't want to miss a moment of President Kennedy on the big screen."

"What's he doing in Germany?" Pop asked before placing a piece of popcorn on his tongue.

"Well, I don't know, Dad. Maybe if we listen, we'll figure it out." Marvel plastered a smile on her face before turning her attention back to the film.

The reporter spoke of "East Berlin" and the "wall of hate." "The miracle" of West Berlin and the "stark desolation" of the east. The shiny motorcade carrying the president rounded a corner, and he stepped out, shaking the hand of a uniformed man.

"Ma," Nick said, hanging down from the roof, his face in the passenger side window, making Marvel jump. "How long you think the news is gonna be?"

"As long as it needs to be," she said, shaking her head. "Have a little patience."

"What's the big deal anyway?"

"Hush," Marvel said.

The music took on an urgent tone, violins screeching and drums pounding.

"What's a dictatorship, anyway?" Nick asked from Marvel's side. "Is that like Hitler?"

"Hitler's dead," Dick said from Stan's side. "Everybody knows that."

"Do not." Nick's face was getting red from hanging upside down. "He coulda escaped."

"Boys, would you please be quiet," Stan said. "If I knew you'd talk all the way through the movie, I would have brought your muzzles."

The twins pulled themselves from the windows, and there was a rustling and bumping from the roof as they got settled once again.

It seemed to me the day the president spent in West Germany was a bright one and warm. I wondered if the sun had shone on the eastern side of the wall that day too. Surely, those on the other side had heard the roar of cheers for Kennedy. Maybe they'd even heard his words.

"*Ich bin ein Berliner.*"

"I am a citizen of Berlin."

I tried to imagine what it might have been like the day the city was partitioned off, east and west. I'd heard stories on the news—we all had—of families separated, not knowing when they'd see each other again.

It had been just about two years. The only thing holding them together, their memories of one another. Even if those memories weren't always happy, I could only imagine how desperately they wanted to be reunited.

I closed my eyes, trying to picture someone on the eastern side of the wall, ear to a gap between the bricks, trying to hear President Kennedy. Straining for hope.

❧

On the way home from the movie, the twins chattered on and on about *Jason and the Argonauts.*

"How did they find somebody with just one eye to play the

cyclops?" and "Was Triton really a giant?" and "Why'd all the men have to wear dresses?" and "Was the skeleton army made of real bones?"

Neither Stan or Marvel could get an answer in edgewise between those two boys and their questions. I wondered just how many Jujubes they'd had.

Hugo, on the other hand, sat on my lap, his sleeping head resting on my chest. In the dark of the ride home, I couldn't see much of him. But every once in a while, the light from a streetlamp would flicker across his face.

All I could think of was how we were on one side of a wall of Clara's making. How she seemed to be very far away even though she was just in the other room.

And I wondered if she knew how much she still belonged to us.

twenty-four

Before I knew it, the end of June had come, warm and sunny. The irises and delphinium of spring were done, making way for the coneflowers and hydrangeas of summer.

The change didn't wait for my permission or for me to even do anything. It came all of its own accord, whether I liked it or not. I was always sad when one plant had to go in order for the new to have space in the soil. But then, when the fresh blooms spread, I was glad for something different.

Lifting my head, I used the back of one of my garden gloves to wipe a bit of sweat off my forehead. I caught a glimpse of Hugo bouncing a ball in the driveway. He had his tongue sticking out the side of his mouth in concentration, and I had to smile at that.

He was such a serious little man at only five years old.

Somewhere in the neighborhood, a radio played at what I had to guess was full volume. I worked to the rhythm of the plinking xylophone that was backed up by smooth strings. A voice joined the instruments singing words I did not understand. Peppy as the song was, I couldn't help but feel sad when I heard it.

Shutting my eyes, I tried breathing against the melancholy that washed over me, heavy and powerful as a tall wave.

For the past few days that song had been playing everywhere I went. One of the disc jockeys had said that it was called "Sukiyaki." I found myself humming along, wishing I knew what made the singer so sad, but unable to understand the words he sang.

Hugo's ball hit his foot, careening off in my direction. Flinching, I put my hands up in front of my face. Clearly, I'd never been much of an athlete. The ball hit my hands and landed right in the middle of the flower bed, breaking half a dozen of the coneflowers' stems.

He stood in the driveway, hands over his mouth and a look of utter horror on his face. Shoulders slumped and tears in his eyes, he waited, it seemed, for me to do something.

"I need a little practice catching, huh?" I said, reaching through the flowers for the ball and rolling it my way. Standing, I bent at the waist, the ball between my knees. I was glad I'd decided to wear my pedal pushers. "Ready?"

Lowering his hands, palms up, in front of his stomach, he lifted one of his eyebrows. The boy had no idea what to make of me. Still, he waited for my throw.

It wasn't any good, my throw, and he had to run into the neighbor's yard to retrieve the ball.

"Oopsy daisy," I called after him. "Sorry."

When he got the ball, he lifted it over his head in both hands and said, "Wanna play catch?"

"Yes," I said.

He made sure I was ready before tossing it to me. I, again,

missed. It was all right, though, because the terrified look on his face was gone, replaced with a slight smile that I liked very much indeed.

Moving just a little bit closer, he made eye contact and nodded to let me know he was going to throw it. That toss I caught.

"Good catch," Hugo said.

"Thank you."

We played like that for ten or fifteen minutes with more catches than misses between us, which I counted a success.

Finished, I bent down to pick up my gardening tools—a spade, gloves, and the like. Hugo looked at the broken coneflowers.

"I'm sorry I broke your flowers," he said.

Hands on my hips, I regarded them. "Hugo, have you ever heard the expression 'when life gives you lemons, make lemonade'?"

He nodded.

"Do you understand what it means?"

"No," he answered.

"It just means that when something happens that you didn't plan on, turn it into something good." I bent down and picked up those flowers, arranging them in my fist. "Let's put these in some water. Maybe your mommy would like them in her room?"

I thought those pink-purple flowers would be a ray of sunshine in her world that was too often dark.

Just like Hugo was.

I took Hugo for an ice cream at Sam's after I got myself cleaned up from my yard work. He didn't even ask if we could invite Clara along. We just hopped into the car and drove away, as if she wasn't there at all.

When I asked him if we should bring something home for her—a sundae or a shake—he shook his head, saying that she wouldn't eat it anyway.

He ordered a cone of Superman ice cream, and I wondered if I'd ever be able to wash the red, yellow, and blue dribbles out of the shirt he'd worn.

It didn't matter, though. He'd enjoyed that treat so much, it was worth the cost of a hand-me-down T-shirt.

On the short drive home, with the windows rolled down and my hair blowing about with abandon, I thought of what a good day it had been. I turned up the radio when the Peter, Paul, and Mary tune came on, the one that had been so popular the year before.

"What do they want a hammer for?" Hugo asked from the seat beside me.

"Well, I don't know, exactly," I said. "But I think it's a nice song anyway."

When we rounded the corner of Deerfield to get home, I noticed something was wrong.

I could see even before we pulled into the driveway that the garage door was open and Norman's Impala gone. I did my best not to let Hugo read my alarm.

"Tell you what," I said, turning down the radio. "I'm going to park on the street for a minute. I'll have you stay in the car until I come to get you."

"Is something the matter?" he asked.

"Not necessarily." I pulled up to the curb. "Roll up your window and keep the doors locked until I say it's okay. All right?"

"Aunt Betty, I'm scared."

I put the gear into park and turned toward him. "You don't need to be, sweetheart. I just want to check something."

After turning off the engine, I got out, making sure that Hugo had his door locked. I turned back to look at him when I was halfway up the drive. He had both hands on the window, his face so close to the glass I could see the steam of his breath. I smiled at him, hoping it didn't show how frightened I was.

In the garage nothing was amiss except for the missing car and the door that led to the kitchen was locked. I used my key to let myself in.

There on the table was a note from Clara.

Birdie,

Went out for a little bit. Be back soon. Keys were in the igni-tion of the black car. Hope you don't mind.

Clara

I never knew I could be so relieved and so furious at the same time.

CHAPTER
twenty-five

J'd stayed up far later than I should have, waiting for Clara to come home. I occupied my time after Hugo went to bed by looking through the old photo album, stopping on a picture of my Uncle Gerald on his tractor, Clara on his lap and me standing beside him. We were so small, and I had absolutely no recollection of that picture having been taken.

Our mother's brother, Uncle Gerald, lived on a farm somewhere called Bliss, a few hours' drive from Detroit. We went there once a year in the summers when we were very young, Mother saying that the fresh air would be good for us.

We'd run through the cornfields with our cousins, Clara moving between the stalks with abandon. I, on the other hand, worried the whole time that we'd get lost or in trouble or that we'd bump into a less-than-savory creature in there.

For a girl only accustomed to a city like Detroit, even a rabbit could be a scary prospect.

Only once was our mother able to convince Dad to let us spend the night on the farm. Clara and I slept on the screened-in porch with our cousins, the cool of the evening so refreshing after a hot day of play.

Never one to sleep well away from home, I'd tossed and turned on the pallet that was my bed that night. The chirping of crickets and croaking of frogs joined with other country sounds, none of which were familiar to me.

Very late, after the rest of the household was sleeping, my mother crept out to the porch, stepping over one sleeping child after another and pushing open the screen door with all the care in the world, slipping out into the night.

I'd followed her, worried that she'd sneak away and that we'd never be able to find her. But she'd just perched on a large rock in the front yard, her knees held tight against her chest. Head tilted back, she stared up at the sky.

"See all of them?" she'd said when I got to the rock. She patted a space beside her, and I climbed up. "We never see this many in the city, do we?"

When I noticed that she was crying, I asked her why the stars made her sad. She told me she wasn't sad. Not at all.

"Beauty makes me cry sometimes," she'd told me.

She let me stay beside her for a long time and she told me the names of the constellations she knew. Those she didn't know, she made up.

It was the closest I'd ever felt to her. That was the most I'd ever felt I really was her daughter.

It was well past two in the morning when lights from a car pulling into my driveway beamed in through the living room window, projecting my shadow on the wall.

I yawned, stretching as I got out of my chair so I could let

Clara in. I had half a mind to explain to her that "be back soon" did not mean twelve hours later.

When I opened the front door, I saw that it wasn't Norm's car in the driveway. It was Albert's. He was next to the open passenger side door, reaching in to help Clara out. She put her hand on his shoulder and stood up, leaning on him heavily.

"Is she okay?" I asked, keeping my voice low so as not to disturb the neighbors, and rushed down the steps.

"Birdie, hi." Clara's voice slurred and she slumped.

Albert put an arm around her to keep her upright.

"Are you drunk?" I asked.

"No," she answered, louder than was necessary.

Albert's wide eyes met mine and he nodded, wincing as if he hated to be the one to give me the news.

Clara's blouse was rumpled and hung on her unevenly, and she was holding both of her shoes in her hand. Her hair was mussed and loose, makeup smudged.

"Are you mad at me?" she asked.

"Maybe a little." I waved for them to come up the walk. "Let's all get inside."

She took a step and then looked down at her feet, her face scrunched in puzzlement. "Where are my shoes?"

"In your hand," I said. "Come inside, Clara."

Her steps faltered, and I met them halfway up the walk. She leaned on both Albert and me as we took the two steps up the porch. Merciful heavens, she smelled awful. Her breath, her clothes, even her skin and hair stunk to high heaven. Alcohol and cigarettes and some other skunky odor that stung my nose.

The screen door creaked, and I let her go inside first. Turning in the vestibule, she looked me right in the eye.

"You can't act like this," I said. "You're a mother. Your son needs you. You have to think of him first."

"I can't control it." She laughed.

"I don't believe that for a minute." I didn't like the scolding tone in my voice. "You're acting like a little girl."

Her smile vanished.

Albert offered to make a pot of strong coffee. I supposed he didn't know what else to do. I told him it was a good idea, even if I did expect to waste most of it down the drain. It didn't matter.

What mattered was getting Clara back to herself. Or at least halfway there.

I took her to the bathroom and had her sit on the edge of the tub while I wiped her face clean with a washcloth and brushed out her hair. Even when I hit a snag, she didn't protest. She didn't complain. When she told me she was going to be sick, I helped her get to the toilet and held back her hair.

"Where did you go?" I asked, drawing hot water into the tub for her bath.

"I just wanted to stop feeling for a little while," she answered.

"So you went to a bar?" I took a fresh washcloth from the closet. "How did you pay?"

"I found a jar of money in the cupboard." She closed her eyes and swallowed, wincing. "I'm sorry."

"Well, it's done now."

I bit the inside of my cheek, not wanting to say anything I'd regret later and not wanting to ask how much she'd taken. That money was for a vacation that Norm and I never got to take. It was just money. That was all.

"How did Albert know to come get you?" I asked.

"I found his number in the phone book." She took in a gulp of air. "I was too scared to drive home."

"Why didn't you call me?"

She didn't answer my question.

The hot water from the faucet steamed up the mirror and window, and I turned off the tap when there was enough of it for her to get a good soaking.

"Can you get in the tub by yourself?" I asked. "Or will you need help? I don't need you falling and cracking your head open."

"I need help," she answered, all the hardness melted out of her voice. "I'm scared, Birdie."

"It's just a bath. It's nothing to be afraid of."

I helped her out of her clothes, trying to avoid seeing too much of her undressed body. What I did see was far too thin, far too angular, and I wondered when she'd last eaten more than a few bites at a time.

She held my arm tight when she lifted one foot after the other to step into the tub. She didn't let go until she was submerged, letting out a hiss at how hot the water was.

"Here's your washcloth," I said. "The soap is fresh there on the side."

"You won't leave me, will you?" she asked, looking smaller than ever, folded up on herself in the bath. "I'm afraid to be alone."

"I'll stay with you for a little bit." I sat on the closed lid of the toilet. "Why are you frightened?"

"I'm scared I'll hurt myself."

"What do you mean?"

She shook her head. "I don't know."

"Let's just get you sobered up," I said. "You need a good night of sleep and you'll feel better in the morning."

She blinked at me slowly, as if it took all her energy to do just that, and let herself sink down all the way into the water. When she didn't come right back up, I lunged toward her, fighting against the water and her slippery skin and the weight of her body to pull her back up. She kept her eyes open the whole time.

When I finally managed to pull her face above water, she sucked in a gasping breath. Leaning her head against the edge of the tub, she parted her lips.

"Why did you do that?" I asked, louder than I'd intended. Nearly a shout.

"Uh, is everything okay in there?" Albert said from the other side of the door.

"Yes," I called back. "We're fine."

I waited until I heard the sounds of Albie moving about the kitchen—a cupboard opening and shutting, the drawing of water from the faucet—before I moved so much as an inch.

"Clara," I whispered. "Please don't do that again."

"I'm losing my mind, Birdie," she said. "Just like Mama."

"No. I can't believe that." I sat on the thin porcelain, wet from the sloshing, afraid that she was right.

She draped her arm on the ledge by the soap holder. That was when I saw the cut that sliced halfway across her wrist. It didn't look deep. But it was enough to make my stomach clench and my heart ache.

"What happened?" I asked.

"I lost my nerve." She swallowed hard. "I couldn't do it."

"Oh, Clara."

"Don't give up on me, Birdie," she said, dropping her hand back into the water. "Promise you won't ever give up on me."

"I never will," I said.

"Do you promise?" She blinked heavily.

"Of course I do."

I helped her clean up, working the shampoo into her hair and scrubbing the washrag across her skin. When she talked, I didn't hear the voice of my sister. When I looked into her face, I didn't see the Clara I'd known all my life.

It was as if something else inhabited her body.

I found that my chest was so tight I could hardly breathe.

twenty-six

The first time my dad took Mother for a stay at the sanitarium he sat us girls down on the couch to explain. Clara and I sat as close together as we could, the lumpy filling uncomfortable under our behinds.

He told us that our mother wasn't well and that it was best for all of us if she went where the doctors could fix her, that they knew just what to do to make her better. When we'd asked how long she would be gone, he said that he didn't know but that it would be a long time.

My sister and I sat on that couch for an hour, arms wrapped around each other and sobbing.

"Would a story make you feel better?" I'd asked her, using the sleeve of my sweater to wipe Clara's eyes.

She shook her head, pushing my hand away.

"What would make you feel better?"

"I don't want to feel better," she said. "I don't want to stop crying."

"What do you want, then?"

"I want to be sad." She frowned. "And I want you to be sad with me."

And so I didn't try to make her forget about the hurt. We just sat together, not leaving each other's side for the rest of the day.

We felt and feared and grieved together.

I didn't leave Clara alone for a moment. I didn't dare. After I got her out of the tub, she couldn't even manage to towel herself dry. She wept as I helped her into a fresh pair of underwear and a clean nightie.

When she spoke, she made little to no sense at all. Her words slurred even long after the alcohol wore off. She moved so slowly and leaned on me heavily when I took her to my own bed to sleep.

While she rested, I bandaged her wrist, grateful that she'd lost her nerve.

By then it was nearly time for Albert to leave for the bakery. I peeked my head out the door to let him know he could go.

"I think I should stay," he said, whispering, and looked past me into the room. "I already called Stan to let him know."

"You don't have to . . ." I started.

But then I stopped, hearing stirring from upstairs. Hugo.

"You go on up," Albert said. "I'll stay with her."

I nodded and passed by him in the hallway. He went into the room, sitting on the edge of the bed and holding his hands in his lap, his eyes on Clara's face.

I might have stayed there, watching, had it not been for Hugo calling out again. I rushed up the steps, feeling light-headed by the time I reached the top.

When I didn't see Hugo in his room—his covers rumpled

at the end of the bed—I put a hand to my chest, afraid for an instant that he'd wandered away somehow.

But then I heard him whimpering. Turning, I saw that Clara's door was open. He was there, sitting on the floor in nearly the same spot as he'd been after she pushed him out of her bed. He had his knees bent, peaks held against his chest by his arms. Rocking, he never took his eyes off the place where his mother should have been.

"Sweetheart," I said.

"She's gone." He didn't look my way. "You said she'd be back when I woke up."

"She is. She's downstairs," I said. "In my bed."

"Can I see her?"

"In a little bit." I took a step toward him. "She's resting right now."

He let go of his shins, letting his legs stretch out in front of him. The fabric of his cowboy pajamas made a whisper sound against the hardwood floor.

"Would you like to go back to bed?" I asked. "Maybe sleep a little longer?"

He shook his head, not moving from his place on the floor. He looked so lonely, I decided to sit with him.

"Can you tell me a story?" he asked.

"If you want one."

"Yes, please."

I tried to think of one to tell, one that might give him comfort or encouragement, but found myself at a loss. Shutting my eyes, all I could see was that picture of Clara and me on the tractor with Uncle Gerald.

That was all it took for a memory to spark in my mind.

"Would you settle for one that's true?" I asked.

"I guess so."

"When your mommy and I were little girls, we'd sometimes visit family at their farm," I started. "They had barns and silos and fields of corn that seemed to go on for a whole mile."

"Did they have cows?"

"I think they only had one for milking." I shut my eyes. "But they did have a whole coop full of chickens. All different kinds. Black ones and orange-colored ones. I think they had a few that were white and another one that was striped."

"Why'd they have them?"

"For their eggs," I said. "My aunt used to send home a couple dozen eggs with us when we left."

"Did they hatch into chicks?"

"No. They weren't that kind of eggs." I grinned at him. "We used to chase the hens around the yard, trying to catch them. All of us kids—your mommy, our cousins, and me—would see how many we could catch in three minutes. Whoever caught the most would get the first piece of pie at dessert."

I could just about hear the clucking of the chickens and see their feet kicking up a cloud of dust as they scrambled away from us.

"Once we caught a chicken, we'd put them in the coop, so we couldn't catch the same one over and over again."

"That would be cheating."

"I guess it would," I said. "Your mommy went last because she was the youngest. She was determined to get every last one of those chickens. You see, nobody else had been able to, not even the cousins who were raised on that farm."

Clear as day, I could see Clara interlacing her fingers, stretching her arms out in front of her and cracking her knuckles, the look on her face fierce, focused.

"She dashed around the yard, grabbing chickens and rushing them back to the coop." I couldn't help but smile. "Faster than anybody else, she got all the hens. I was happy for her and clapped my hands. My cousin Paul, though, was madder than the dickens."

"Why?"

"Because he was very competitive and hated losing to girls." I leaned down to whisper in his ear. "She loved to beat him at games because of it."

This made Hugo smile.

"Just as your mommy was about to let us congratulate her, she saw something near the barn," I said. "She took off like a shot for the chicken she'd missed, even though the cousins called after her to leave it alone."

I hadn't understood why they tried to make her stop and hollered after her to get it, thinking the cousins just wanted her to lose.

"She ran at that bird, hands out in front of her and ready to snatch it," I went on. "When she got closer to it, I expected it to turn and run away from her. But it didn't. Instead, it took off toward her."

Clara had let out a ferocious cry, like a warrior dashing into battle. The chicken had equaled her scream.

"That was when Paul yelled, 'It's gonna get her,'" I said. "And he took off running to help her. I followed, not having any idea what the fuss was all about."

Hugo shifted so he was facing me and crossed his legs in front of him, leaning forward.

"I ran after Paul until we were just a few feet away from your mommy and the chicken," I said. "That was when I saw the spurs."

"What's that mean?"

"It wasn't a hen. It was a rooster." I caught his eyes. "Just then, that mean old coot spread his wings and jumped into the air, aiming those sharp spurs at your mother. I yelled for her to run, but she thought I meant to go after that bird harder, which was what she did."

Clara went even faster, spreading her own arms and leaping until she met that rooster in the air. Her body weighing more, she knocked him down on the ground.

"I've never seen anyone wrestle harder or longer than your mommy did with that rooster," I said, shaking my head. "It put up a fight. That rooster was mean. But your mother was meaner."

Hugo's smile widened, a good sight for me.

"We tried to pull her off him, but she wouldn't give up. She was going to win." I stopped, I had to. The memory had me choked up in a way I hadn't expected it to. Swallowing hard a few times, I tried to ease the tightness in my throat.

"Did she win?" Hugo asked.

"Of course she did," I answered, even though the words were pinched. "That rooster eventually let her pick him up. She lifted him over her head and yelled, 'I win!'"

"And she got dessert first?"

"Yes. But not until after she got a few of her scrapes and scratches tended to," I said. "Goodness. Did that wrestling match ever make her dirty."

"I like that story," Hugo said.

"I do too."

He crawled into my lap, grabbing my arm and wrapping it around him, his head on my chest. His little body was warm, and I didn't want him to leave even if I melted into a puddle from the hot room. I could have let him stay there for the rest of the day if only he'd sit still that long.

"I've never known anyone as strong as your mommy," I whispered. "She doesn't give up easily."

I kissed the top of his head, feeling his soft hair against my lips and breathing in the still-fresh scent lingering from the bath he'd taken before bed.

Closing my eyes, I pictured Clara standing next to that red barn, rooster in hands raised over her head. Hair a mess and falling out of its braid, dirt scuffed on her arms, legs, and face, dress torn from the scuffle.

Clara the conqueror.

Let there be a little fight in her yet, I prayed.

twenty-seven

*M*arvel's car was parked in the driveway, and she waited behind the wheel, patiently, for Hugo to come out so she could take him home with her for the day. Nick and Dick sat in the backseat, equally still but—I imagined—less than patient.

We all knew that Hugo needed time with Clara. Just a few minutes.

Albert and I waited in the kitchen, cups of coffee going cold on the countertop.

"Why do you have to go away?" Hugo asked, his voice so sad it broke my heart. "I can take care of you."

"You shouldn't have to," she told him. "I should be able to look after you."

"Will you come back?"

"Yes, baby. As soon as I'm better."

"Are you sick?"

"Yes."

They were quiet for a handful of minutes, and I struggled not to stick my head into the room to make sure everything was okay.

"Aunt Birdie will take good care of you," Clara said after a few minutes, her voice thick. "You do as she says, all right?"

"Yes."

"Will you draw me pictures?" she asked.

"Uh-huh."

"Okay. You'd better go."

Again, quiet.

"I love you," Clara said. "Don't forget."

"I love you too," he answered.

He stepped out of the bedroom, rubbing at his eyes. Eyes that were rimmed with red and swollen from crying.

What a strong little boy, our Hugo.

So much like his mother.

Albert offered to drive, and I was glad for it. I could barely see straight to walk let alone keep a car on the road. He helped Clara out of the house, holding her steady just like he'd done the night before. This time, though, she let her head rest on his shoulder as if it was too heavy to hold up herself.

I'd never had a hangover, but I could only imagine how greatly unpleasant it was.

"Watch your head," he said to her, easing her into the back of the car. "All right?"

He waited for her to answer before shutting the door.

"Thank you," I told him. "You're so careful with her."

He nodded but didn't say anything, which was not a surprise to me.

I went around to the other side of the car, climbing in beside my sister and taking her hand in mine.

"I'm sorry, Birdie," she said. "I'm such a problem."

"You aren't," I said. "Don't be sorry."

Albert drove slowly, as if worried about jostling us too much. Every once in a while he'd check his rearview mirror, never looking in my direction, but in Clara's.

The hour it took to get there seemed to go fast even with all three of us riding silently. I thought over all the things I wanted to say to her, but they all left my mind when we pulled into the parking lot outside the imposing building of dark brick and barred windows.

Albert drove up to the doors and rushed around to Clara's side to help her out. I sat in the car by myself for only a moment, not able to shake the idea that this could be the last I'd see of my sister. Stomach clenched and bile working its way up my throat, I feared that I was walking her into a death sentence.

"I don't know what I'm doing," I whispered. A prayer.

I took a deep breath and got out of the car.

I waited with Clara until we could be seen by a nurse. She kept her head on my shoulder the whole time, humming a song that was vaguely familiar but that I couldn't quite place. It sounded like a lullaby, and I wondered if it was comforting for her.

Then I wondered if she even hummed it to calm me.

When the nurse at last came to take her away, I doubted my decision. I thought of how I could take care of her at home. That she'd be fine if only I could love her enough. I was tempted to jump up from my seat and shoo away the nurse, telling her we didn't need her after all.

But then I remembered the cut on Clara's arm and realized it would take more than love and prayers and gentle words to help her get better.

"Miss Clara?" the nurse called into the room. "Will you come with me?"

My sister lifted her head. "I'm scared, Birdie."

"I am too." I took her hands. "Together?"

I stood first, and when she was up, I took the first step. We walked together, her arm over my shoulder and both of mine circled around her middle.

The nurse smiled when we reached her but didn't budge from the middle of the doorway.

"I'm sorry," she said. "Only Miss Clara today."

"Oh, of course." I loosened my hold on my sister.

"Take care of Hugo," Clara said, shuffling away from me.

"I will." I grabbed her hand, kissing the back of it. "I love you."

She nodded, letting the nurse lead her away.

When the door clicked behind them, I wished that Albert had stayed inside with us.

I wasn't sure I had the strength to walk out to the car.

twenty-eight

Hugo's bed-wetting started again that night. He woke several times with terrible dreams, calling out for me and crying until I feared he'd make himself sick. When I came to his room, he wouldn't tell me what he'd dreamed or what had frightened him.

I spent the last few hours of the very early morning sitting on the top step, head leaned against the wall, falling into shallow sleep until he cried out again.

On my second day with barely a wink of sleep, I felt my own sanity slipping.

"Oh, Lord," I whispered once the morning sunshine started flooding through the windows. "Help."

The Almighty's help came by way of a strong cup of coffee and an early call from Marvel checking in on me.

I was still exhausted to the point of tears and ill at ease.

I checked the clock and saw that it was time to get Hugo up. If ever there was a Sunday that I needed to get to church, it was that one.

Hugo came downstairs, dressed for church but with his shirt buttoned all catawampus, and I offered to help him. I could tell by the way he stuck out his bottom lip—just a little—that he was not happy about it. But he endured my help anyway, even telling me thank you after I'd finished.

"How about some oatmeal and peaches?" I asked, getting the Quaker Oats down from the cupboard. "I could make you an egg too. We have time before we have to leave for church."

"Yes, please," he said, pulling at the collar of his shirt.

"Is something wrong?" I asked.

"It's itchy." He pulled it harder and then scratched at the back of his neck.

"Oh, don't scratch too hard, you might hurt yourself."

"I don't like this shirt." His voice took on a tone I hadn't heard from him before. It was lower, edgier, aggravated.

"Is it the tag?" I stepped toward him. "Let me see."

"No!" he yelled. "I don't want you to."

"Hugo, I can help you."

"Don't touch me!" He stomped his foot on the floor. "I don't want you."

"Now, this is no way to behave," I said. "I only meant to help you."

"I want to do it myself," he shouted. "Leave me alone."

"I won't have you yelling at me, young man."

I put out my hand to touch his shoulder, hoping to calm him. He flinched, backing away from me, a very angry scowl on his face.

"Leave me alone!" he yelled before shoving a chair in between us.

He screamed, his little face so red and his teeth bared. He kicked the table and stomped his feet again and again, yelling and flailing and throwing things on the floor. My pink coffee cup smashed into shards, my Bible fell, splayed on top of the puddle of coffee.

I stood as tall and straight as I could, refusing to walk away from him, even as he screamed for me to leave. As anxious as I felt, I didn't let him see my hands shake or my face change from anything but calm.

Eventually his anger cooled. When it did, I knelt down, careful not to put my knees on a fragment of glass. When I reached for him, he flinched, putting up his arms as a guard. I dropped my hands, putting them on my knees.

"I love you, Hugo," I whispered. "I would never hurt you."

He looked at me, his hands still in front of his face.

"I know you're scared for your mommy. I know you miss her," I said. "This must be so confusing for you. But I am not going to hurt you and I am not going to leave you."

The anger cracked away, showing me the face of a very sad and very scared little boy. His sobs took the place of screaming. His body fell into mine, and I held him as he shook with crying.

"I'm not mad," I said. "It's all right. I understand."

He let me lift him, and I carried him to the living room, his arms tight around my neck like he was holding on for dear life.

"I miss my mommy," he said between cries. "I want her back."

"I know, sweet pea. I know."

We didn't make it to church that morning. Neither of us were in a state to be seen by anybody.

What we needed was a warm breakfast and a day to heal.

He had the old picture Bible open on the floor in front of him, and he pointed to a painting of a man sitting outside the mouth of a cave, his head in his hands.

"What's this story?" he asked, voice raspy after his outburst.

I lowered myself to the floor beside him and squinted at the picture.

"This is Elijah," I said, pointing at the bearded man. "What do you think happened to him?"

"He fell down?"

"Hm. I don't know about that," I said. "He had a very important job. He had to give messages from God to the Israelites."

"Like mail?"

"Sort of."

"Is he sad?" Hugo asked.

"I think he was scared." I skimmed my fingertip over the page. "Some people didn't like the message, so they chased him, trying to hurt him."

I turned the page to show Hugo the painting of Elijah running from soldiers with drawn swords and angry faces.

"He had to hide from them," I said. "God told Elijah to stand on the mountain."

Hugo turned the page for me. Elijah stood, his robes and hair rustled by the wind.

"A very strong wind blew him around, but God wasn't in the wind. Then an earthquake shook the mountain, but God wasn't in it. Then a fire blazed, but God wasn't in the flames."

"Where was God, then?"

"I think Elijah wondered the very same thing." I lowered my head close to Hugo's and made my voice very quiet. "Then God came in a whisper to promise Elijah that all would be well and to give him the name of a helper."

"What's his name?"

"Elisha," I answered.

"They had the same name?"

"Close. But not exactly the same."

Hugo flipped a few pages and saw a picture of Elijah riding in a chariot of flame. In the picture, Elisha knelt on the ground with his arms outstretched, and I couldn't tell if it was in praise or grief.

For a moment, even, I thought it could have been both.

God was in the whisper.

But sometimes that whisper burned like fire.

twenty-nine

The last time I'd watched the fireworks in Detroit was just a handful of months before we moved to LaFontaine. That morning our dad had told us he wouldn't be home until late and that we weren't to leave the apartment.

"I guess we'll just have to watch the show out the window," I'd said to Clara, letting my shoulders slump.

"We'll see about that," she'd answered.

When it was finally dark enough, Clara pushed the window open as wide as it would go, lifting one leg up and over, her hard-soled shoe clunking on the iron landing of the fire escape.

"What are you doing?" I asked.

"Going to the roof."

"No." I'd crossed my arms and made my sternest face but didn't move to stop her. I knew better.

I could never win in a fight with my sister.

"Why not?" she asked.

"We aren't supposed to leave the apartment."

"The roof is part of the apartment," she said. "Come on."

"We'll get in trouble." I let my arms fall to my side. "I don't think it's a good idea."

"Well, I don't care what you think." She swung the other leg out the window before turning her face toward me. "You can come watch with me or you can be an old fuddy-duddy and stay here."

She was up and out before I could say "boo."

Against my better judgment, I'd followed behind her.

"It's the best place to see it all," she'd said, several rungs ahead of me on the ladder.

I'd just tried not to look up, knowing if I did, I would see her skivvies.

She had always thought it was so funny that I was embarrassed by such things.

We sat on a couple of old, overturned wooden milk crates and watched the explosions only a few miles away. The booming blasts seemed to shake the whole city, filling the sky with every color I could ever have imagined.

About halfway through, she covered her face, putting her head between her knees and sobbing. I knew without asking what it was about.

It was the last time I saw my sister cry over the death of our mother.

I watched the rest of the fireworks with my hand resting on my sister's back, the tears in my own eyes blurring the edges between the bursts of light and the pitch-black sky.

⁓

LaFontaine simply did not have the budget to put on a firework show every year. So, they reserved their display for even years. The odd years, everyone went to Detroit or Lansing. But the idea of the traffic in or out of the city was more than enough to make my eye start twitching.

So, I formulated another plan.

I put my old picnic basket on the table beside where Hugo worked on a coloring page.

"How would you like to go on an adventure?" I asked.

"I'd like that a lot," he answered.

"All right," I said. "But first we have to pack our supper."

I pulled out the makings for sandwiches and let Hugo slap the ham and cheese on his own bread and spread mayonnaise and mustard all over the top of it. When he'd asked if he could please have a few pickles on top, I told him that he was a boy after my own heart.

"How about I tell you a story while we work?" I asked, getting the jar of dill slices from the refrigerator.

He nodded his head and licked a smudge of mayonnaise from his thumb.

"There once was an ogre who lived underground," I began, turning the lid of the jar and fishing out a few pieces with a fork.

"Why'd he live underground?" Hugo asked, climbing up on a kitchen chair and kneeling on the seat.

"Because he didn't like people." I held up the fork, five pickles speared on the tines. "Is this enough or would you like a few more?"

"Maybe two more, please?"

"Oh, your manners are so nice." I dug out a couple more slices. "The ogre thought that people were cruel and nasty and smelled badly."

Hugo grinned at that.

"He couldn't be blamed for thinking such a thing. Whenever

he saw a newspaper, he read about wars and crimes and the horrible things some people do to one another."

"Why'd he think we're stinky?"

"Well, because right along with the articles about bad things were advertisements for cologne and soap."

He covered his mouth and giggled.

"I'm glad you think that's funny." I held up a golden delicious in one hand and a banana in the other. "Which would you like?"

"Apple, please."

I put it into the basket.

"You see, this ogre never took the time to get to know people."

"His name's Rocky," Hugo said. "Okay?"

"Of course, okay." I tore strips of wax paper off the roll to fold around the sandwiches. "One day, while spying on the people, Rocky noticed how they were attracted to color. He watched a woman sniff a red rose and a child licking a yellow lollipop. A man drove a green car and a little girl played with a pink doll."

I made my voice deeper and said, "'They don't deserve the colors,' the ogre cried. 'They're wretched! Evil! Gross!' And so he began to make plans to steal the color from the world."

Hugo's eyebrows knit and his forehead wrinkled. "That's not nice."

"No, it isn't," I said. "But Rocky wasn't concerned with being nice. So, little by little, he took the colors away. First, he plucked green, taking it with him to his underground home."

"Then what happened to the grass?" Hugo asked.

"It turned a dull gray," I answered. "Can you imagine walking outside to see the leaves and yards weren't colorful anymore?"

"No." He lowered one side of his mouth. "I wouldn't like it."

"Neither would I. The next day he took red." I sighed, grabbing a tin of Goldfish crackers from the cupboard. "The cardinals lost their brightness, poppy flowers darkened to black, stop signs were no longer easy to see."

"What did he take next?" Hugo asked. "Blue?"

"He did." I pointed out the window. "The sky became a big dome of white. He took yellow and then orange and then purple. Last he stole away brown and pink, and everything was in black and white."

"Like TV."

I nodded. "Rocky stood outside the door of his underground home where he'd hidden all the colors. He called for the attention of the people in the town, saying, 'I have taken all the colors, you horrible and stinky people. And I'll never give them back!'"

"I bet they chased him," Hugo said.

"They didn't," I answered. "Instead, they decided to show that they weren't awful or mean or smelly. Every morning, when the ogre woke up, he found a tray with breakfast on it. What do you think they made for him?"

"Scrambled eggs and toast," Hugo answered.

"That does sound good, doesn't it?" I went on. "And in the middle of the day, they would bring him flowers of all kinds. While they couldn't see the colors, they remembered them, and picked the prettiest they could find."

I finished packing the basket and let the top clap shut.

"And at night, they stood near the doorway to Rocky's underground home, singing lullabies for him as he fell asleep."

"Why were they being nice? He was mean to them."

"Because if they were mean back, all that would have done was prove that the ogre was right about them," I said. "They were trying to prove him wrong."

Hugo sank down on the chair until he was sitting flat on the seat. Then he leaned on the table, propping his head on his hands.

"One day, while Rocky was enjoying his fluffy eggs and crisp toast, he understood something." I lowered my tone again. "'These people aren't as bad as I thought they were. In fact, they're good people.'

"That very day, he stepped outside and, once again, called for them all to pay attention."

"Did he give them back their colors?"

"I'm getting there." I winked at him. "He spread his arms wide and said, 'For your kindness, thank you. For your generosity, thank you. And your forgiveness I ask, please.' But before anyone could say a word, bursts of light broke up from underground where Rocky had it tucked away. The colors flowed like a fountain, reds and greens and purples. And as they broke free, they took their places back in the trees and sky and flowers. They returned to the faces of the people in town and the houses along every street."

Hugo sat up, his eyes smiling.

"Rocky was so pleased to see the joy of the townsfolk that he used magic to make sure the colors flowed like a fountain every night after the sun went down."

"Why?"

"Because he realized how seeing something beautiful can be like food for the soul."

Hugo clapped at the end of the story, and I picked up the picnic basket.

"Are you ready for our little adventure?" I asked.

Hugo helped me carry our picnic basket out to the car.

thirty

When Norm and I got married, we'd hardly had money enough to pay our bills, let alone go on a proper honeymoon. While I wasn't bothered by such a thing— but then I hadn't ever been on any sort of vacation to speak of—Norman felt badly.

So he'd scrimped and saved for a one night vacation to the simple and everyday town of Jackson, Michigan.

It was nothing fancy, but I was excited to have reason to pack an overnight bag, and he'd felt proud of himself, pulling into the parking lot of the roadside motel. We ate our supper of sandwiches that I'd packed from home before going out to explore.

We ended up at a man-made waterfall, walking up and down the steps beside it for hours. As soon as darkness fell, the spurts of water were lit up with lights of every color. Red and orange fanned like a rooster tail or yellow like a sunbeam. Purple and green and blue flowed down the tiers.

We talked, held hands, kissed under the light of a well-placed lamp, and enjoyed being Norm and Betty.

Eventually we ended up sitting on the soft grass, watching the rainbow-colored lights shine up through the water that seemed as if it erupted from the very earth below it. Norm lowered his shoulder for me to rest my head on, and he sang to me in his off-tune voice that I'd already come to love so well.

When I hold you in my arms, doll, I feel a certain charm.

Our eyes met, and the way he looked at me made my heart feel as if it swelled.

It's a special kind of magic. Not just any kind of magic.

He reached his arm around my shoulder, pulling me even closer to him.

When I look into your eyes, oh my love, I can't disguise;
It's a special kind of magic. Not just any kind of magic.

The rush of water tumbled over the hand-cut stones. Splashes sprayed around the people still milling about. Kids ran past us, and a mother called out to scold them.

But sitting beside Norman, all that mattered was my head on his shoulder and his voice.

It's a special kind of magic,
Your love.

I should have known that the Cascades Park would be full to the brim with people on the Fourth of July. The only parking spot I could find seemed to be forever far away from the entrance, and the picnic basket I'd packed was heavier than I'd realized.

Hugo, ever the tiny gentleman, offered to carry it, but I was afraid that he'd wind up hurting himself carrying something nearly as heavy as he was. By the time we made it in, I was more than a little grouchy.

The only spot we could find to sit and eat our supper was out of sight of the fountain, and I felt put out. My disappointment was more for Hugo than me. But the boy was blissfully unaware of what he was missing and seemed quite content to watch all the people around us while he nibbled on his sandwich.

By the time day began to fade and the fountain lights were turned on, I took Hugo by the hand. We left the basket and our picnic blanket where it was and made our way to the fountain.

"Where are we going?" he asked.

"You'll see," I answered.

When we turned the corner and the boy got his first look at it, I realized that all the hassle had been worth it.

"Rocky's fountain," Hugo said, his words riding along a gasp that I couldn't help but smile at.

We walked up the side of the falls, him holding my hand tight while watching the water turn every color of the rainbow. We took it slow despite the crowd pushing past us in a hurry to get to the very top, I supposed.

When we reached the third tier from the top, I looked at the light pole to my right and remembered kissing Norman in that very spot years before. He'd been so tender with me, so kind and gentle. I'd thought that nothing bad would ever happen again.

Oh, how silly I'd been. How very optimistic.

I wanted more than anything else to stand under that lamp just one more time, to rest my hand on the cool stone of the railing where the beam of light shone.

But I couldn't have reached it, not while holding on to Hugo, not against the crowd.

"Aunt Betty," Hugo said, tugging at my hand. "Can you take a picture of me by the fountain?"

He stood against the railing, his back straight and his head held tall and proud.

"Very nice," I said after snapping the photos.

I turned to a man walking by, asking him if he wouldn't mind taking a picture of Hugo and me together.

"Of course," the man said.

I showed him how to work the camera before rushing to stand beside Hugo, putting my arm over his shoulder and placing my hand on his chest.

The man's face changed when he saw the two of us side by side, and I worried that he might say something untoward. But he put the camera to his eye and snapped the shutter. When I thanked him, he flashed me an uncomfortable smile.

When I turned back to Hugo I saw that he'd gotten himself up on the ledge.

"Don't worry, Aunt Betty," he said. "I won't fall in."

I sat beside him, hand on his shoulder to be sure.

"What's your favorite color?" I asked, nodding at the fountain.

"All of them," he answered

He made my heart smile.

thirty-one

My very earliest memory was of my little sister tottering around the apartment, holding my mother's pointer finger to steady her balance. After a few steps, Mother took her finger from Clara's tiny fist, leaving her to stand on her own.

Chubby arms held out on either side, she flapped them up and down as she walked by herself.

That was the first time I feared that my baby sister would one day fly away.

My fear returned periodically over the course of our childhood but had been tucked away in the dusty corner of my memory once we'd grown up and lost touch.

But when the telephone rang in the wee small hours of Wednesday morning, I felt that old anxiety again. Without even picking up the receiver or hearing a voice on the other end, I knew it was about Clara.

In my mind's eye I saw her with arms moving up and down,

graceful as ballet, and rising off the ground, aiming herself for the sun.

Forcing the image away with much blinking, I made my way to the telephone in the kitchen, forgoing my formal response for a simple hello.

"Mrs. Sweet?" the high voice on the other end asked. "This is Nurse Jones from the State Hospital."

"Yes?" As much of a chill that coursed through my veins, my hands grew sweaty and I was afraid I'd drop the receiver. I lifted my other hand so I could have a firmer grip.

"Your sister, Clara, had a bit of an . . ." She paused, leaving a silence that felt as if it was strangling me. "An incident."

"Is she all right?" I asked, interrupting.

"She's in the hospital wing," she went on. "It seems she's tried to hurt herself."

"Will she be all right?"

"We expect that she'll survive." She cleared her throat. "Recover, rather. We expect that she'll recover."

"Can I come see her?" I asked.

"She's been asking for you."

"I can be there first thing in the morning."

Clara's bed in the hospital was curtained off from the other five in the room, and for that I was grateful. Even though a thin piece of fabric didn't provide much privacy, at least I didn't have to look at the other patients and wonder what it was that had brought them to that place.

Curled up and laying on her side, Clara looked so very small under the crisp white bedsheet. Her hair was a mess, greasy from at least a week of not being washed.

I was tempted to march out to the hallway and insist that they take better care of my sister. That they make sure she was clean and safe and looked after. I had half a mind to let them know that she wouldn't have hurt herself if they'd done their jobs.

An unfamiliar urge nearly overtook me, making me want to yell and slam and kick and growl.

But the other half of my mind didn't want to raise a fuss. Not that way, at least. That other, calmer, meeker side of me knew that more flies were caught with honey than vinegar. I'd talk to the nurse in charge, but I'd do it with gentleness even if it took all my power to offer it.

What Clara needed was not a raging bull. I shut my eyes and breathed slow and deep until my temper was eased. When I opened them I focused on my sister.

Her skin was so pale, she almost blended in with the sheets.

I sat on the edge of her bed, remembering when she was small and I'd check on her in the nighttime to make sure she was okay. Of course, then she'd have her thumb stuck in her mouth and her rag doll held tightly in her arms.

If she'd stir, I would run the backs of my fingers across the inside of her arms, soothing her until she fell back into a nice and steady sleep.

I reached over and did so then, surprised by how dry her skin felt against mine.

Clara rolled over, upsetting the sheet that had been pulled over her. Before I had the chance to fix it, to straighten it back over the curve of her hip and pull it up to her shoulders, she took my hand and looked me right in the eyes.

"How are you feeling?" I asked.

She turned her face away from me. "I'm sorry, Birdie."

Her voice was hoarse, and I thought she could have used a cool glass of water. I thought of offering to find a nurse to get her something to drink, but I didn't want to leave her even for a minute. Not yet, at least.

Her wrist was wrapped thickly with white bandages, her arm unmoving on the bed.

"You don't have to be sorry." I tilted my head, trying to catch her gaze again.

Her eyelids were heavy, and I expected her to fall asleep at any moment.

"I couldn't bear it anymore," she said, her voice sounding as dry and cracked as her lips.

"What do you mean?" I lowered myself so that my top half was closer to the bed, almost lying down beside her.

She licked her lips and shut her eyes.

"Living is too hard, Birdie." She grimaced when she swallowed. "This would have made everything so much easier for everyone."

"That's not true."

"It is."

"Maybe it feels like that right now," I said. "But we need you, Clara."

"I'm just a problem."

"No. Clara, we love you." I squeezed her hand. "You have to know that."

"I'm suffering, Birdie." A tear ran down her face sideways. "It will never stop."

I lifted my hand, putting it on her cheek and feeling how cold she was. "Do you want a blanket?"

She didn't answer, so I got myself up out of the bed, pausing until the starburst in my eyes cleared from getting up too fast.

Parting the curtain, I tried to catch the attention of a nurse to ask for a couple of blankets. There were none in sight.

"I want to die."

It was so matter of fact, so frank. There wasn't a hint of emotion behind it, and that was what startled me most.

"Don't say that . . ." I started to say.

But when I turned toward her, I saw she'd rolled away from me and I knew she was done talking.

I stayed at the foot of her bed as if keeping watch over her would fix her, would convince her of my love. There I would have remained until the end of the day were it not for a nurse bustling in, a stack of tightly folded linens across her arm.

"Visiting time is over," she said to me. "She needs some rest."

"Five more minutes," I asked. "Please."

The nurse looked at Clara before placing a clean set of sheets at the foot of the bed.

"Five minutes," she conceded. "Not a second more."

I waited for her to leave before I sat back down beside my sister.

"Hugo needs you, Clara," I said, keeping my voice quiet and calm.

"But he has you now, Birdie," she answered, not meeting my eyes. "He doesn't need me anymore."

"I'm only his aunt." I reached for her hand, trying to be as gentle as I could so as not to hurt her. "He needs his mommy."

She breathed in through her nose, and for a moment I thought she might cry, that she might let an ounce of emotion crack through the flat exterior.

But she didn't.

"Do you remember the dog you and Norm had right after you got married?" she asked. "Mitzi?"

"Of course I do," I answered. "She was a good girl."

"Remember how her hips got bad and she had a hard time walking?" She swallowed hard, flinching at the pain of it.

"Do you want a drink of water?" I asked.

She shook her head, shutting her eyes. "Do you remember how much pain she was in?"

"Yes. It was awful."

"And Norm took her to have her put down."

"That was a horrible day, wasn't it?" I put my free hand on the center of my chest where the regret still settled from the loss of that good dog.

"But it had to be done."

I nodded.

"Norm said she needed to be put out of her misery," Clara said. "Because it's cruel to make an animal suffer."

"I remember how hard you cried."

"But you said it was the right thing to do, and I believed you."

The nurse pushed through the curtains, that time empty handed, and consulted her watch, sighing, I assumed, because our time was up.

I had no plans to leave Clara's bed until I was good and ready. The nurse must've sensed that, and she exited the room.

"Do you still think it was right?" Clara asked.

Lowering my eyes to my lap, I sighed and told her that I did.

"What about when people suffer?" She met my eyes and I nearly gasped at the fierceness, the cutting in those ice-blue irises. "Life is more than I can bear, Birdie. It's too hard and I don't want to fight anymore."

"Don't say that," I said again, my voice weak and anemic. "Please."

She closed her eyes, turning her head so that her face was hidden in the pillow.

I didn't wait for the nurse to come get me. I leaned over Clara and kissed her cheek before taking my handbag and walking out the door.

The nurse stood at a desk, her eyes focused on a file she held in her hand.

"Excuse me," I said.

She looked up at me. "Yes?"

I couldn't remember ever seeing anyone who looked more worn out than that woman.

"I wondered how often my sister will get a bath." I smiled. "I hate to complain, but her hair seemed a bit dirty."

"We try to get them into the showers once a week." The nurse glanced toward the room I'd just come out of. "It was her turn a few days ago, but . . ."

I raised my eyebrows.

"But she resisted," she said.

"I'm sorry?"

"She wouldn't let the orderly go in with her." The nurse sighed. "She said she was perfectly capable of taking a shower by herself."

"Then why didn't you let her?" I asked.

"That's not our policy." She looked down at her paperwork. "Your sister is . . ."

She paused and let out a stream of air between her lips.

"Yes?" I asked.

"Your sister is a fighter."

She said it as if it was a bad thing.

thirty-two

One of the advantages of having a west-facing house was that I could sit on my front porch and watch the sunsets. That night had offered a good sky full of color, making the humid Saturday evening worth sitting outside in. I lingered there even after the last of the orange and pink had faded.

Leaning my head back against the wooden pillar, I let my eyes close and realized that I was so exhausted I could have fallen asleep right there.

Forcing my eyes open, I noticed a pair of headlights coming down the road. The car slowed as it reached my house, parking out front. It was Albert's Buick. Holding my wristwatch in a thin beam of light that streamed from the living room lamp through the drawn curtain, I could see that it was well past time for any reasonable person to be out and about.

"Now, what are you doing here?" I asked as he came up the walk.

"Oh. Is this a bad time?" He stopped about a yard in front of the porch.

"It's never a bad time." I rubbed my eye with the knuckle of my right hand. "I don't want to talk about Clara, though."

"All right," Albert said. "We can talk about something else."

"In that case, have a seat." I nodded at the pillar opposite the one I leaned on. "Would you like a 7 Up? I have a few bottles in the refrigerator."

"That would be nice, thank you."

I went inside, going up the stairs to check on Hugo before getting the pop bottles. By the glow of the night-light I could see where he lay, curled up in his bed with his thumb in his mouth. Flannery looked up at me from her place by his feet.

He slept so peacefully, so sweetly in the cool air of his bedroom.

I was glad.

I pulled the covers up over his shoulders and kissed his temple before going back downstairs, feeling the conflicting desires for him to sleep and for him to wake up so I could hold him a little bit.

I wondered if that was something that real mothers felt. There were so many mysteries about motherhood that I'd not yet figured out how to ask Marvel to explain. Then again, it little mattered if I ever understood them.

At best, I was just playacting the part of mother. Mine was a temporary role.

Albert sat on the porch waiting for me. When I handed him his bottle, he thanked me.

"I hope you don't mind that I didn't bring you a glass," I said.

"Not at all." He took a conservative sip and closed his eyes in appreciation for the cool drink. "How's Hugo doing?"

"All right for now." I lowered myself to the porch, wishing there was at least a little something to cushion my behind and kicking myself for not thinking of that when I was inside.

He nodded and lifted his head. "I'm glad."

"And how are you?" I put my bottle on the porch. "Anything happy you can tell me? I sure could use some good news."

"Well, I might." He closed his eyes. "I was saving it for when things settled down a bit."

"Don't wait." I clapped my hands in front of my face. "Please tell me."

"I auditioned for the LaFontaine orchestra." He looked at me out of the corner of his eye. "I was accepted. I'm the very last chair, but it's something."

"Well," I said. "How wonderful. I didn't know that you still played."

"I figured if I was going to keep the thing around, I might as well put it to use." He shrugged. "I'm rusty. But I can only get better, right?"

"Haven't you told anyone?"

"Just you."

"I'm proud of you." I put my hands on my chest. "This is the best thing I've heard in a week."

"I'm glad I could make you happy." He opened his mouth to say something else, but shut it, swallowing hard.

I decided not to press him on it. If he wanted to tell me, he would in time.

A car drove by, pulling into the driveway three doors down. The man who got out looked our way as if checking to be sure I was all right. I waved at him to let him know I was.

"You were brave to audition for the orchestra," I said.

"I don't know if it was brave or stupid." He grinned at me before looking back to the sky.

"Did you know that I've only heard you play once?" I leaned against the pillar once again, drawing a long drink of my 7 Up.

"It was right before Norman and I got married, and I'd come to the house to get something from your mother. She wasn't there yet, and you thought you were all alone in the house."

He'd been in the basement, and the tremulous, mournful tones of his cello traveled up the stairwell and into the kitchen where I'd let myself in. Pressed up against the wall, afraid to move an inch and make a noise, I'd listened to the song, rich and luxurious as velvet.

For weeks after, I felt odd around Albert, as if I knew a secret about him that he'd have rather kept to himself.

And it felt as if I was being ungrateful for not thanking him for the gift of that song.

That was what it had felt like. A gift.

"It bothered Mom that I was such a shy cellist," he said. "I wish I would have played for her more than I did."

"Albie, don't you think that when you do something that makes the world a better place that it's worth pursuing?" I asked. "When you make a delicious pie or say hi to someone on the street, it's good. Every time you drive past my house to check on me, it's good. Even if you always find me at my least dignified state."

He grinned.

"How could it be selfish for you to play your cello when music gives others such joy?" I sniffled, nearly embarrassed by how emotional I was becoming in that moment. "It would be selfish if you kept it to yourself."

We sat in quiet a few minutes, after which Albert got up, saying he needed to get some sleep before work the next day.

I took his empty bottle, holding it in the crook of my arm and watching him walk down the path toward his car. He opened the door, but before getting in, he said my name.

"Yes?" I asked.

"Would it be all right . . ." He paused. "Do you think it would be okay if I visited Clara next week?"

"That might be nice for her," I said.

He patted the roof of his car twice. "Well, good night, Betty."

I lifted my free hand in a wave to him.

He waited until I was inside before driving away.

thirty–three

J found Hugo in the living room with my old photo album open on the coffee table, Flannery curled up in the chair behind him. His head was propped up on his hands, and he focused his eyes on one particular picture. When I got closer, looking over his shoulder, I saw it was of Clara and me, sitting on the steps of our apartment building.

"Who's that?" he asked.

"Why, that's your mother and me," I answered.

"You had short hair?" He turned his face toward me, his lip curled and forehead furrowed.

"Most girls had their hair like that back then." I knelt beside him. "It was called a pageboy."

"I like your hair better now."

"Thank you. I do too."

He leaned back, resting against the couch. "Where's my mommy?"

"Don't you remember? She's in the hospital," I answered. "She's sick and they're going to help her get better."

"Is she going to die?"

"Is that what you're afraid of?" I put an arm around him.

He nodded and pinched his lips together. I thought he was trying hard to be strong, to not cry.

"Oh, Hugo," I said, holding him close. "You don't need to be scared of that. The doctors are helping her get better."

"Can I visit her?"

It was the same question Clara had asked our dad years and years before when Mother was in the asylum. Dad had looked her straight in the eye then and told her that it was no place for children.

That was the right answer. But I couldn't bring myself to say it.

"Not now, sweetheart," I said instead. "But you can draw pictures for me to take when I go."

He nodded and reached out, closing the photo album.

"I think I want to be alone," he said.

He got up, left the room, and climbed the stairs. I heard the door close.

When his crying traveled through the vents to the living room, I had to fight against myself to not rush up and comfort him.

Some grieving needed to be done alone.

At least at first.

———

Norm had always prided himself on keeping the yard trimmed and presentable. I, on the other hand, clearly hadn't given the grass a second thought in the months since he passed. The wet beginning of summer had made the grass a glorious shade of green and completely unruly. The blades came up well past my ankles when I stepped off the back porch.

He would have been disgusted by the patches of dandelions that had sprouted up, unchecked. He'd have shaken his head at how his careful edging along the pavement had grown over.

It had only been a week since the boy down the street had last been over to cut the grass. But with all the rain we'd had, it grew faster than I could ever remember it doing.

I couldn't stand being inside and hearing Hugo's crying, so I thought I'd make myself useful and get busy doing something productive outside.

So I put on a pair of slacks and headed to the backyard.

I stood at the door of the shed, staring down the Simplicity Wonder-Boy 400 riding mower, trying not to be intimidated by its cherry red paint job and shiny chrome wheels. The blade didn't bear a single fleck of grass, and there wasn't a clod of dirt to speak of in the tread of the tires.

When I looked at the knobs and levers and switches, I felt a little light-headed at the prospect of having to figure the thing out all by myself. For a moment—just a flicker of a second—I considered marching myself back inside to forget about the whole thing and wait for the neighbor boy to come around to do the job.

But then I thought better of it.

"You are Betty Jane Sweet," I whispered, hands on my hips, feet just slightly apart to make me feel more powerful. "You can do anything you put your mind to."

So, I put my mind to pushing the miniature tractor out to the yard. And then I put my mind to starting it.

But no matter how much of my mind I applied to the task, I simply could not figure it out. Even consulting the manual gave no clues.

I'd never been one prone to fits of temper. That day, though,

I swung my foot back and kicked the doggone Wonder-Boy, aiming for the tire.

Unfortunately, I'd never had much practice in kicking things and hit the hard metal frame. Instantly, I regretted my tantrum, feeling a sharp pain shoot from my big toe up through my foot and calf.

"Oh!" I yelped, bending at the waist and feeling as if I might pass out.

I let myself drop to the grass on my behind, holding the toe of my canvas tennis shoe with both hands and bawling like a little girl.

It wasn't so much the pain or the frustration of not being able to get the Wonder-Boy to work. I wept because I was alone and because my purpose was gone. I cried because Norm and I had wanted so much from life and he'd gone too early to realize much of it. I cried for Clara and Hugo and how really hard life can be.

Little did I care how loudly I sobbed or what a wrenching I did to my face. What did it matter? It wasn't as if anyone could see me there on the ground in my backyard, leaning against a riding lawn mower.

At least that was what I thought.

A car door slammed, and I sucked in my breath, suddenly aware that I wasn't the only one around at that time of day. I bit my lips between my front teeth, hoping that would remind me to be quiet, at least for a minute.

But I'd been spotted.

Stan stood at the gate, eyebrows lifted high and looking at me as if I'd lost my ever-loving mind.

"What in the world are you doing, Betty?" he asked. "Are you all right?"

"Yes," I said, trying to smile but failing miserably. The best I managed was a grimace. "I'm fine."

"You're sure?" He let himself in through the gate.

"No." I stood up, using the mower to steady myself. I was glad to find that my toe didn't hurt nearly as much as it had moments earlier. "I, apparently, can't figure out how to turn on a lawn mower."

"Did you try—"

I didn't let him finish.

"My husband's dead. I'm only forty. That's too young to be a widow." My voice rose in volume and pitch as I went on. "My sister's in an insane asylum, and I'm trying to take care of her little boy. I have no idea how to raise a child. I've made a mess of everything. He's upstairs bawling his eyes out, and there's nothing I can do to make it better. And I can't even figure out how to start this stupid lawn mower!"

I took in gasps of breath, rapid and shallow. The air never seemed like it was enough. It felt a whole lot like drowning. Sparks of white popped in my eyes, and I was so dizzy I thought that I would fall down.

Stan's hand steadied me, holding me by the elbow and leading me to the back stoop.

"Easy now," he said. "Simmer down a little, will you?"

It took more than a handful of minutes before my breathing slowed down, deepened. My hands shook when I lifted them to my face.

"Better?" Stan sat beside me, hands in his lap.

"No," I answered. "Maybe a little. I don't know."

"You want a glass of water or something?"

"Just stay with me for a couple of minutes, would you?"

"I can do that," he answered.

A squirrel bolted across the backyard, stopping just before reaching the fence. He raised up on his hind legs, sniffing the air in our direction before taking off again to scamper up a tree.

"Betty . . ." Stan started.

"Don't tell me that it's going to be okay." I rubbed my temples, hoping to ease the throbbing in my head. "Because I'm not entirely sure it will be."

"I wouldn't." He cleared his throat. "What I was going to say is that I'll mow the lawn for you."

"You don't have to do that."

"I know," he said. "I will expect a shiny quarter when I'm done."

A very quiet laugh worked its way out of me. As small as it was, it felt like sunshine after a long rain.

"Can you believe I've never mowed a lawn before?" I let my shoulders relax. "Norman never wanted me to ruin the grass, I think."

Stan shook his head. "He didn't think you should have to do that kind of work."

I bit my lip hard, feeling it tremble against my teeth. The last thing I needed was to have another sobbing fit. One a day was plenty.

Stan put his hand on my shoulder. It was a warm hand and thick. But he didn't rest its full weight on me. He was gentle.

"He was a good man," I whimpered. "I miss him."

"Me too." He nodded. "Best friend I ever had."

"Oh, Stanley."

"Now I'm just stuck with Al," he said, smirking. "Ah well. Beggars can't be choosers."

I used the collar of my blouse to wipe the tears from under my eyes.

"Goodness gracious," I said, sniffling. "You'd think a girl could do a little yard work without dissolving into tears."

"You have every right to cry." He stood, dropping his hand from my shoulder and letting it hang at his side. "Now, let me see what's wrong with that beast over there."

Stan circled the Wonder-Boy, fidgeting with this and wiggling that. He got on hands and knees, looking up under it. After a handful of minutes he came back, a glint in his eye.

"Welp, you could've messed with that all day long and not gotten it to work," he said. "Don't worry. I know what's wrong."

"What is it?" I asked.

"It doesn't have any gas in the tank." He smirked.

"For the love of Pete." I smacked my forehead.

"Rookie mistake." He turned toward the mower. "You go on inside and rest a bit. All right?"

Body sore and weary, I managed to get myself up and to the door. I turned to see him carrying a gas can out of the shed.

"Thank you, Stan," I said before going inside.

"It's what Norm would have wanted me to do." He flashed me his understated smile. "I don't mind."

It wasn't long after Norman came home from the war that Marvel brought Stan to supper to meet all of us. Marvel was sixteen and so clearly taken with Stan that Norm was just sure he'd break her heart.

"She's too young to have a boyfriend," Norm had said.

"I was fourteen when we met," I said. "You didn't seem to have a problem with that."

"It's different." He stormed across the room, adjusting a picture frame on the mantel.

"How?"

"I knew my intentions," he answered. "I don't know if this Stan guy is honorable."

"Give him a chance, honey."

"I don't want to."

"Well, you'll have to," I said. "Because I invited Marvel over for Friday night. And she's bringing him."

"Betty! Why would you go and do a thing like that without asking me?"

"Because I knew you'd say no."

Norm grumped around the rest of the week, stewing over having to spend time with a young man he wanted nothing to do with. When Friday came, he resisted putting on a fresh shirt and pulling a comb through his hair.

"Oh, Norman," I'd said. "Try to be nice. For Marvel's sake."

"I'll try."

"Besides, he's bringing the bread."

"He's buying it?" Norm squinted at me.

"No. He's making it."

"Oh for goodness' sake."

When Stan pulled his ancient pickup truck into the driveway, Norm watched to make sure he got Marvel's door. When he did, Norm shrugged, allowing the boy at least a few points. When Stan came in, one hand on the small of Marvel's back, Norm shook his head, subtracting all of them.

But it was when Stan handed the loaf of bread he'd made to me, wrapped in a cloth, that Norman really paid attention.

"You made this?" Norm asked.

"I did," Stan answered, beaming and completely unaware of how he was being scrutinized. "It's an old family recipe."

"What is it?"

"Challah bread." Stan nodded at it. "You ever have it?"

"Sure I have," Norm said. "I've made it a hundred times."

"Well, I've made it about three times." Stan grinned. "I hope this one passes muster."

Needless to say, the loaf won Norman over. As soon as Stan finished high school, he took a job at Sweet Family and saved as much as he could to buy a diamond ring for Marvel.

Norman was in the wedding as best man.

It was a miracle, the good a loaf of bread could do.

thirty-four

Friday morning was already muggy by eight o'clock. I opened up the windows, hoping for a good breeze. All that did was let the humidity inside. By nine I already felt like a wilted pansy.

Hugo didn't seem to mind the heat so much. He sat at the kitchen table with a book that Nick and Dick had sent over. He couldn't quite read the words, but the pictures were colorful and told enough of a story all on their own.

Flannery had found a sun spot in the middle of the room, and I tried to remember she was there so I wouldn't trip over her. As many times as I stepped over her, she didn't seem to even notice. Of course she didn't.

"Did you get enough breakfast?" I asked Hugo.

"Mmm-hmm," he answered, not looking up from his book.

The honking of a horn in the driveway caught our attention. Hugo sat up straight, and I stepped into the living room to see who it could be.

The turquoise station wagon was parked out front, the engine idling. Marvel rushed to the front door, waving at me when she saw me looking out the window.

"Get some shorts on," she said when I opened the door, the strong smell of her Coppertone wafting in through the screen. "And I've got swim trunks for Hugo."

She peered in around me and waved at Hugo before holding up a pair of shorts. She opened the screen door and handed them to me.

"Where are we going?" I asked.

"Just come on." She flashed her biggest smile. "It's too hot to be inside all day. Let's go."

"All right," I said. "Give me five minutes."

"Oh, and no pedal pushers, Betty," she called after me. "Wear your Bermuda shorts."

I sighed, worried about showing off my chubby knees to the whole world, but I put them on anyway.

I nearly always did what Marvel told me to.

❧

Just about everyone in mid-Michigan had the same idea Marvel had about coming to Lake Lansing to cool off. It was no easy task, finding a parking spot, and when we finally did, Nick and Dick burst out of the car doors, hopping on the grass, impatient for us to get going.

Hugo, on the other hand, waited for me to hold his hand.

"I want you to have loads of fun," I told him. "All right?"

He nodded, his brow furrowed like he was paying special attention to my instructions.

"I'm riding the roller coaster until I get sick," Dick said.

"Why would you want to do that?" Marvel asked. "Don't run too far ahead, boys."

"Did you know Al Capone used to come here?" Nick said. "Somebody told me he didn't die like everybody thought he did. They say he works here, selling hot dogs and popcorn."

"None of that is true." Marvel sighed, adjusting the bag that was slung over her shoulder.

"Could be," Nick said, shrugging. "Carl Lange told me it was."

"And who do you think is smarter, me or twelve-year-old Carl?" Marvel asked, then put up her finger. "On second thought, don't answer that."

Nick gave her a smirk and skipped ahead of us, catching up with Dick.

"Are you excited?" I asked Hugo. "What are you most looking forward to?"

"The pony ride," he answered. Then he whispered to me, "Do you think it'll talk to me? Like Mr. Ed?"

"Oh goodness, I don't know." I winked. "Wouldn't that be something?"

"Hugo," Dick called from half a dozen paces in front of us. "Come on!"

"Go ahead, sweetie," I said. "You know I'll keep my eye on you all day, right?"

"You promise?"

"Of course I do."

We let them go on the rides—roller coaster, Ferris wheel, the Fly-O-Plane—all morning, denying them cotton candy and taffy until after. Then, once they were good and sticky, we headed to the lake. They were by no means the only ones in the water, but the twins didn't seem to mind. They splashed and wrestled and stood in line to go down the tall slide into the deeper part of the swimming area.

Hugo, though, only went shin deep, watching all the other kids run past him and dive under the surface.

I made to get up off my beach towel, but Marvel told me to hold on. She stuck her fingers in the corners of her lips, letting out a shrill whistle that could have gotten the attention of the man running the carousel clear across the park.

Nick and Dick perked up from where they were, looking our way. She waved her arm in the air and then pointed at Hugo. Those boys—those good boys—went running toward their younger cousin.

Somehow they convinced him to go in just a little deeper, patiently inching in alongside him until they were to mid-thigh and he was waist high. They let him splash them, pretending to get knocked out by the spray of lake water, and I delighted in how he giggled at them.

"You have raised two fine boys, Marvel," I said, settling back onto my towel, the warm sand forming to the shape of my backside.

"I can't take all the credit. Stan helped a little." She watched the trio of boys with a smile on her face that looked the very definition of proud. "They think a lot of Hugo."

"He's something, isn't he?"

Nick bent down a little bit, his arms out in front of him at a ninety-degree angle. Dick had his hand on Hugo's back, talking to him and nodding. I didn't know what they were up to until they helped Hugo ease onto Nick's arms, belly down. Dick crouched so he was at Hugo's level and showed him how to move his arms, how to kick his legs, how to keep his head above the water.

They moved forward, Hugo kicking up a whole lot of water in his wake.

"How are you holding up? It's been a hard summer, hasn't it?" Marvel said. "I've been praying for you, honey."

"Thank you." I took in a good-sized breath, letting it out in a long puff. "I've had a hard time praying lately."

"I can see why." She took off her sunglasses and looked me in the eyes. "Can I be honest with you?"

"Have you ever done anything else?" I smiled.

"This is how my mother raised me to be." She winked at me. "Betty, I don't understand what you're going through with Clara."

"I don't either."

"But even though I don't understand, will you let me be there for you?" she asked. "Please."

I nodded. "I won't be able to ask, you know."

"I know."

I swallowed and turned to once again watch the boys. Nick kept moving with Hugo across his arms. But when he got jostled by someone who came up from the water unexpectedly, he fumbled Hugo, dipping him under the water. Dick scooped him right up, hands under his armpits, pulling him back into the air.

Hugo coughed a little, and Dick patted him on the back a couple of times before helping him onto Nick's arms again.

"Do you think they'll be able to help her at the . . . ?"

"Sanitarium? Oh, I hope so."

Nick took one arm out from under Hugo, putting it behind his back, I thought, so Hugo wouldn't know. Even without the two arms to support him, my littlest nephew stayed level, bobbing along on the surface of the lake.

"When will you visit her next?" Marvel asked.

"Maybe next week," I answered.

"I'll watch Hugo."

"Thank you."

"It's no trouble," she said. "He's a good boy."

We watched the boys for a little while, the swimming lesson continuing. The sun warmed my skin, and I hoped that it would give my pale flesh a nice glow, conveniently forgetting that it only ever turned me into a lobster.

In the water, Hugo tottered and Nick slid his arm back under his belly, saying something into his ear.

After just a little while, the three of them ended the swimming lesson, running to shore and dropping in the sand to dig a channel, using their hands for shovels.

When Hugo noticed that I was watching, he cupped his sand-covered hands on either side of his mouth.

"Aunt Betty," he yelled. "Did you see me swimming?"

"I did!" I called back. "You were amazing."

"It was like flying."

"Oh, I brought the camera." I scrambled up off my towel, with no small lack of grace. "You boys, I want nice smiles, all right?"

They posed for me, Hugo grinning brilliantly while Nick and Dick flexed their muscles on either side of him. I couldn't help but laugh, calling for them to stand this way or that. I spent more frames on them than was probably necessary, but those nephews of mine were hams and I couldn't help myself.

By the time we left for home I was gritty from sand, burned by the sun, and I hadn't thought of my chubby knees once all day.

thirty-five

It was very early in the morning, and I woke with a crick in my neck. Rolling from my side to my back, shifting my head on the pillow, I remembered I'd slept on the floor in Hugo's room. Every bone in my body ached.

Goodness, I certainly was getting old.

The night-light shone just enough that I could see that Hugo still slept soundly, his little body so close to the edge of the bed I feared he'd fall off. His lips were parted just slightly, and his fingers curled in a fist, holding the silky part of his blanket. It was hard to believe that this sweet one, so calm and peaceful, had woken in the middle of the night screaming for me to come and help.

It had been a whole week since his last bad dream, and this one had caught me right when I thought they were done for good.

Managing to get myself up off the floor, I saw that it was still dark out. I thought I could get an hour more of sleep in my own bed. I folded the blanket I'd pulled atop me and grabbed the pillow just before I heard a little voice.

"Aunt Betty?" Hugo said, his voice barely a whisper.

"It's not time to get up yet, dearest," I said. "You can sleep a little longer."

I bent over him, kissing his temple and feeling his curls on my face.

"Did my mommy die?" he asked.

"Oh, honey," I said. "No."

He let go of a deep breath, and I could see his little shoulders relaxing as if he'd carried a far too heavy weight for much too long.

"Is that what your bad dream was about?" I asked.

He nodded. "Would you tell me if she was dead?"

"Yes. I would." I touched his forehead. "I would never keep something like that from you."

"Do dreams sometimes come true?"

"Not in the way you're thinking." I sat on the edge of his bed. "I think that means that sometimes wishes and hopes come true. Not that nightmares do."

Worry creased the space between his eyebrows. "Is she still at the hospital?"

"Yes." I cupped his cheek with my hand.

"When can she come home?"

"Just as soon as the doctors say she's better."

"What if she doesn't ever get better?" Hugo asked, his little eyelids blinking so heavily and slowly. "What if she stays sick forever?"

"Sweetheart, I don't know," I said.

I smoothed his hair. It was getting long, and I thought I'd need to find a barber soon to give him a trim.

"Can I tell you a story?" I asked. "A very short one?"

"Okay," he said, sniffling.

"There was once a turtle named Sam," I began. "He lived near a river filled with crayfish and frogs and minnows. The sun shone through the leaves that hung over the water like a canopy, and a gentle breeze was always blowing so that it didn't get too hot."

"That sounds nice," Hugo said. "I want to go there sometime."

"Maybe Nick and Dick would too." I winked at him before going on. "But even as wonderful and special as that riverside was, Sam was too afraid to enjoy it. Can you believe that?"

"What was he scared of?"

"Everything. When the leaves rustled in the wind, he'd gasp. If a minnow darted through the water, Sam would yelp with fright. If one of the frogs croaked, Sam would run as far away as he could get—which wasn't far or fast, if you want to know the truth."

I grinned at him, and he smiled back.

"Sam decided one day that the world was just too scary," I went on. "He pulled his arms into his shell. Then his legs. Last his head. He thought that if he could hide from the world, he'd be safe."

"Oh, Sam." Hugo shook his head.

"The trouble was, Sam was so worried about getting hurt that he missed all the wonderful things around him. He didn't see a rainbow that crossed the entire sky after the rain. And he never got to meet the brand-new baby bunnies that were born in the warren near the edge of the woods. When the hummingbirds came to visit the honeysuckle near where he hid in his shell, he missed them completely."

"That's sad."

"It is," I said. "One day a tiny ant crawled into Sam's shell and told him about everything he was missing out on because he was hiding. So, Sam stuck his pointy nose out of the shell and right away smelled the sweet lilacs in the bush nearby. Then he poked his head out so he could see the pretty blue sky above him. Then his ears next, and he heard the delicate song of the chickadee."

Hugo blinked slowly and yawned.

"Sam let his arms and legs push out of the shell and felt the cool grass and warm sunshine against his skin." I pulled the sheet up over Hugo's shoulders. "Sam stepped toward the water and slid on the dirt until he was in the river, feeling it rushing around him."

I stood as quietly as I could, the tingles in my toes turning to stings as I put weight on my feet. Backing away, I watched the gentle rise and fall of Hugo's shoulders, his heavy eyelids closed and his mouth opening again, just a little.

"Don't let the scary things of the world keep you from seeing the good," I whispered, as much to myself as to him. "Even the darkest night can't put out all the light."

The sunrise had just turned the sky a deep indigo. Instead of going back to sleep, I sat on the steps next to an east-facing window and watched, trying to see the coming sun the way my mother might have. Glory upon glory. Color more brilliant than any painting.

Just along the horizon I saw the birth of the morning.

This was the gift God had for me right that moment.

I saw hope.

thirty-six

All week long the *Peanuts* comic strip in the newspaper had given advice for how to safely view the eclipse. Hugo had me clip each of them so he could paste them onto a piece of thick paper. We read them together about half a dozen times each, Hugo listening intently, not getting the jokes.

He took them as serious instructions from Linus for how to avoid going blind on the day of the eclipse.

The very last strip which ran on the morning of the eclipse showed Lucy and Linus standing in the rain, the marvelous event blocked by heavy rain clouds.

"I don't want that one," Hugo told me, scowling. "That one makes me sad."

I folded up the paper and put it in the junk drawer, saving it for whenever he'd change his mind.

"Nick said he was going to look at it," Hugo said from where he sat, looking over the cartoons at the table. "With his bare eyes."

"He did, huh?" I shook my head. "He'll be sorry if he does."

"Will he go blind?"

"Maybe." I turned my watch around to remind myself to keep an eye on my nephews. The last thing Marvel needed was for one or both of them to burn their eyes out.

"I won't look. I promise."

"That's good of you." I wiped down the counters. "Are you almost ready to go?"

He slid down from the seat and put the *Peanuts* comics under his arm. I could just imagine him telling Nick and Dick the rules of how to safely enjoy the moon blocking out the sun. Just the thought of it made me smile.

"Don't forget your box," I called after him.

He ran into the living room for the old moving box that we'd turned into a pinhole viewer. Carrying it, he hardly fit through the door out to the garage.

I nearly lost my composure, watching him move through that old house as if it was always where he'd belonged. Where he'd always been meant to be.

My heart seemed to swell first with love for that little boy. Then it ached because he wasn't mine. Not truly. I wouldn't have him there with me forever.

I cleared my throat and picked up my car keys from the hook on the wall and followed behind him.

He might not be mine forever and always, but he was for that day.

It would have to be enough.

⁓

Stan and Albert had lugged a half dozen lawn chairs onto the roof of the bakery. Marvel and I put down a picnic blanket for the boys to sit on. We had a plate full of special cookies that

Albert had made just for the occasion, yellow frosting on one side with a crescent of chocolate on the other.

Pop came out on the roof following Nick and Dick who, true to fashion, elbowed one another to be first up.

"Beat ya," Nick said.

"Did not," Dick said back. "Grandpop, who won?"

"I don't know," Pop said. "I can't tell you apart."

Hugo stood beside me, watching their shenanigans and shielding his eyes with one of his hands. It was a mightily sunny day, but I knew that wasn't why he shied away from the brightness.

He was afraid that the sun would blind him even before the eclipse began. Nothing I said could convince him otherwise.

It seemed that Linus and Charlie Brown had adequately warned the poor boy to distraction.

The kids put their heads in their boxes, letting the light come through the pinhole on one side and reflect on the white paper they'd pasted on the inside. Whenever Hugo took his off, he insisted on sitting on my lap, curled into a ball, his face buried in my chest. Eventually he told me that the sun made him feel weird.

"What do you mean?" I asked, keeping my voice to a whisper.

"It makes me afraid," he said. "And sad."

"Why?"

"What if the moon swallows the sun forever and we never see it again?"

"Oh, sweetie, the moon won't swallow it. It just blocks it for a few minutes." I showed him, moving one hand in front of the other. "Then when it passes, we'll have our sun back."

"Do you promise?"

"Yes. I promise." I rubbed his back. "There's nothing to worry about. Remember Sam? Don't hide in your shell, sweetie."

But the closer we got to the time for the moon to block out the sun, the stranger I felt. The sky seemed to be the wrong color. I got goose bumps on my arms even though the day was warm. Something in me felt off.

Just about four o'clock the moon approached the sun, moving slowly toward it as if it meant to sneak up on it. We warned the boys over and over not to look directly at it. Marvel even made sure to remind Pop.

"I'm no imbecile, you know," Pop said, but still turned his face so as not to be tempted.

The boxes on the heads of the boys were quite comical, and I was glad I'd brought my camera so I could snap a picture of it. They'd used such big boxes that sat awkwardly on their shoulders and dwarfed their bodies.

Marvel held a colander over the cream-colored blanket on the roof; a hundred crescents made incomplete dots all along the fabric.

Even though I knew I wasn't to look, it seemed like such a sad thing that I couldn't witness this event that would never happen again. Not quite like that, in my lifetime.

It took all my effort not to turn my face sunward to see the most incredible thing I ever could. But I knew that it would have left me blind.

What a world, that the full glory of it was more than we could bear.

It took my breath away, to think how much greater the majesty of the One who moved the moon across the sky, who held the sun in place, and who allowed us to enjoy every bit of it.

How he must have loved us so.

thirty-seven

Hugo wore his bow tie to church with a white button-up shirt. I'd used a little bit of Brylcreem left over from Norman to slick his hair back. Still, the curls wouldn't be completely tamed, looking like tight finger waves that reminded me of Cab Calloway.

He raced up the steps behind Nick and Dick to their Sunday school classroom, and I stood at the bottom, watching them go and fighting the urge to call out for him to hold the railing.

Sometimes being safe wasn't the most important thing.

"He'll be fine," Pop said, coming up from behind me, his cane thudding on the hard floor. "He's got to spread his wings a little."

"I know." I drew in a deep breath, holding it a few seconds before letting it out. "I just worry about him."

Pop patted me on the shoulder then nodded at the stairs. "Want to sit with me for a spell?"

"What about Sunday school?"

"I got kicked out for bad behavior." He winked at me.

"Well, I can't say that surprises me."

Pop made a groaning sound when he sat down. When I asked if he was all right, he grimaced.

"Yeah. Getting up will be a whole lot harder." He rested the cane against the wall under the railing. "How are you holding up, kiddo?"

"Well, I'm still alive," I answered, sitting beside him.

"That's got to count for something." He patted my hand, his arthritic swollen knuckles looking sore. "You're doing a good job with that little boy."

"I'm trying." I bit my lip. "Half the time I have no idea what I'm doing."

"I remember those first years of having kids. It's a lot of work, isn't it?"

"Well, I'm not sure that I would know exactly."

"Sure you would," he said. "You might not have given birth to Clara or Hugo, but you've been a makeshift mother to both of them."

It was generous of him, and I was grateful.

"Now, I don't want you thinking I'm a scaredy-cat, but I was so afraid when my three were all little," he said. "I was scared the bakery would go broke or that our house would catch fire or that I'd be a terrible dad to them. I wore myself out with the worry. It made me mean more times than I like to admit."

"I can't imagine you being mean."

"Sometimes that's how a man deals with his anxious thoughts." He shrugged. "Lacy cornered me one day."

He shook his head and laughed at the memory, rubbing his clean-shaven face with the palm of his hand.

"She said if I didn't knock it off, she'd have me sleeping in the back room of the bakery until I did." He caught my eyes and raised his brows. "When I told her it was because I was scared, she said I was wasting my time."

He wiped under his nose with the back of his hand.

"She told me something that's stuck with me. And I'm going to say the same thing to you today," he said. "The people in our lives, they were God's before they were ours. And just because we've got them doesn't mean they stop being his."

I folded my hands in my lap, trying to keep from fidgeting.

"When I married Lacy, I didn't take her from God and I wasn't borrowing her. She belonged fully to him before and above anything." He squeezed his hand into a fist and released it, a few crackles sounding in the process. "It's the same with the kids."

"Did that work?" I asked.

"Well, sometimes." He chuckled. "But you better believe she reminded me whenever I forgot."

"I'm sure she did." I felt a pang of missing Mom Sweet.

"I will tell you that it didn't make losing Lacy or Norm any easier," he said. "Nothing could have made that easy."

He knocked a tear out from under his eye.

"Oh, Pop." I took his hand.

"Nothing that can happen to any of us is outside of God's hand." He looked me straight in the eyes. "He knows we'll suffer, Bets. He knows because he has suffered. And I believe he feels the pain right along with us."

He turned his hand over and wrapped his fingers around mine.

"I know that's not the most comforting way of saying what I mean." His grin was the exact one he'd passed down to Norman. "What I'm trying to say is that we're going to have trials of all kinds. But we can't lose hope, Bets. We can't. If we can just believe, we might just see him overcome it all."

From the classroom at the top of the stairs the kids sang "Jesus Loves Me" just like they did every week.

Pop smiled as he hefted himself up. When he offered me his hand, I took it even though I didn't need his help to stand.

We walked down the hallway together, my arm tucked into his.

He sang along with the kids with every bit of earnestness as they did.

We were God's little ones.

We belonged to him.

It didn't take away all the worry.

But it made it easier to bear.

thirty-eight

I t was a warm day with clear skies, and a nurse told me that my sister was in the courtyard, sitting in the shade of her favorite tree.

"It's an apple tree," the nurse said. "She says it smells good."

She walked with me outside, and I hesitated as soon as we stepped out the door, my legs feeling as if they'd turned to lead, my stomach upset.

"That's her," she said, pointing. "Right there."

We continued on, my feet falling heavy on the cobblestone walkway, my shoes making loud noises.

"Wait here." The nurse grabbed my arm, stilling me. "I'll let her know you're here."

I stayed in place like I'd been told and watched the nurse approach Clara. So gentle, so kind.

"Miss Clara?" the nurse said, her voice full of sweetness. "You have a visitor."

She pointed in my direction, and Clara turned her head.

At first her expression held no recognition and I feared that whatever treatments they'd been giving her had ruined her brain. But then she breathed in and tried for a smile, even as much effort as it took.

"Birdie," she said.

My shoes clonked on the stones and I was glad when I stepped off into the grass. It was too peaceful of a place for such a hard sound. Clara moved to one side of the bench so I'd have room to sit beside her.

"You came." She looked at me with eyes round with surprise. "I thought you'd forgotten about me."

"But Clara, I was here just last week," I said. "Don't you remember?"

She blinked hard a few times, wrinkled her brow.

"Are you all right?" I asked, putting an arm around her and pulling her close to me, if only for a moment.

"I'm fine." She opened her mouth as if adjusting her jaw. "How's Hugo?"

"He misses you," I said. "I brought some pictures he made for you. The nurse said she'd take them to your room."

"Maybe she'll tape them to the wall."

"Would you like that?"

She nodded. "That would be nice."

Her lips twitched to the side and she shrugged. As far as I could remember, I'd never seen her behave so fidgety before.

"Did you get to see the eclipse?" I asked.

She shook her head. "We stayed inside."

"That's too bad."

Clara folded her hands in her lap, and I tried not to stare at her wrist. The wound was healing, I could see. But it would leave an angry-looking scar. I turned away from it when I realized she was watching me.

"I brought a photo for you," I said, unclasping my purse. "Hugo said you'd like it."

It was a square, glossy print of Hugo in his Sunday suit, standing next to the front yard flower beds. Flannery was perched in the window, staring at him, her mouth open mid-meow.

Clara held it on her open palm, not blinking as she drank the image in.

"My handsome boy," she whispered. "He looks so grown up."

She smiled even as a tear tumbled down her cheek.

"He needs a haircut," she said. "Can you take him to a barber?"

"Yes." I nodded.

"Don't try to do it yourself." She turned her attention to me, her eyebrows raised high. "Last year when we were low on money, I decided I would cut it. I didn't realize how hard it would be to get it even. I had to shave it all off."

She caught a giggle in her hand.

"He was bald as a cue ball," she said. "I felt terrible."

Her laughter shifted to crying and her smile dropped. She held the picture to her chest so hard that I worried she'd wrinkle it beyond recognition.

"I've been such a horrible mother," she said between sobs.

"No, sweetie," I said, putting an arm around her.

"I don't deserve him."

"Please, don't cry." I bent at the waist so I could talk into her ear. "Do you remember the tree in the park when we were younger? The one you named?"

She nodded. "Roberta?"

"That's the one. You loved that tree, didn't you? You'd climb it and stay in her branches for hours on end."

"She was beautiful."

"Yes. She was," I said. "And remember when you heard they were going to cut it down?"

"They had no right," she said between gasps. "There was nothing wrong with her."

"So, what did you do?"

"I tied myself to her trunk with twine." She turned her face toward me. The old spark of determination was there in her eyes, even if it had grown dim. "I told them they'd have to cut me down first."

"You always were a firecracker."

She raised her head. "I knew they'd cut her down anyway. I just wanted to fight them."

"And you did," I said. "You've always been a fighter."

She nodded.

"Now you have to fight, all right. You have to fight to get better." I used the pad of my thumb to wipe away a tear from her face. "Can you try?"

"I won't win," she said, her voice so small I nearly didn't hear it.

"You might."

The nurse came around and told us that our time was up. Before I let her escort me out, I put my arms around Clara, feeling more sharp edges under her skin than I had just weeks before.

"Please try to fight," I whispered in her ear before kissing her on the cheek. "I love you."

I turned around once before I was out of the courtyard to see that she'd watched me walk away.

I kissed the tips of my fingers and blew it her way.

By then, she'd turned away from me.

For years I did the very same thing on the morning of July 29. I would get up before sunrise to brew strong coffee to pour into a thermos and make sandwiches with egg salad or lunch meat. I would pack the picnic basket to the brim with all of Norman's favorite foods. Pickles and potato chips and celery sticks.

Fixing a plate of scrambled eggs, bacon, and toast with tomato slices on the side, I'd carry it in to Norman, singing "Happy Birthday" and waking him with a kiss on the mouth.

"My favorite day of the year," he'd say every single time, his eyes bright and his smile wide.

We'd drive to someplace out of town. I'd let Norm pick where we'd go, and I'd say yes to his every request.

Ice cream three times in one afternoon? Yes.

Wading to our knees in the fountain at the zoo? Yes.

Staying up well past our bedtimes to talk after we'd been together as husband and wife? Yes.

And every birthday night, just as he was drifting off to sleep I'd whisper in his ear, "My favorite day of the year too."

I didn't set my alarm to go off early that July 29 and I didn't have plans for a picnic or any sort of getaway. I intended to live that day as if it was just any other. Not as a way of forgetting Norm. Never would I have wanted that. Rather, it was so that I'd make it through without bawling my eyes out every other minute.

Still, I woke early and got out of bed. Taking a deep breath to bolster myself, I pulled open the curtains.

Outside my window, the sun was rising.

"Aunt Betty," Hugo said, climbing up into his chair for breakfast. "Are you sad?"

I put the two plates of scrambled eggs and toast on the table and sat down across from him. "Why do you ask?"

"You're quiet." He leaned his elbows on the table. "And you aren't smiling. You usually smile a lot in the mornings."

"Oh, sweetheart." I found myself at a loss of what to say. "I'm sorry."

"You don't have to be sorry for being sad."

"Well, you're right about that," I said, dropping a little jam onto my toast and spreading it with the back of my spoon. "I suppose I am sad. We all have days like that, don't we?"

He got up from his seat and walked around the table. Up on his tiptoes, he planted a soft kiss on my cheek.

"Thank you," I said. "Would you like me to tell you a story?"

"Yes, please," he answered before going back to his seat.

"Once upon a time there was a girl named Ella," I started. "She lived in a little house at the edge of the sea."

"What color was it?"

"Ella's home was painted pink, her very favorite color in all the world. She was happy there, every day swimming in the sea with her friends."

"Were her friends people or fish?" Hugo asked.

"They were fish of every color and size. Fast fish and slow, big and small. And they all loved Ella so very much."

I went on to tell him about how there had been less rain that year, that little by little the sea began to dry up. The fish all moved away, looking for a new place to live where there was plenty of water for all of them.

"When they left, Ella was all alone," I said. "And that made her so sad."

"Why couldn't she go with them?" Hugo asked around a mouthful of eggs.

"Because she couldn't swim as long and as far as they could. Remember, she wasn't the same as them." I half frowned. "So she stayed in her little pink house by the sea, missing her friends every day and collecting her tears in a little bottle."

"Why'd she do that?" Hugo asked, curling his lips and squinting his eyes.

"Well, I suppose so she'd know just how much she missed them all."

Hugo shrugged. "All right."

Flannery jumped next to Hugo on his chair and nudged his shoulder with the top of her head before sniffing at his plate.

"Shoo, kitty," he said, but with a giggle.

She hopped off and sat at his feet, grooming herself.

I went on to tell about how Ella stayed in her house, no longer venturing out because she saw no purpose in it. There was no one around to play with or visit for miles and miles. All Ella did was look out the window, missing her friends.

She was so very sad.

"One day someone knocked on her door," I said. "It rattled her shutters and made Ella gasp."

"Is it a bad person?" Hugo asked.

I only shrugged and went on with the story. "Ella answered the door to see an old man with wild gray hair and gaps between his teeth." I tried for an old man's rasping. "'Little girl,' the old man said, 'why are you all alone?'"

"Was he a bad man?" Hugo asked, eyes wide. "She shouldn't talk to bad men."

"Well, you're right," I answered. "Just remember that this is only a story, all right?"

"Is he a bad man or a good man?"

"If it matters so much to you, he's a good man." I winked at him before going on. "Ella told him about her friends and her worries that they'd not be able to find a new home. She told him how much she missed them. By the time she finished telling her story, it was dark outside. 'Will you help an old man see?' the man said. 'Will you give him your lantern?'"

I told of how Ella went inside and took out the only light she had, offering it to the man.

"But then how will she see?" Hugo asked.

"Ella wondered about that too," I said. "But she knew that it was the right thing, to help the man. Soon, he began to yawn and asked if he could rest for a little bit in her yard. Ella said he could. 'Will you comfort an old man?' he asked. 'Will you warm him with your blanket?'"

I told of how Ella took the beautiful green blanket from her own shoulders and spread it out on the man, feeling the chill of the air herself instead.

"But then wouldn't she be cold?" Hugo asked.

"Yes. But she knew that it was the right thing to do, to help the old man. In the morning, when he woke up, he asked for something to drink. But all she had . . ."

"Was the bottle of tears?" Hugo finished for me.

I nodded. "But those she didn't want to give up. Those she wanted to keep, a reminder of the friends she missed."

I told about how Ella held the bottle to her chest. It was the only thing she had left, but she knew that it was right to help the poor old man. So, she handed it to him.

"What do you think he did with those tears?" I asked.

"Did he drink them?" Hugo cringed. "I hope he doesn't drink them."

"He didn't," I answered. "But he took the lantern and the green blanket and the bottle of tears and disappeared."

"I don't like the old man," Hugo said, frowning. "He shouldn't have taken her things."

"Well, there's more to the story." I leaned my elbows on the table. "Ella went back into her house, shutting the door, thinking that all she had was lost. Her friends, her lantern, blanket, and tears. But she was surprised to find that her sadness was still with her."

I told of how just as she closed the door there was a strong earthquake, one that made her almost lose her footing. When she looked out the window, she saw a building growing up from the ground, erupting from the dirt.

Hugo slid off his seat, coming around the table and climbing up on my lap.

"The old man stood on the steps of the building, his gap-toothed mouth pulled into a wide smile," I said. "He called to her, 'Come see! Come see!' And Ella did."

Hugo leaned into me.

"Ella followed the man into the building, not believing what she saw when she entered. The walls were full of water," I said. "More water than she'd ever seen in her whole life. Glass held it all in, and Ella touched it with her fingertips. There, on the other side, swam fish of every color, shape, and size. Goldfish and pikes and barracudas. There was even a tank with a very small shark."

"Her friends?" Hugo asked.

"Yes. All of her friends were there. They swam behind the glass, laughing and telling her how happy they were to see her." I smoothed his hair with my hand. "Do you have a guess about what the water was made of?"

He leaned his head against my chest. "Was it rain?"

"No. Close, though," I said. "The water in all of the tanks was made of Ella's tears."

I continued on, telling of how something above her caught Ella's eyes and she looked up, gasping for the beauty of it.

"What was it?" Hugo asked. "Was it the ceiling?"

"Sort of. But it looked to Ella more like the sky. A sky of the most brilliant, bright, shiny green," I said. "It was a fresh green, like the very first grass of spring, just the very same shade as her blanket. And hanging from the center of the sky was a lantern exactly like the one she'd given the old man. She kept her face tipped upward, not daring to take her eyes off the sky for fear that it would fade away."

"It was real, though, wasn't it?"

"Of course," I answered. "It was then that she felt a hand on her shoulder. It was a warm touch, tender."

"Was it the old man?"

I nodded. "He said, 'Welcome home.' And she smiled, all her sadness fading away."

"Did she live happily ever after?" Hugo asked.

"I hope so."

"Aunt Betty?"

"Yes, dearest?"

"That place isn't real, is it? It's just make-believe."

"The land of the glass fish houses and green sky?" I asked. "Why, of course it's real. How would you like to go there?"

"When?"

"Right now."

He turned his face, and I loved the way his eyes sparkled.

Nestled in the Detroit River—right between the shores of Michigan and Canada—was an island of wonders. Some of my very earliest memories were of Belle Isle, taking the trolley there with my mother and sister when I was very small to spend the day.

I thought that if I tried, I could think of a memory in every inch of that place. All of them happy. Every single one.

I drove around the island the long way around so Hugo could see the luxurious fountain and the statues and the wide-open waters. I pointed across the river to Windsor and slowed when we drove past the old ships.

Hugo was turned in the passenger seat to look out the window, saying "wow" more than I thought any human had ever done in the history of the world.

"We'll see all of it," I told him. "We've got the whole day."

When I saw the glass dome of the conservatory, I knew we were nearly where I wanted to stop first. Not too far off, we found a parking spot that was just wide enough for the Bel Air. I made sure to have Hugo lock his door when he got out.

"What's that?" he asked, waiting for me to get the camera from the trunk of the car. "That big glass building? Is that where Ella's friends live?"

"That's where they have all sorts of plants," I said, nodding at the smaller building beside it. "That's where we're going first."

"Is that it?"

"Yes," I answered. "Take my hand while we cross the parking lot."

He did, looking both ways for traffic like I'd taught him.

"Are you excited?" I pointed at the small, box-like building of brown brick with ivy climbing up the sides.

He nodded.

I squeezed his hand.

"What does that word spell?" Hugo asked, pointing at the letters engraved above the doorway.

"It says 'Aquarium,'" I answered. "Do you know what that is?"

He shook his head.

"It's a place for underwater critters to live."

"And who's that man?" he asked.

I knew he meant the bearded face that peeked out from the very top of the archway over the doors.

"That's Neptune," I answered.

"Is he the old man from the story?"

"Huh. Might be."

Hugo nodded as if satisfied with the answer.

We reached the steps up into the aquarium and I hesitated, worried for a moment that he wouldn't think it as spectacular as I had when I was a girl. Scared that it wouldn't live up to his expectations.

But after we stepped inside, I realized that it had been silly for me to worry. I watched Hugo's eyes widen to the size of quarters and his mouth drop open.

"This is Ella's home," he said, just loud enough for me to hear him. He pointed up and around him and at everything he saw. "Her blanket, her lantern, her friends."

The arched ceiling was made of jade-colored tile. Yellow light flickered on the polished green, making it look like the surface of a lake on a sunny day. Lining the walls were glass fish tanks housing gar and sturgeon and trout. I lifted Hugo at each glass square so he could see inside. Eels and pike and fish of many colors zipped and floated and dove in the water, and Hugo's eyes kept track of every movement.

At each tank, Hugo spoke to them, not seeming bothered when they didn't answer him. He asked if they'd seen Ella, if she was doing all right, he asked them to tell her hello for us.

I refused to hurry him. I let him take his sweet time. When he asked to go back to the puffer fish, citing the need to tell him just one more thing, I gladly obliged.

There was no telling how long he might go on believing in the workings of magic. I wanted to help him hold on to it as long as he could.

When he finished with the fish, he stood close to the middle of the aquarium, other visitors passing us by. He tipped his head back and gazed up at the green sky above us for so long, I wondered for half a minute if he'd fallen asleep.

But then he whispered up at me, moving his eyes from the jade-colored tile to my eyes.

"Thank you, Aunt Betty," he said.

I put my hands on his shoulders and tipped my head up, enjoying Ella's green sky.

We wandered around the conservatory next, letting the palm trees shield our faces from the sun that shone through the domed glass ceiling. We had our picnic lunch in the gardens, soft grass beneath the checkered blanket I'd brought to sit on. We strolled through the children's zoo and dipped our fingers in the cool water of the fountain.

I made sure to take pictures of Hugo standing by the clock tower and in front of the yacht club and beside the ancient cannon at the Great Lakes Museum. I planned to take the nearly full roll of film to be developed right away.

Clara would want to see them when next I visited.

We got home late. Hugo was already asleep in the seat beside me, and I had to struggle to carry him inside and up to his bed.

Completely worn out, I decided I would climb into my covers too, leaving the day's chores for another time. But while I crept down the stairs, a long-forgotten memory triggered in my mind.

Forgetting to walk quietly, I rushed down the second half of the steps and to the living room, clicking on the light and grabbing the photo album. Flipping through the pages, I eventually found the exact picture I'd hoped was there.

"Oh, it is true," I whispered. "I didn't make it up."

The year I was born, the schoolchildren of Detroit brought their pennies from home—milk money from their mothers and dads—and donated them to buy an elephant. When I was a little girl, I believed that elephants came from Germany because that was where Sheba had come from.

It wasn't until much later in school that I learned otherwise, with quite a bit of embarrassment.

When Mother was well enough to take Clara and me to Belle Isle, she'd let us spend all the time we wanted at the elephant's area of the zoo.

I never grew tired of watching her roll around in the mud or catch peanuts from the crowd. Clara, on the other hand, lost patience quickly—too quickly, in my opinion. She'd whine at me to move along, tugging on my arm until I relented.

Which I always did.

The last thing I had ever wanted to do was make a fuss and upset Mother. Nothing had upset Mother quite like seeing her girls argue. As the older and more mature sister, it was up to me to cave to Clara's wishes.

My, but did I resent her for it.

Even though I didn't think she noticed, my mother had.

For weeks before my eighth birthday my mother had made promises of the best birthday present a girl could want. She'd made hints that I'd be amazed, surprised, and otherwise shocked.

Dad just shook his head and warned me not to get my hopes up, that we didn't have money for gifts or even the amount of sugar that a birthday cake would require.

"Don't expect anything," he'd said more than a handful of times.

But it was too late.

When my birthday came, Mother kept me—just me, not Clara—home from school and took me on the streetcar in the direction of Belle Isle.

The zoo had been all but empty; most people were either at school or work. But Mother marched us in as if we owned the place, her chin held high and her smile unfading. And when we walked right up to the zookeeper, she put out her hand and looked him right in the eye.

"I'm Etta Johnson," she said. "May I have a word with you? In private?"

He lowered his brows and turned his mouth down into a frown, but followed my mother several feet from me. She spoke to him behind her hand, and they both looked at me a few times.

When the keeper nodded, my mother smiled.

Oh, what a beautiful smile it was.

"I hear you like elephants," the man said, walking toward me. "Would you like to meet Sheba?"

"Yes, please," I'd answered.

"Well, come on, then."

When he offered me his arm, I'd reached up to take it, letting him lead me inside the elephant enclosure, Mother following behind us.

He'd given me a handful of peanuts to feed her, which the elephant took happily. Then he told me I could touch her, and I put the palm of my hand on her trunk, feeling the dry roughness of skin.

She had the most tender eyes, gentle and kind. I could see that even though she towered over me.

Mother stayed on the other side of the room, hands to her mouth and crying quietly. A smiling kind of cry.

"Don't you want to pet her?" I'd asked. "She won't hurt you."

Mother shook her head. "This is just for you, Betty," she'd said.

The man helped me use a ladder to climb up on the elephant's back, and I sat with my legs on either side of her, my feet dangling several feet above the ground. I touched her back, surprised by the little line of fur that grew up, darker than her skin, along her spine.

The keeper led Sheba in a circuit around the pen, and the elephant stepped carefully, jostling me with her movement.

Every once in a while, I'd turn my head to see Mother standing with her hands still drawn up to her mouth, a look of absolute delight on her face.

The zookeeper asked Mother if she wanted him to take a picture of me. When she told him she didn't have a camera, he offered the use of his.

"I'll send it to you if you give me your address," he'd said. "I'll need you to hold the lead rope, though."

The photo he sent was of me, sitting astride the elephant, my hands on her back and the happiest kind of smile spread on my face.

But what caught my eye more than anything was the image of my mother, tall and lean. She hadn't faced the camera, and I wondered if she'd expected to be in the photo at all. Her face was turned up toward me, her smile lighting up everything.

"She loved me," I said out loud, holding the album in my hands. My voice crackled over the words and my eyes stung with tears.

I was forty years old and finally realizing the love of my mother.

This is just for you, Betty.

This story is just for you.

"She really loved me," I said one last time. "Thank you."

forty-one

It had drizzled for three days straight, and Hugo and I both felt more than a little stir crazy. I'd cleaned everything that could have possibly needed a scrubbing and he'd filled in every page in the coloring book I had for him. There was nothing worth watching on television, and I couldn't think of a single thing to do with the boy to keep him entertained.

We needed to get out of that house. There was no way around it. But with the rain coming in downpours like it did, I was at a loss for special places to take him.

"Is there any place you'd like to go today?" I asked, standing in the doorway between the kitchen and the living room. "Anything you'd like to do?"

"Can we go to the bakery? Please?"

"The bakery? You really want to go there?" I narrowed my eyes. "What would we do there?"

He shrugged. "See Grandpop."

Even though he'd started calling Pop that a few weeks before, it still warmed my heart every time I heard it in his little voice.

"Well, I suppose," I said. "You better put your book away."

He popped up, picking up the book, and dashed to the shelf to put it away. I didn't think I'd ever seen a child so excited to go watch a few old men work.

I thought maybe the hope of a couple of cookies didn't hurt matters at all.

I parked as close to the bakery entrance as possible. The ability of my plastic rain bonnet to protect my freshly set hair was questionable at best, even if the downpour had slowed a little since we left the house.

"Let's run to the bakery real fast, all right?" I said, turning toward Hugo. "Don't forget to close the car door."

I got my umbrella up as fast as I could after opening my car door, and I waved Hugo to come out my side so he wouldn't get wet. But instead of rushing to the sidewalk, I stopped in my tracks.

Across the street, where the old fabric store had long before gone out of business, was a sign posted in the window.

Future Home of Lazy Morning Bakery!

"Oh, the nerve," I barked. "The nerve."

"What's wrong?" Hugo asked.

"Nothing." I turned, putting my hand on his back and leading him to Sweet Family. "Let's just get inside."

We dodged puddles and managed to make our way inside without getting completely drenched. It didn't hurt that Stan saw us coming and held the door when we got near.

"Well, would you look at who came for a visit," he said. "Pop, we've got some troublemakers out here."

Pop hobbled out from the back and clapped his hands together, knocking a dusting of flour from them.

"Well, you're just in time," he said. "Hugo, wanna try to make some bread?"

"Yes, please," Hugo said.

"Maybe you could teach your Aunt Betty once you get it figured out."

"Now, I have no desire to ever learn to bake," I said, swatting the air in front of my face. "That's why I married into this family."

"Do you see what I have to deal with?" Pop asked Hugo. "All the women in this family are headstrong and sassy."

Hugo looked at me to see if I would laugh. When I did, he covered a small giggle with his hand.

"I'll let you in on a little secret, kiddo. Come here," Pop said, leaning down and faking a whisper, winking in my direction. "I wouldn't want these women any other way. Now, come on. Let's get our hands in some flour."

They headed to the back, Hugo keeping pace with Pop even though he could have gone faster. Just as they went through the doorway, Hugo turned and looked up at Pop, a grin on his face that nearly melted my heart.

"You see what's going in over there?" Stan asked, nodding to the Lazy Morning sign. "They just bought the place yesterday."

"How dare they?" I shook my head and even thought of raising my fist.

"That's business."

"What are you boys going to do?" I asked.

"Just keep baking." He winked at me. "It's all any of us knows how to do."

Hugo stood on a step stool pushed up to the counter where Pop had showed him to sprinkle flour on the kneading board.

The spare apron we'd hung around his neck and tied behind his back reached well past his knees, halfway to his ankles.

I wished for all the world that I had brought my camera so I could have gotten a picture of that.

"There's nothing in the world as soft as flour," Pop said, taking a pinch of it between finger and thumb, rubbing it, letting it sift through back to the board. "You try it."

Hugo did and smiled.

"Isn't it nice?" Pop asked. "Now this is what's going to keep your dough from sticking to everything."

He nodded at a bowl with a puffy lump of dough.

"Can you lift that out of the bowl?" Pop said. "Just grab the whole thing and plop it on this flour. Just like that."

Hugo dug his fingers under the dough, pulling it from the bowl and lifting it.

"It's sticky," he said, making a face.

"It won't be after you knead it a little bit. Now put it down. That's it," Pop said. "And sprinkle just a little flour on it."

The front door opened, letting in a cool rush of air. I turned to see Hazel Crawford, the minister's wife, walking in. She shook the rain out of her umbrella before folding it closed and dropping it into the bucket by the door.

"Betty," she said, feeling of her hair with both hands and walking to the counter. "I haven't seen you in ages."

"Hi, Hazel." I put my hands in front of myself, clasping them. "I must have missed you at church on Sunday."

"Were you there?"

"I was."

"I'm glad," she said. "The reverend and I have been worried about you."

"Well, thank you for your concern. I'm doing all right."

"And the little boy?" She raised her eyebrows.

"Hugo? He's all right."

"He's Clara's, isn't he?"

I nodded.

"What's she up to these days?"

"She's away." I put a hand to my stomach, where it seemed a rock had settled. "Hugo's staying with me for a little bit."

"How nice."

"Yes, well," I said, pulling my mouth into a smile.

It was the same smile I'd used when I was a girl and someone asked after Mother. It was the smile I'd always hoped was believable enough to convince others that everything was fine.

Clearing my throat, I let the smile drop. I was so tired of straining to keep it up.

"Did you come in for some bread today?" I asked. "Or some rolls?"

She nodded. "You know how Jim likes his baked goods."

It had been years since last I'd stood behind that counter and helped a customer buy a few loaves of bread. Surprisingly, I remembered how to use the cash register and make correct change.

Loaded down with her purchases, Hazel met my eyes.

"Betty, I want you to know that we're praying for you," she said. "I know people like to say that to make someone else feel better. But Jim and I really are. If you need anything—anything at all—please let us know."

I told her that I would and we said our good-byes.

Minutes after the door closed, I heard uproarious laughter from Pop and a belly giggle from Hugo.

"I guess that's one way to knead the dough," Stan said. "Pop, where'd you put that ladder? Or do you just want to wait for it to fall down?"

A thunk and another bout of chuckles.

"Well, that answers your question," Pop said. "All right, Hugo. Let's try that again."

The rain was letting up, and I walked around the counter and to the photo of Mom and Pop on the day they opened the bakery. I wondered what she would have thought about everything going on in our lives right then.

When the doctor told her she didn't have long to live, she didn't cry and she didn't get angry. Instead, she got up the next day, went to work, and smiled at everyone who walked through the door. She gave cookies to the children who came in with their mothers, whether they behaved themselves or not. And she let people talk her ear off, complaining about troubles that weren't half as severe as her own.

She didn't do all of it to convince everyone that she was all right. She did it because she wanted to squeeze every last joy out of living.

Eventually she was too sick to get out of bed, and I spent as much of my time with her as I could, spooning broth into her mouth when she could stomach it and dabbing her forehead with a cold washcloth when the fevers flared.

"You're going to be all right," she'd said to me just a few days before she passed. "No matter what happens, you'll be okay."

"It's going to be hard." I tried to hold in my tears but failed.

"Of course it will be." Her eyes were dull by then, her words thick. "But not too hard for God."

The picture of her on the wall had captured her undying determination.

Goodness. How I missed her.

forty-two

My father's refusal to tell Clara and me what our mother had died of did little to put her death out of our minds. In fact, the unknown only made our imaginations go wild. At the library Clara would ask to see books with lists of ailments from cancer to tuberculosis to the plague. She even kept a notebook of symptoms for each disease, asking me over and over which of them our mother'd had.

"Do you think she could have passed the sick down to us?" she'd asked one day while we sat on our shared bed in the apartment over the bakery.

"No," I answered, plaiting her long blonde hair so that it wouldn't be a nest of tangles the next morning. "Would you stop moving, please?"

"Well, if you didn't pull so hard, I'd sit still." She'd breathed in deeply, raising her shoulders. "What if I end up with the same thing she had? What if I die?"

"You aren't going to die," I'd said. "Not anytime soon, at least."

"How can you be sure?"

She'd turned to me, and her hair slipped from my hands, the braid coming loose. At the very first, I'd been tempted to scold her for undoing all my work, but then the way her wet eyes met mine let me know it was more than just a hobby, all of that research she'd done.

"You're really worried, aren't you?" I'd asked, lowering my voice.

She pushed her lips together and creased the space between her eyebrows.

"Sometimes I don't feel . . ." She closed her mouth again and turned her eyes toward the ceiling. "I don't feel right."

"What do you mean?"

Without looking at me, she touched her temple with the end of her pointer finger. "Sometimes I don't feel right here."

"Headaches?"

She shook her head, and I racked mine trying to figure out what she could mean. But then she turned her back to me, flipping her hair over her shoulder once again.

"You can braid my hair," she said. "I'll be still."

I fretted over her the next few days, watching her closely and trying to see if she was ever sick the way our mother was.

But where Mother's moods flipped at the toss of a coin, Clara's stayed a long and sustained sadness with rests of happiness every so often.

I chalked it up to the moodiness that came with growing up. Nothing more.

⌒

I sat in the crowded waiting room at the sanitarium where an orderly had directed us—me and a handful of other visitors—

telling us it would just be a few minutes. A few minutes had become nearly an hour, and it didn't seem we'd ever be let out of the room.

A man across from me checked his watch, huffing a sigh out of his nose before turning and looking out the window. I presumed he was wishing that he could crack that window a little to let in some fresh air and that he resented the bars across it on the inside.

I'd always felt sorry for men in their suits during the summer months. Sure, I had on my support hose and girdle, which were warm enough—not to mention constricting—but at least I could let my arms remain uncovered.

Lifting my visitor's pass, I fanned it in front of my face. It did little to displace the humidity in the room, but just having something to do was a small comfort.

"What do you think the holdup is?" a woman asked from the other side of the room in a voice just above a whisper.

The man beside her—her husband maybe—shrugged, not looking up from the newspaper he held like a shield in front of his face.

"I hate coming here," the woman said, an edge to her tone that I could feel even from ten feet away.

"Yes, dear." The man's indifference was only punctuated by the turning of the page.

Shifting in my seat, I tried to stifle a desire to give both of them a piece of my mind. I wondered who exactly she thought enjoyed visiting a state hospital.

My fingers interlaced in my lap and resting on my handbag, I felt a pang right in the center of my chest that was a lot like homesickness, a feeling that I couldn't wait to get out of that room, away from the building, back to where I belonged.

The pang turned into a spreading swell that nearly crushed me with hopelessness of ever feeling anything different.

I pulled in breath through my mouth, letting it settle in my lungs before releasing it.

"Who are you visiting?"

I turned toward the voice to see a woman who was sitting one chair away from me. If I'd had a guess, I'd have thought she was just a few years older than I. Her face was kind and her voice gentle, both so necessary in that difficult place.

"My sister," I said.

"I'm sure she'll be glad to see you," the woman said.

"And you?" I asked.

"My son." Her soft eyes looked right into mine. In them I saw understanding that made me want to cry. "He's been here for five years."

"That's such a long time." I swiveled on my behind so that I was facing her more fully.

I tried to imagine Clara in that place for so many years. Hugo would be nearly eleven years old by then and getting ready to start junior high school. The crushing feeling in my chest grew stronger.

"I come every week," she said and glanced out the window. "He doesn't always know me, but that's all right. Sometimes it's enough just to see his face."

"That must be awfully hard."

"Yes." She nodded. "But at least he's still alive."

I put my hand to my chest to show her how moved I was by what she'd said. The tears in my eyes possibly told her that well enough, though.

The woman across the room was once again griping at the man I took for her husband, and I gave it my utmost to block her voice out.

"You must really love him," I said to the woman with the kind face.

"Of course I do." Her smile was winsome, full of motherly pride. "He's my boy."

Tears prickled the corners of my eyes, and I blinked wildly to keep them from tumbling loose.

"The first year he was here I felt so helpless," she said. "I thought there was nothing I could do for him."

She reached over the space between us and took my hand.

"Eventually I realized that there was one thing I could do." Her smile reached her eyes. "I could love him."

"Yes," I said, as if in answer.

"No matter what happens to him here or outside these walls, I can love him." She sniffled. "Even if he passes before I do, I can love him."

I pulled in a breath through my mouth.

"You've just got to love her."

***

My visit with Clara that day was short. The nurses told us we'd only have a few minutes, and I felt rushed when I sat across the table from my sister. When she didn't seem to recognize me, panic fluttered in my chest.

"Clara?" I said. "Are you all right?"

At the sound of her name, she turned toward me, her eyes not registering my presence.

"What's happened?" I asked.

She didn't answer me, and when I reached across the table for her hand, she didn't respond. Still, I kept my fingers wrapped around hers and told her everything I could think of about Hugo. That he'd learned to swim and made his own loaf of bread. That

I'd taken him to get a haircut and that he asked for a canary when we went to the pet shop afterward.

"I told him that it might not be such a good idea," I said. "Not with the cat and all."

I told her how much I loved her and that we all hoped she'd be able to come home soon.

When the nurse came to let me know it was time to go, I asked if my sister was all right.

"She had a treatment yesterday," she told me. "She'll be better after a day or two."

"What kind of treatment is that?" I asked, trying to keep my voice from sounding too frantic. "Don't you think it's making her worse?"

"I probably shouldn't be telling you," the nurse said. "The doctor won't like it."

"I promise not to tell."

She leaned closer to me. "It's called electroshock therapy," she whispered.

"You're electrocuting her?" I crossed my arms so I wouldn't be tempted to grab the nurse by the shoulders and shake her.

"It works, I promise. But sometimes it takes them a little while to bounce back."

"She doesn't know me, though. I'm her sister."

"That's normal." She checked a sound over her shoulder. "Her memories will come back. But it will take a little time."

I entertained the thought of taking Clara home right then. I'd get rid of the shapeless gown she wore and the socks dingy from the grimy floor. I'd burn them if I had to. Then I'd wrap Clara in a soft robe and let her sleep it off in her clean bed. Hugo and I would keep the house quiet for her and bring her cups of chamomile tea whenever she wanted them.

But then I thought of Hugo seeing his mother in that state. Of her not knowing him. How that would hurt him.

It was then that I realized that her being in that hospital was as much for him as it was for her.

"Visiting time is over, ma'am," the nurse said. "I'm sorry."

I didn't even have a chance to tell Clara good-bye.

Sitting in my car, not even able to start it for how my hands shook, I remembered what the woman had told me. Even when I couldn't do anything else for Clara, I could love her.

You've just got to love her.

I prayed that I could know that it was enough.

forty-three

The agreement was that Hugo would spend the day with Nick and Dick while I visited Clara. What was meant to be a few hours of play had turned into a sleepover—another of Marvel's spontaneous notions. When I asked if she needed me to stay over too, she'd practically pushed me out the door.

"Go have a nice evening," she'd said.

"But what am I supposed to do?" I'd asked, planting my feet on the threshold.

"That's not my problem." She'd winked. "Whatever you do, make sure you enjoy it."

On the short drive home, I realized what I wanted to do more than anything else. I wanted to write. With all the stories I'd been telling Hugo, I'd had very little time to write any of them down.

At the stop sign just down the road from my house, I decided that I'd make those stories a gift for Hugo, something for him to remember me by when life went back to normal.

Traffic cleared, yet I didn't go. Not until the car behind me honked twice.

I pressed on the gas pedal, rolling through the intersection and nearer to home.

I wasn't sure life would ever go back to normal.

The realization settled like a pit in my stomach.

I took a shower, put my hair in curlers, and brewed a good strong pot of coffee. Drinking a cup of joe that late in the afternoon was a little dangerous for a woman my age—I'd either never fall asleep or be up all night going to the restroom.

Either way, it was a risk I was willing to take.

I put on a Frank Sinatra album, the big band one he'd released the year before. Humming along to "Goody, Goody," I swayed my hips, watching the record go round and round.

Norman had never been a fan of Old Blue Eyes. He'd thought he was arrogant, which may very well have been true. But with a voice like that—strong and brassy—he had a right to be a little stuck on himself.

I turned the music down so I could just hear it in the background and sat at my writing desk. Curling my fingers around the sides of it, I thought about the day Norman had brought it home for me just months after we moved to the house on Deerfield.

He'd been so pleased with himself.

My Norm may not have had a voice like Sinatra or the wealth either. He wasn't smooth and wasn't altogether interested in charming the ladies—other than me, at least. But he'd been kind, thoughtful, sweet.

With a heart like that, he had a right to be proud. He never was, though. Not once.

Sitting at my desk and smoothing the blank page then picking up the pen, I couldn't bring myself to make so much as a stroke of ink on the paper. Fear of doing poorly paralyzed me.

Dropping the pen, I stretched fingers that hadn't even had the chance to cramp up or grow sore from too much writing. I blew air out of my mouth and got up from my seat to look out the window.

From where I stood, I turned back to the white page with its blue lines. I decided that the music was all wrong and changed the record to something slower with no singing that could distract me.

"That's better," I muttered, hearing the orchestral music, slow and sonorous, flooding through the speakers. "Just write something. Anything."

I sat back down, once again taking up the pen.

"It's only a story. How hard could it be?" I asked myself.

As it turned out, it could be quite hard.

"Just write," I whispered through clenched teeth.

I put the tip of the pen on the paper and wrote, "Jimmy and the Yellow Castle."

Then I popped back up out of my seat to check on the coffee. A cup poured and steaming, I went back to the desk only to remember that I needed cream and sugar. That done, I decided I should have something to nibble as I wrote.

Before I knew it, I'd wasted an entire hour by avoiding the work I wanted more than anything to do.

The spirit was willing, but the flesh was one nervous Nelly.

"Do not even think of getting up from this chair until you have written a full sentence," I said, grabbing the pen and letting it wiggle up and down between my thumb and finger.

Flannery lay in Norman's chair, grooming herself. Every once in a while she regarded me and blinked at me slowly. She took that opportunity to go into the kitchen. Even from where I sat in the living room, I could hear her jump up on the counter. A light clinking of dishes made me think she'd found the butter dish.

"Get down from there," I called, trying to shoo her with my arms while staying in the seat a whole room away. "Oh, never mind. Enjoy the butter, naughty kitten."

Puffing out my cheeks with air, I shut my eyes and decided that it did not matter if what I wrote was good or garbage. No one would ever have to see it.

I wrote the first part of the story and then the next, surprised by how the ideas came from my head and somehow moved my pen across the page.

When I made a mistake or misspelled a word, I found the little bottle of Liquid Paper I kept in the junk drawer to be quite helpful.

By the time I'd finished writing that first story, it was just after six o'clock. I had a thought of making something to eat, but that was fleeting. I didn't want to disturb my momentum.

"Which one next?" I whispered, turning the page. "The turtle."

I drank through the whole pot of coffee, feeling the jitters race through my arms and legs and into my fingers. I filled so many pages on the pad of paper, not with perfect stories, but with ones that were good enough.

By the end of the evening I'd managed to write three stories. It wasn't as much as I'd originally expected, but I was pleased with myself nonetheless.

When I fell into bed at midnight, body spinning from too much caffeine, I knew Norman would have been proud.

The few hours I was able to sleep were deep and easy.

My dreams were in full color.

CHAPTER

forty-four

It was another rainy day. Just one more in a month that had already been so wet. It almost seemed like we'd all end up floating away if it didn't settle down after a while.

Every light was on in Marvel's house, and I thought if Stan could see that, he'd rush through, turning them all off. But the warm glow of lamps coming out of the windows made me feel at home as I drove up the road. Parking in the driveway, I let the car run just a moment before shutting it off and rushing to the side door that would lead into the kitchen, letting myself in as usual.

"Good morning," Marvel said, turning from the skillet on the stove. "I'll have these done in ten seconds. Blueberry, just the way you like them."

My stomach rumbled, and I realized I hadn't eaten since lunch the day before and those pancakes smelled awfully good.

"The boys are in the dining room," she said. "I told them to set a place for you. I'll be right there."

My three nephews sat at the table, already eating the first

batch of pancakes Marvel had made. I walked around the table, behind the chairs of each of them, leaning down to kiss their cheeks as I made my way to my place.

It made me smile when not one of them squirmed away from me.

"Oh, you all smell like campfire," I said, sitting and pulling my chair up under the table.

"Dad made a fire in the backyard last night," Nick said.

"He did?"

I looked at Marvel, who had just come in behind me, a tall stack of pancakes on a platter.

"All the wood was wet from the rain," Dick said after stuffing a hunk of sausage into his cheek.

"Don't talk with your mouth full," Marvel said, sitting beside me. "It was more smoke than fire."

"That's too bad." I used the knife and fork Marvel had brought me to cut my pancakes into small squares.

"It was neat," Dick said. "It started raining, so Dad put up the tent in the basement so we wouldn't miss out on our campout."

"I wanted to have a fire down there, but Mom said no." Nick pushed his mouth to one side of his face and shrugged one shoulder.

"Well, it sounds like you had a fun sleepover." I looked at Hugo and smiled. "Did you enjoy yourself, Hugo?"

He nodded eagerly. "We told ghost stories."

"Not scary ones," Dick added. "Funny ones."

"Well, I'm glad to hear that," I said.

The boys polished off the last of their breakfast and dashed away to play in the tent again with Marvel calling out to them not to run in the house. Hugo doubled back and stood beside me.

"Did you miss me?" he asked.

"Oh, I did," I answered, taking his hands. "But Flannery and I were all right because we knew you were having a good time."

He grinned at me.

"Now, go wash your hands before you find the twins, all right? You're pretty sticky."

He used the kitchen sink to rinse his hands and then headed for the stairs that led to the basement. He didn't even take a second to dry them.

"He was good for me," Marvel said, dipping a piece of pancake into a puddle of syrup.

"I'm so glad."

She got up quick from her seat. "I forgot coffee. How could you have let me forget?"

"Oh, dear," I said, turning in my seat to watch her bring the pot and two mugs to the table. "Thank you. I sure need it."

"Cream and sugar's already right there." She nodded at the lazy Susan in the middle of the table while she poured the rich-smelling coffee into the cups.

We both fixed them the way we liked them, and Marvel left the pot close at hand, knowing that we both needed as much of it as we could get on a gloomy day like that.

"What did you do with your evening?" she asked, blowing into her mug before taking a sip.

"Nothing much," I answered, careful not to make eye contact with her.

Had Marvel DeYoung known that I was writing stories down, she would have asked to see them, not understanding why I would be so hesitant to share them. So, I stirred my already sufficiently blended coffee and cream and tried to be as nonchalant as possible.

"Sometimes it's just nice to relax, huh?" she said. "You know, I've been thinking. School starts in just two weeks."

"It does?" I asked, holding the fork over my plate.

"Nick is not excited about going back." She pursed her lips together. "He's already threatened to run away five times."

"Just tell him he can't run away to my house again."

"Actually, I think that's his plan exactly." She sipped her coffee. "Are you thinking about getting Hugo registered for kindergarten?"

"Oh, goodness. I hadn't even thought of that."

"You probably should do it sooner than later, Betty." She rested her elbows on either side of her plate and let her shoulders slump. "I know you didn't expect Clara to be gone so long."

I shook my head.

"I can make a call to the principal if you'd like," she said. "Don't take Nick's word for it. Mr. VanZee is a good man."

"Thank you."

All three boys came racing through the house, sounding like a stampede of wild horses. For some reason, they all had their shirts off and bandannas tied around their foreheads. Hugo's slipped down over his eyes and he stopped to push it back up before taking off to catch up to the bigger boys.

He'd grown so much since coming to my house just two months before. And I didn't mean taller or broader, although I was sure that was the case too.

He'd grown in other ways. Ways that mattered even more.

I was sure that if I checked, his nails would be filthy.

Just the thought of it brought a smile to my face.

forty-five

The first time I met Norman's mother was two days after we'd moved into the apartment over the bakery. I'd been sitting on the steps outside our door while Clara sat inside, pouting over something our dad had said to her earlier in the day.

Instead of tolerating her mood, I'd decided to enjoy the fresh air, library book resting on my knees. It was October and seemed like the perfect time to reread *Anne of Green Gables*.

I'd just gotten to the chapter where Anne Shirley met Gilbert Blythe for the first time, my very favorite part. Sometimes, when I knew no one was around to hear me, I'd read Anne's words aloud as if in a play. I liked how sure of herself she was—or at least seemed to be. And I wished I could be sassy just like her.

Thinking I was quite alone, I parted my lips, just about to whisper the lines.

"Now, Miss," a voice called up to me from the alley below. "Shouldn't you be in school?"

Startled, I clapped the book shut, losing my place. I peeked over the side of the iron stairs to see a round woman with her hands on her hips looking up at me.

"I'm sorry, ma'am," I'd called down to her.

"What are you sorry for?"

"Oh, well," I stammered. "Hello? Sorry."

"My son Norman told me there were a couple of girls living upstairs," she said.

My cheeks burned just to know that the handsome boy had spoken of me. To his mother, and in the same breath as my little sister, but still, that was something.

"Yes, ma'am."

"Well, how old are you?" she asked, crossing her meaty arms under her more than ample bosom.

"I'm fourteen, ma'am," I answered, holding one of the iron rails. "My sister's twelve."

"Haven't you gone and registered at the school yet?"

"No." I took in a quick breath. "My father said he would sign us up later."

"Why not now?" She gaped at me. "I see you can read all right, so you aren't dumb. And doesn't that father of yours work at the school?"

I'd tried explaining that our mother was dead, and that Dad wasn't always one for staying on top of things. What I hadn't told her was that we had no money for proper clothes or shoes, not to mention any books and pencils we might have had to buy.

That, I was sure, she could have figured out all on her own.

"I'll set it to rights," she'd said.

And she had.

By that evening, she'd made a call to the school, ensuring that both Clara and I could go to class the very next morning.

She'd marched up to our apartment as soon as my father came home from work and told him that was how it would be.

When he'd balked about the money to pay for new clothes, she'd asked him to come down to her car and help her carry up what the ladies in church had collected for us.

They'd brought in half a dozen dresses each for Clara and me, collected from the closets of a few women at the church who could each spare one. Not a single word had passed her lips about the abominable state of the clothes we'd come to LaFontaine in, and I was grateful.

The fresh-smelling and perfectly pressed dresses were the most beautiful I'd ever hoped to have. I'd worn a pink one with tiny white flowers to my first day of school.

Norm and Albert had walked Clara and me to school that first day, escorting us right to the front steps. And they'd met us there once school was over to make sure we got home all right.

Before Norman went inside the bakery to work, he'd turned to me and smiled.

"You look nice in pink," he'd said.

I was sure my cheeks flushed enough to match my dress.

It only made me feel better to see that he had blushed too.

When I was in school, all of the grades—from kindergarten to high school—were in the same building. Of course, that was before LaFontaine grew and they put up a new building for the older students.

The elementary took over the old, and when I pulled open the door for Hugo on the day we were to register him, I was surprised to find that it smelled the same as always. But exactly.

It was a little wax crayon mixed with newly sharpened pencils with just a little chalk dust for good measure.

"Are you nervous?" I asked, my voice echoing off the walls.

"No," Hugo answered. "I like to learn."

Still, he held my hand tight as we walked through the halls, big eyes inspecting everything we walked past, drawing closer to my side with each step.

The school secretary had Hugo and me sit on a bench in the hallway to wait for a meeting with the principal. The walls were the same shade of cream that I remembered and the floors just as shiny and slick as they'd been then.

"Aunt Betty," Hugo whispered, wiggling in his seat. "I have to . . ."

"Okay," I said, understanding his urgency. "It's right across the hall there, do you see it? It's the door that says 'boys.'"

He nodded, and I was proud of his ability to recognize the word by sight.

Of course, as soon as the door closed behind him, I was called into the office. The secretary stood in the doorway, smiling down at where I sat on the bench.

"Just one minute, please," I said. "My nephew is in the rest-room."

"I'm afraid Mr. VanZee can't wait too long," the secretary said. "He's a very busy man."

"I'm sure he is."

"Why don't you go in and I'll wait for your nephew." She smiled at me from behind a pair of glasses that were far too large for her face. "Hugo, right?"

"Yes." I stood. "You'll send him in?"

She nodded and extended her arm to show me the direction to the office, following behind me.

"Right through there," she said, stepping around her desk.

I hesitated, half turning back toward her. "I really should wait for Hugo."

"He'll be fine." She rolled a sheet of paper into her typewriter. "He'll know where to find you."

As uncomfortable as I was, I still went into the principal's office and shook his hand over the desk, taking a seat when he asked me to.

"Mrs. Sweet, it's nice to meet you," he said. "Now, I see you're wanting to enroll . . ."

He consulted the papers in front of him.

"Hugo Johnson," I answered. "My nephew."

"I see." He squinted at the papers in a way that made me think he could have used a pair of glasses. "Does he live with you? Is this his address?"

He showed me the paper, and I nodded.

"He's lived with me most of the summer," I answered. "I'm unsure how long he'll be with me."

"Hm. I don't understand," the man said, rubbing his chin, which only made the cleft even more pronounced. "He's just staying with you for the summer?"

"That was what I'd originally thought."

"His stay is extended, then?" He squinted at me.

"Yes. So, I thought he should start school." I pointed at the paper. "He's old enough. And very smart."

"Uh-huh. But he needs to be registered by a parent or guardian." He put the papers on his desk, using thumb and finger to square them with the edge. "I'm afraid we can't enroll him otherwise."

"Well, I'm not sure what to do exactly," I said. "I'm afraid my sister is unwell."

"I'm terribly sorry to hear that." He said it in such a way that I believed him.

I swallowed hard. "She's in the hospital. Indefinitely."

"I see." He sighed. "Did his mother leave him in your care?"

"Yes," I answered, looking toward the door, nervous that Hugo hadn't come in yet.

"That does change matters a bit, doesn't it?" He made a clicking sound with his tongue. "Tell you what, I'm going to consider you his guardian and let you enroll him. Once his mother is well enough, you bring her in and we'll have her sign some papers."

"Thank you," I said. "May I be excused?"

I felt absolutely foolish as soon as the words came out, and I put a hand to my mouth, knowing that I was blushing.

"You may." He grinned at me. "We'll be happy to have Hugo join us in just a week and a half."

I stepped out, expecting to see Hugo standing at the secretary's desk or sitting on the floor with a book. But he wasn't there.

"Did he come in here?" I asked.

The secretary stopped her click-clacking on the keyboard to look around. "Oh, I guess not."

I rushed out of the office, my heart beating so fast it hurt. In the handful of steps it took for me to reach the hallway, my mind had constructed every bad thing that could have happened to Hugo.

When I reached the hall, I saw him sitting on the bench, bent at the waist and holding his face in his hands, crying quietly, his shoulders bobbing up and down. My heart that had been racing then felt as though it might break for him.

"Sweetheart," I said, crouching down beside him and putting my hand on his back. "I'm right here. I'm here, Hugo."

He jumped at me, throwing his arms around my neck so hard I nearly fell over, but I caught myself on the bench.

"It's all right," I said again. "I was just in the office."

"I thought you left me," he said with stuttering words and shuddering breaths.

"No, Hugo. I would never do that." I held him tighter, closer. "I wouldn't leave you like that."

I stood, holding him close and carrying him down the freshly waxed floor, his muffled sobs echoing off the walls.

forty–six

Hugo stood at the window, still wearing his nice outfit from our trip to the school. It had taken a peanut butter sandwich and a good nap to calm him after getting home. Even so, he hadn't felt in the mood to play a game or watch television.

So, he stared out the window, standing perfectly still.

"What are you looking at?" I asked, crossing the room to stand beside him.

"The rain," he answered, taking my hand.

"It's peaceful, isn't it?"

He nodded. "I like watching it."

"Me too."

"I like it when the worms come out," he said. "Do you like worms, Aunt Betty?"

"Well, I'm not sure that I do." I squinted my eyes. "When I was a little girl, I was afraid of them."

"They don't bite."

SUSIE FINKBEINER

"You're right, sweetie." I sighed. "I suppose it was because of how wriggly they are."

Hugo lifted his hand, making his pointer finger wiggle like a worm.

"Why do they come out when it rains?" he asked, putting his hand down.

"Hm. I don't know. Why do you think they do?"

"'Cause they like the way the rain feels on their skin."

"That's a really good idea," I said. "Do you like the way rain feels on your skin?"

He nodded. "Maybe I'm part worm."

It was a joke. A joke deserving of the laugh I gave it. A joke that gave me a dose of hope that his heart was going to be all right.

"Can we listen to a record?" he asked.

"Well, of course we can." I left him to find one he might like.

But looking at my selection, I realized I was sorely lacking in what I thought boys would like. I had no Elvis or Spike Jones. He picked one with Doris Day on the cover, smiling widely.

"Why did you pick this one?" I asked.

"She looks like Mommy."

I winked at him, not knowing what about Doris Day reminded him of Clara, but put the record on anyway.

Peppy, bouncy, tinkling music came out of the speakers as Doris sang of a bright and shiny love.

Hugo's head bobbed with the rhythm, and I put out my hands to him, which he took. We tap-stepped along to the song, swayed one way and then the next. I spun him and we twirled and at the very end I picked him up off the ground, dipping him up and down as he laughed until tears gathered in the corners of his eyes.

At the end of the song he wrapped his arms around my neck, holding me as tight as his strength allowed.

The next song—"I Want to Be Happy"—started and I hummed along with it, wishing my voice was smoother, prettier. Wishing my voice was more like Clara's. But Hugo didn't seem to mind; he kept his grip on me as if his life depended on it.

Trying not to allow my voice to crack, I sang, only fumbling on a few of the lines about wanting to be happy and wanting to make someone else happy too.

The weight of sweet Hugo made my arms sore and my body tired, but I didn't want to let him go. I knew, though, that I couldn't carry him all day long, so I let him slide down to the floor. When I released my hold on him, I felt a little pang of something I could not have defined.

But then he took my hand again.

After the rain, Hugo convinced me to go outside with him. We treaded gingerly, careful not to squash any of the worms on the concrete path that cut through the yard. He squatted down by each one, taking it in his hand, letting it move itself into curlicues on his palm. Before depositing them back in the grass, he whispered something to them, so soft and so gentle that I couldn't hear.

Once we reached the sidewalk, Hugo went up and down in front of the half dozen houses between us and the intersecting road, rescuing worms from drying up once the sun came out and giving them what I imagined was a benediction.

A good half an hour later, his work done, Hugo and I went inside to wash up for a little supper. When I asked him what he'd said to the worms, he shrugged as if suddenly shy.

"You don't have to tell me if you don't want to," I said.

He crooked his finger, beckoning me to come near and putting his mouth close to my ear.

"I said, 'stay off the sidewalk,'" he whispered.

"That's all?" I asked.

"Yes. I don't think worms are very smart."

He pulled the step stool to the kitchen sink and scrubbed his hands clean under the faucet.

Oh, how that little boy enchanted me.

forty-seven

The dayroom of the sanitarium had a heavy smell of urine that day, and no matter how long I sat there, I couldn't seem to get used to it. Clara, sitting across the table from me, didn't seem to notice it.

I knew that as soon as I got home I would take a very long, very hot shower. But I knew it would do nothing to erase the stink from my nose. That would take a few days, I was sure.

"Albert's been to visit me," Clara said, eyes on a word scratched into the tabletop. She traced it with her fingers.

"He told me," I said.

Her words came out slower than usual, her movements delayed. But at least she knew me.

"He reads to me."

"What does he read?" I asked.

She met my eyes. "Something about a hobbit. I don't like it, but I don't want to hurt his feelings."

"I'll see what I can do about that."

Clara reached through the bars on the window, tracing a raindrop on the steamed glass.

"Birdie, do you still think about our mother?" she asked, not turning toward me.

"I do," I said. "Probably every day."

"I've forgotten so much about her," she said, breathing in deeply.

"Maybe I can refresh your memory." I leaned forward. "What do you want to know about her?"

"What color were her eyes?"

"They were blue," I said. "And her hair was the same shade of blonde as yours."

"How did she wear it?"

"Either braided down her back or twisted into a bun." I crossed my arms against a chill I wouldn't have expected on that warm day. "Sometimes she'd put a little rouge on her cheeks. Dad didn't like it, though."

"Why not?"

"He said she was prettier without makeup."

"Was she a good mother to us?"

"I think she did her very best," I answered. "She told us stories."

"I do remember one of them," she said. "At least part of it."

"Which one?"

"There was a girl who turned into a bird." Clara's eyebrows rose, just the slightest bit. "It was because she was afraid of something."

"The dark," I said. "She wanted to follow the sun. Do you remember?"

"But she got tired."

"And she needed to land."

Clara put both hands on her cheeks, and I saw how ragged her fingernails were. "Where did the bird-girl land?"

"On a mountain . . ."

"So high it was in a cloud." Clara nodded. "I remember that part."

"What happens next?" I asked.

"She made a wish that she wouldn't be afraid anymore." She lowered her hands. "But the wish didn't work."

The rest of the dayroom blurred, out of focus. The sounds quieted. Even the stinging smells dulled. All I knew in that moment was Clara, her voice so much like Mother's.

"It didn't," I whispered, remembering the way I'd told the story years before and how it had made Clara so angry. I'd changed it from the way my mother told it so it would have an easy ending. All I'd wanted was the happily-ever-after.

But that wasn't the story. Not the true one.

I understood that it wasn't the ending that Clara had needed.

"The bird was so scared." Clara's voice trembled and she sniffled. "But she knew she had to fly anyway."

"But this time she couldn't chase after the sun," I added.

Clara shook her head. "She had to learn to live with the darkness even if it would never stop scaring her."

Tears in my eyes, I nodded. "So she spread her wings," I started.

"And flew home."

Clara smiled.

And in that smile I saw the little girl who beat the rooster and the one who refused to let the men cut down her favorite tree. I saw my sister.

And she was beautiful.

forty-eight

Albert Sweet made the best chicken pot pie in La-Fontaine. In fact, I thought that if there was ever a pot pie contest in Michigan, Albie would bring home the blue ribbon. He always managed to get his crust flaky, keeping it from becoming soggy under the rich gravy.

Even just the thought of it made my mouth water.

So too, the thought of it could put my nerves on end.

It was the kind of meal that the Sweets had along with family meetings. We'd had it the day Mom told us she had cancer and when I told the family I wasn't able to have children. The comfort of pot pie was forever linked in my mind to bad news.

When Marvel told me we were having family dinner at her house and that Albie was making supper, I knew we were in for a difficult discussion.

I was just glad that she'd thought to set up a table in the basement for the boys—next to the tent that was still pitched down there from the sleepover weeks before.

"Stan, Al, and me had a little talk with the fella from Lazy

Morning today," Pop said, pushing his fork into the top crust. "They're opening the day after Labor Day."

"I offered to bake a cake for their big day," Stan said.

"Stanley . . ." Marvel scolded with a laugh in her voice.

"I thought it was the neighborly thing to do."

"The man didn't seem too amused," Albert said, smirking.

"Hey, I said I'd add raspberry filling, no extra charge." Stan shrugged. "What kind of person would turn that down?"

"All joking aside," Pop said, "we've got to figure out what we're going to do. Now, this man brought over a flier with their prices listed. I don't know how they can sell bread for so cheap and stay in business. But I do know that we can't match what they're selling for."

"I bet you dollars for donuts their bakes aren't half as good as ours." Stan leaned back in his chair and crossed his arms. "Can't be."

"That may be. But it won't matter to somebody who's got to tighten their belt." Pop put his fork down. "That person's going to go where they can save a few pennies."

"I'm not willing to let them win," Albert said.

Stan thumped him on the back.

"What do we have that Lazy Morning doesn't?" Marvel asked. "The Sweets. Us. I say we out-charm the socks off of them."

"I like the sound of that," Pop said. "How do we do it?"

"Well, I've been told that I'm charming." Stan winked at Marvel.

"Oh you." She swatted at him. "But I was thinking more of Betty and me pitching in. Running the front and helping the customers. We both still have aprons in the back, don't we?"

"You sure do, kiddo," Pop said.

"Betty and I can take turns working while the boys are at school," she said.

"I would like that," I piped in. "Unless you gentlemen wanted me to help bake the bread."

"No," Stan answered, a little too fast. "You can be the charmer. I'll let you."

"Another thing to think about is offering some of Lacy's special recipes," Pop said. "Now, I know. I know. She didn't want to make them to sell. She liked keeping them just for us. But maybe it's time we started sharing a little bit."

"I don't know, Pop," Marvel said. "Would it feel like we're giving away too much?"

"They're just cookies. Maybe some sweet rolls and a couple fancy pies," Pop said. "That's all. They aren't who we are or what makes us a family. I know your mom had stories to go along with all of those recipes, and I still treasure that. I think it's nice. But who says those stories were only meant for us anyway?"

"Mom said," Albert answered.

"Yup. She did." Pop pulled his hanky out of his pocket and scrubbed it under his eyes. "But she's also the one that said we'd stay open until God told us it was time to close. I haven't heard that from the Lord yet, and I don't expect to anytime soon."

"Should we take a vote?" Stan asked.

"No." Pop shook his head. "Lacy wouldn't have liked that. Either we all agree or we don't do it."

"I don't know if I have much say in it," I said. "But I don't think it could hurt to try."

"Yeah." Stan grinned at me. "What's the worst that could happen? People like Al's cinnamon rolls so much we sell out of them every day? That doesn't sound so bad to me."

"I do like making Mom's recipes," Albert said. "It helps me remember her better."

"Oh, Albie," Marvel said, her eyes full of tears. "How can I not want that for you? Okay. I agree."

"What do you think Norm would want?" Pop asked me.

I clenched my teeth, finding myself unable to speak without falling apart. Instead of saying anything, I nodded my head.

We finished our dinner, not bringing up Lazy Morning again the whole evening.

Albert's pot pie had never tasted so good.

forty-nine

Norman and I had gone through a rough patch around the time Mom Sweet died. Neither of us had done anything wrong and we hadn't entertained the idea of divorcing. Still, we'd struggled. Hindsight told me he was in the throes of grief and that sometimes it made a man pull away.

At the time, though, I worried that the good years we'd had together were a thing of the past.

One night, after a month of silent meals and even more distant bedtimes, I couldn't hold it in any longer. I'd sat in my chair and cried my eyes out over my plate of roast chicken and broccoli. Norm had stayed in his chair, a potato wedge speared on his fork.

"Don't you even care that I'm crying?" I'd asked, hands over my mouth.

"Of course I do," he'd answered, although his voice certainly hadn't sounded like it to me.

"Then *do* something!" My voice had been shrill, wildly out of control. "Isn't there anything you can think of to say?"

"No. I don't know what you want me to do."

"Maybe ask me why I'm crying." Although it was meant as a suggestion, the tidbit had tumbled out of my mouth more as an accusation.

"Why are you crying?" he had asked, putting the potato in his mouth and chewing.

Oh, but that chewing had driven me over the edge.

I'd let him have it. He sat in his chair, eating bite after bite and taking everything I could dish out at him. Not batting an eyelid.

The very last of my rant was to claim that he didn't care.

"I'm sorry you feel that way," was all he'd come up with in reply.

That night he'd slept on the couch.

In the morning, he'd called Pop and said he needed the day off. He made me breakfast, carrying it to me on a tray and refreshing my cup of coffee when it grew tepid. We'd dressed and gotten into the Chevy he owned at the time and went for a drive.

We'd ended up at Greenfield Village, just twenty minutes or so west of Detroit.

While I didn't remember any of the buildings we'd seen that day or the streets we'd walked, I hadn't forgotten the conversations.

Norm had admitted to being heartbroken over his mother's death. I let him know how unloved I'd felt over the months. We listened to each other all day. We'd held hands and I'd let him kiss me for what seemed like the first time in forever, his small act of apologizing and mine of forgiving.

We'd ended the day riding on the top deck of the steamboat called *Suwanee*, going lap after lap around the man-made lagoon, swatting at mosquitoes and listening to the man play banjo. Norm stood behind me, his arms wrapped around my waist as we watched the paddle wheel go around and around.

"I never want you to feel like you aren't loved," he'd said.

Then he'd paid for one more trip around the lagoon for us, the last of the day.

Marvel had wanted one last hurrah of summer before the boys went off to school and we started working at the bakery, so we put together a plan and packed a whole bunch of sandwiches. It was the first time I'd been back to Greenfield Village since that day with Norm, and I felt no small measure of missing him because of it.

After a while, though, I determined that I would enjoy my day. The sun was shining, it wasn't humid, and the boys were patient enough to stop and listen to the prepared speech of each of the actors dressed the part of an engineer or housewife from 150 years in the past.

When we traveled from one exhibit to the next, Hugo kept up with Nick and Dick, laughing at their silliness.

"I'm not ready for summer to be over," Marvel said. "But don't tell my boys that. They'll try to convince me to let them quit school and stay home all the time."

"I wouldn't dare betray your secret." I grinned. "I'm sad for it to end too."

"Is he excited for school to start?" She nodded at Hugo.

"I think he is," I answered. "It surprises me that he isn't more nervous. I certainly am."

"I felt the same when Nick and Dick started kindergarten."

"It's more than just that." I stopped, watching the three boys staring up at a sign. "What if the other children are mean to him because he's different? What if they say something about the color of his skin?"

Marvel heaved a sigh. "I thought about that too."

"Kids can be so nasty."

"Yup. They can," she said.

"There's nothing I can do if something happens to him at school." I shook my head. "I wish I could shield him from every ugly thing."

"Honey, we can't keep them safe all the time," Marvel said. "All we can really do is pray our hearts out and be there for them when someone is cruel."

"I guess so."

"You know, I told my boys they needed to watch out for him." She crossed her arms. "They're already so protective of him."

"They're good boys."

"When they want to be." She raised one eyebrow. "They know that if they need to defend him, I won't punish them. They just can't throw the first punch."

"Do you think it might come to that?" I asked, hand to my chest.

"Oh, I hope not."

"Me either," I said.

One of the twins pointed into a mess of tall grass, and the other hopped over the wooden fence.

"What are you doing?" Marvel called out to them.

"Snake!" Dick yelled. "We saw a snake!"

Then he hurtled into the weeds.

Without looking to me for permission and without so much as a moment's hesitation, Hugo followed after him.

"He's changed so much over the past few months, hasn't he?" I asked.

She nodded. "You've been good for him, Betty."

"Well, I don't know about that." I moistened my lips. "But I do know that he's been good for me."

We didn't go on the *Suwanee* that day—the boys opted for a ride on the train instead. That was all right with me. When Hugo slid onto a seat smack-dab in the middle of the train, he patted the space right beside him for me to sit in. As the train chugged along with its jerky motions and slow-moving pace, the little fellow took my hand and smiled up at me.

"I never want you to feel like you aren't loved," Norm had said.

I thought he would be quite pleased to know that his wish had come true.

fifty

The more time Hugo spent with Nick and Dick, the grimier the tub was after his evening baths. The more effort I had to put into washing his clothes. The more socks and pants and shirts I found in need of mending.

For the first time in my life, I understood what Marvel had meant when she said that her boys were like wolverines.

After I put Hugo to bed, I collected all the worn and hole-ridden clothes, carrying them to the living room along with my thread and needle. I turned on the light next to my chair and got busy. Stitching for a few minutes, I decided it might be nice to have a little background noise, so I got up and turned on the television.

By the time I sat down, the set was still warming up, so I focused my attention on my sewing.

At first I didn't really pay attention to the words of the baritone voice that came through the set. I assumed it was just a part of whatever program was playing that evening. As that voice went on, it took on an urgency, an intensity that made me look up from my work, letting the shirt drop to my lap.

Even in the blurry picture of my television screen, I could tell that the man was Martin Luther King Jr. He'd been in the news and on magazine covers and talked about quite a bit. Not being one to understand all the happenings in the world, I'd not paid a whole lot of attention to what they called civil rights, as embarrassing as that might have been.

Then again, I lived just about as far north as one could get. We didn't have the Jim Crow laws like they had in the South and I didn't know a single person who would have considered themselves a bigot or a racist.

Still, I heard the prejudiced things people said in hushed tones. I'd seen the way a white woman might cross to the other side of the street when she saw a dark-skinned man coming her way.

As much as I hated to admit it, I'd done the same. Out of fear? Yes. But that hadn't made it right. And when I heard someone say something cruel or ignorant or just plain ugly about another person I stayed quiet, not wanting to upset anyone.

My reluctance to speak up was every bit as offensive as the nasty words the other person had said.

Sitting in my chair, I felt ashamed of myself. I grieved that I never thought twice about it until I had to.

I have a dream.

Still holding the shirt, and careful not to poke myself with the needle, I got up, turning the television volume just a little bit louder so as to hear him better.

The camera panned out, showing a hundred men—at least that was my guess—standing at the feet of the giant-sized Abraham Lincoln. The crowd clapped and the screen zoomed in to the statue of the long-past president's carved-in-stone face.

Instead of sitting back in my chair, I lowered myself to the floor, folding my legs up under me.

I have a dream.

Dreams of equality, of the end to racism, that children of all colors would hold hands, that they would be brothers and sisters.

Turning my eyes away from the television, I looked at a picture that Hugo had asked me to put on the mantel in a new frame he had picked out at the dime store.

It was one that Stan had snapped on the night of their backyard campout. Nick and Dick had Hugo between them in a two-handed seat carry that they'd learned in Scouts. Hugo had his arms around their shoulders, and his mouth was open in a glorious laugh.

We will be free one day.

Slumping, I thought of how I hadn't understood the bus boycotts and the lunch counter sit-ins and the marches. After all, why wouldn't they all just move to places where they might be accepted, why not go to diners where they would be served? Why did they have to go where people would treat them badly?

Maybe it hadn't been a lack of understanding in me, but an unwillingness to listen and learn.

Let freedom ring.

Sitting on the floor, listening to the crowds cheer on Dr. King, keeping my eyes fixed on the little brown boy being held up by his older pink-colored cousins, my thinking shifted.

How would it be for Nick and Dick to be able to go to a good school that Hugo could never attend? For the twins to enter through the front door while Hugo was made to walk in the back? Two sit in the front of the bus and one in the rear, the twins use one drinking fountain while another is put to the side for Hugo. Nick and Dick could stand up against injustice and be lauded as heroes. Hugo would suffer the spray of fire hoses and the bites of police dogs for the very same stand.

All because of the tone of their skin.

Sitting on my living room floor, a mending shirt in my lap and Martin Luther King Jr. still speaking through the television, I realized why it was worth the fight.

All it had taken was loving someone like Hugo to clear my vision.

It should have mattered to me all along.

Right around ten o'clock Hugo came downstairs for a drink of water, his bear dangling from his hand and dragging along the floor behind him. He found me in the living room, my pad of paper on the writing desk.

"What are you doing?" he asked.

"Oh." I put the pen on the table beside me. "I was just writing down one of our stories."

He sidled up to my chair, looking down at the book. "You write pretty."

"Well, that's very nice of you to say." I touched the back of his neck, feeling where the barber had cut it close to the scalp, but glad he'd left the top just a little bit longer. "Are you all right?"

He nodded but didn't smile.

"If you aren't, it's okay to tell me, you know."

Shrugging, he looked away from me. "I miss my mommy."

He tried keeping himself strong, I could tell by the way he

pressed his lips together and clenched his jaw. But he couldn't fight off the sadness. His little face scrunched up on itself and the tears came.

"Oh, buddy," I said, dropping the book to the floor and reaching for him, pulling him onto my lap. "It's all right."

He let me cradle him in my left arm. With my right hand, I pushed the tears off his cheeks as they came. Once his crying slowed, softened, released, he looked into my eyes.

"Aunt Betty?" he said. "Can you tell me a story?"

I nodded at Hugo, and he shifted on my lap, sitting up and turning so he could look right into my eyes.

"There was once a young boy . . ." I started.

"Can his name be Hugo?"

"I thought you already knew your stories." I pulled back my face from his to look into his eyes.

"Maybe not all of them."

"All right," I went on. "Hugo was the kind of child who had lots of dreams. Not the kind he had at night while he was sleeping. No, he had the kind of dreams that someone has when he believes the world can be a more beautiful place."

"I do have those dreams," Hugo whispered. "During the daytime."

"I know you do." I adjusted my arm, resting it against the chair. "The thing about these dreams, though, is that they don't come true on their own. They never do."

"How do they come true, then?"

"They come true with a lot of hard work, and gumption, and so much love." I leaned down and kissed him on the forehead. "So much love that sometimes it hurts."

He didn't ask me what that meant, and he didn't argue that love didn't hurt.

I thought that in his five-and-a-half-year-old heart, he knew that what I'd said was true.

Love hurt sometimes.

But it was always worth it.

fifty-one

The elementary school was close enough for Hugo to walk all by himself—just around the block and at the end of a dead-end street—and he knew the way. Still, I went with him on that first day, holding his hand not because he needed me to reassure him.

I was the one who was nervous.

"It's only half a day," I said, more to comfort myself than him. "You'll be home before lunch."

"I know," he answered.

We reached the sidewalk that led to the front steps of the building. "You remember where your classroom is?"

"We saw it last week." His forehead wrinkled. "Are you scared, Aunt Betty?"

I sighed and smiled.

"It's okay to be scared," he said.

Bending my knees, I met eyes with him and put my hands on his shoulders.

"You don't need to worry about me," I said, straightening his collar.

I looked right into his smiling eyes and wished that Clara could have been there to see her brave boy.

"One last picture?" I held up the camera and caught his handsome smile. "Thank you." I turned his little body toward the building. "Have a good morning, Hugo. I'll be right here waiting when you're done for the day."

He looked at me over his shoulder once as he raced his way to the school.

My heart only ached a little.

I made it to the bakery just a few minutes after leaving Hugo at the school. But in those minutes of driving, I'd boo-hooed more than I'd expected to.

No one had prepared me for how hard that morning was going to be.

Harder yet was trying to find a parking spot. It seemed most of the town had shown up for the grand opening of Lazy Morning.

Tenderheartedness turned to feelings of being betrayed turned to downright frustration when I had to park two blocks away.

"Stupid, stupid, stupid Lazy Morning," I said.

But only in my car and quiet enough that no one would be able to hear me through my rolled-up windows.

"How'd our guy do?" Stan asked when I finally rushed in through the back door. "First days are always a little scary."

"He had no problem," I answered. "I'm proud of him."

"Glad to hear it." He nodded at the back wall. "Marvel washed your apron so it would be ready for you."

There on the wall, hanging from a hook, was the apron Mom Sweet had made me years before when Norm and I first got married. It was a pretty pink color—nearly coral—and had a frill along the bottom in white. Along the neck, Mom had embroidered a swirling stem in green that unfurled into a little daisy.

I traced that embroidery, remembering how excited Mom had been to give it to me and how touched I'd been to receive it.

I'd been delighted to own something so pretty.

I put the apron over my head, surprised to find that the strings still reached around my waist after all those years.

If I pretended hard enough, I could almost imagine it was a hug from Mom.

Pop was out front, standing on the other side of the display case with Mrs. Brown. She was the only customer in the store, and when I looked out the front window I could see a line coming out the front of Lazy Morning.

I wondered if Mrs. Brown had come to Sweet Family after losing patience with waiting.

"Now, you know Orville better than I do," Pop said. "But if I'm right about what bread he likes, that's a new one he should try. Nice and crusty on the outside and chewy on the inside."

"He just might like that," Mrs. Brown said, taking her change purse from her handbag. "How much would you like for it?"

"Tell you what, Betty there's going to get it wrapped up for you." He nodded at me. "How about you and your husband try that for your supper. No charge. If you like it, I'll let you buy the next loaf."

"Well, I can't let you do that," she said, but she dropped her change purse into her handbag just the same.

"Sure you can," he said, watching me put the loaf into a brown bag. "I know you'll like this so much, you'll want to buy one every week. Maybe even twice a week."

"I'm sure that I will." She took it from me when I extended it over the counter, giving Pop her thanks in return.

When she walked out the door, he sighed, turning to go back to the kitchen.

"She would have paid for it," I said, calling after him.

"Oh, I know, Bets," he said, stopping in the doorway and holding the jamb for support. "But do you think she'll get that kind of treatment across the street?"

"I don't think she would." I tried for a smile, but all I could manage was a soft sigh. "Did you know that years ago, when my father, Clara, and I first moved to town, Norm gave us a loaf of bread every week?"

"Said it was part of the rent?" Pop asked, grinning. "Yes, I knew about that."

"Was it?" I asked. "Part of the deal?"

"Nope. It was not." Pop shook his head. "The boy insisted on paying for every loaf out of his own pocket change even though we told him he didn't have to."

"Why did he do that?" I asked.

"He said it was something he wanted to do by himself." Pop's eyes grew every bit as watery as mine. "That's his mother in him, you know."

He went to the back, and I heard the squeak of his office chair when he sat down.

I never thought the man gave himself enough credit.

fifty-two

Hugo wouldn't get out of school until right at noon. I'd known that for more than a week. I'd written it on my calendar so I wouldn't forget. I had even turned my watch around backward for a reminder. Still, I feared that I'd forget somehow to meet him in the schoolyard.

Because of that, I left the bakery the moment Marvel came to relieve me and ended up at the school with plenty of time to spare.

I was thankful for the bench under an old oak tree.

Just a few minutes after I sat down, a younger woman asked if she could join me.

"Of course," I said, inching over to one side.

"Thank you." She exhaled when she sat. "I guess I got here a little early."

"At least the rain hasn't started yet," I said, peeking out from under the overhang of leaves to see patches of blue sky among the gray clouds. "Do you have a kindergartener?"

She nodded. "Sally. She's my oldest."

"How many do you have?"

"Four." She shook her head. "And another on the way."

"I never would have known," I said, looking at her as-of-yet flat stomach. "You aren't even showing."

"Thank you." She touched her middle absentmindedly. Then she pulled a cigarette from her purse, lighting it and inhaling deeply. "You have a kindergartener too?"

"It's my nephew," I answered, nodding toward the building. "Hugo."

"What an interesting name." She bit at her lip, holding the cigarette close to her face. "Are your children all grown up?"

"Well." I crossed my ankles, suddenly feeling quite elderly. "No. I don't have children of my own."

I saw her glance at my left ring finger where I still wore my wedding band and felt the urge to assure her that I was not a spinster. A widow, yes. But that was an entirely different story. One I didn't quite feel up to telling.

"Oh," she said. "It's nice of you to help your sister. My mother is home with my other three."

Trying not to be too obvious, I checked my watch. We still had ten minutes until the children were dismissed. A painfully long amount of time to sit and not know what to say to the woman.

Somehow, the time did pass and the bell rang. Holding the seat of the bench, I forced myself not to get up just yet, as much as I wanted to run to the school to find my boy. It seemed the woman beside me did the same thing.

"I've never been so nervous in all my life," she said. "Is it silly that I missed her?"

"It's not silly at all," I answered.

When I spotted Hugo, walking slowly from the building with

his little jacket folded neatly over his arm, my heart skipped a beat.

There he was, whole and looking fine.

Beside him was a little girl with pretty blonde hair pulled back into a red ribbon. The two of them giggled at something, keeping pace with each other as they made their way down the steps.

The woman beside me stood quickly, rushing over to the girl with the red ribbon, taking her by the hand and pulling her from Hugo's side. The little girl looked over her shoulder.

"But, Mama," the little girl said, her voice tiny and sweet. "He's my new friend."

I stood as they came near, watching them and not understanding.

"Do you know what your daddy would say if he saw you playing with someone like him?" the young woman said. "We don't mix. You know that."

"But Hugo's nice," the little girl said.

"That may be, but white and black don't go together."

The woman stopped, not too far from where I stood, and looked directly at me, her mouth agape. Red rose in her face and she worked her mouth as if there was something she was thinking of saying.

"What an awful thing to teach a child," I said. Keeping my spine straight, I held my head up.

I braced myself, ready for something ugly to come out of her mouth, thinking plenty of things I could have said as well.

Instead, she broke eye contact with me and pulled the little girl away.

Turning toward Hugo, I tried my very hardest to cover my anger with a smile. I hoped to keep my hand from shaking when I extended it for him to take.

"Did you have a nice day?" I asked, hoping he didn't hear how my voice quavered.

"Why'd she say that?" Hugo looked up at me, his eyes round.

"I don't know." I shook my head.

Out of the corner of my eye I could see the girl with the red ribbon walking away, holding the hand of her mother.

fifty-three

I woke that morning to little fingers tapping on my forearm. When I opened my eyes, I noticed that it was far too light out for it to be my usual time to get up. Gasping, I sat up fast, holding the covers over my bosom as if the sheets could protect me from being as late as I was certain I already was.

"Aunt Betty, it's Monday," Hugo said, standing at my bedside. "Are you up?"

"I am now." Nearly breathless, I turned and glanced at Norm's old alarm clock. We had half an hour before the first bell of the day would ring. "Gracious. We've got to hurry."

"I got myself dressed." He looked down at his clothes as if making sure they were still there.

"Very nice, sweetie." I nodded at the door. "How about you let me get ready? Close the door behind you, please."

As soon as the door was latched, I threw the covers off and hopped out of bed.

Heavens. It was unlike me to oversleep like that.

Rushing about and not caring as much as usual about how

my face and hair looked, I somehow managed to get Hugo to school on time. Granted, he had to eat toast and peanut butter on the way there, but he said he didn't mind that at all.

By the time I bustled my way into the bakery, I was already exhausted from the morning.

"Sorry, sorry," I said, putting the apron over my head. "My alarm didn't go off."

"Well," Pop said from his desk. "Sometimes a woman gets a little absentminded when she reaches a certain age."

"Oh boy," Stan said, carrying a tray to the cooling rack.

"If I'm old, what does that make you?" I tied the strings behind my back.

"A classic." Even at his age, the man still had dimples when he grinned. "Don't sweat it, kiddo. We managed all right without you."

"So, you're saying you don't need me?"

"I'd never say something like that," he said. "Not to your face, at least."

"Oh, you." I winked at him.

Turning, I saw Albert coming through the front door, a newspaper open in one hand, the other rubbing his chin. Lips slightly apart, they moved along with what he was reading.

"Good morning, Albie," I said. "How were your deliveries?"

"Fine," he answered, not looking up from the paper.

"Is something the matter?"

It was only then that he looked up at me, as if he hadn't known I was there. He took a step toward the counter, setting the paper down and turning it to face me.

"They bombed a church," he said, his voice weak and trembling, either from disbelief or grief or rage. Maybe even from a mix of all three. "Four little girls died."

"Where?" I asked, trying to focus my eyes to read the article.

"Birmingham." He took in a halting breath. "Alabama."

It was wrong of me, but my first instinct was to shut my eyes and push the newspaper away. I wanted to pretend that I hadn't heard what he'd said. I wanted to go on with my day, not knowing about something so horrible as what was in that article.

But I simply did not have that luxury.

The first line of the article had said that the four girls "blasted to death" were "Negro," and at the very first, I wondered why it mattered what color they were. It was the "blasted to death" that turned my stomach, broke my heart, and made my head throb all at the same time.

But it did matter, I realized.

It mattered that the little girls had brown skin and dark eyes and hair. It mattered that they lived in Alabama where people who looked like them weren't afforded the same dignities as people who looked like me.

It was of great importance that less than a week before, children who had the very same skin color walked into public schools in that very same state, screamed at and threatened and spit upon.

"Who would do something like this?" I whispered, meaning all of it. Every last bit of it.

Albert shook his head, eyes still on the paper. "It's horrible."

I thought once more about Dr. King's dream.

It seemed so far off.

Impossibly far.

fifty-four

Kneeling on the floor beside Hugo's bed, I rubbed his arm with the tips of my fingers. He'd told me it would help him fall back to sleep. Oh how like his mommy.

As much as I'd tried to shield him from the story of the girls in Birmingham, he'd heard someone talking about it at school. And, as children have often been known to do, they created a mythology around the facts. They inflated it, made it personal, turned an already horrific evil into nothing short of a ghost story.

Every night that week, Hugo had woken several times, sweating and crying and certain that the bad men would come for him, despite my promises that he was safe there with me.

It was Thursday, and I wondered how long we could go on with such disturbed sleep. All I could think of to do was tell him stories every night—some of my own, some borrowed from the Bible.

"There was once a king named Jehoshaphat," I began. "Isn't that a funny name?"

Hugo's smile told me he thought so.

"Jehoshaphat was the king over a land called Judah a very long time ago." I pushed myself up and sat beside him on the bed. "One day he heard that three whole nations wanted to go to war with his country. Do you think one army could survive if three attacked it?"

"No, ma'am," Hugo answered.

"Jehoshaphat didn't think so either. He was very afraid."

"Did he hide?"

Shaking my head, I raised my eyebrows. "Nope. Even though I think he might have wanted to. Instead, he told everyone in Judah to stop eating."

Hugo pulled his chin down and scowled.

"It sounds funny, doesn't it?" I pinched a bit of the fabric of my nightie, rubbing it between my finger and thumb. "He did that so that the people would pray."

I told Hugo about how every person in Judah prayed, calling out for God's help. The king beckoned them all together, and he put his hands in the air, asking for help.

"Jehoshaphat reminded all of his people about how God had helped them before," I said. "He asked God to take care of them again."

I imagined the crowds in front of the king, all of them with heads bowed and lips begging God to save them.

We don't know what to do, Jehoshaphat had cried out. *But our eyes are on you.*

"Everyone in Judah was quiet, waiting to hear what God would say," I went on. "All the men and women and children listened as closely as they could."

Closing my lips and putting a shushing finger in front of them, I moved my eyes from one side to the other. Hugo giggled at this, and I gave a quick "shh," making him giggle even more.

"Eventually, a man put his hand up, just like he wanted to be called on at school." I lifted my right. "He said, 'God gave me an idea!'"

"What was his name?" Hugo asked.

"Well, I don't remember." I put my hand down. "That's what a normal, everyday guy he was."

The everyday guy went in front of the whole nation, standing right beside the king, and told them God's plan.

"What was the plan?" Hugo asked. "Were there cannons?"

"There weren't," I answered. "In fact, God told them that they wouldn't have to fight at all."

"Then they would lose." Forehead wrinkled, Hugo shook his head. "That's not smart."

"Oh, but wait." I rubbed the pad of my thumb between his eyebrows, hoping to ease the creases bunched up there. "God made them a promise that he would be with them the whole way. He told them they didn't need to be afraid."

As I told Hugo about the nation of Judah assembling to go to the battlefield, I thought of how quiet it must have been. How difficult it would have been for me to swallow past the lump of fear in my throat, had I been there. I imagined standing shoulder to shoulder with the people I'd known all of my life, hoping that God's promise would hold true.

Praying that I'd have the faith to believe that the Lord would be with us all the way.

"Jehoshaphat sent the singers to the very front," I said.

"Singers?" Hugo narrowed one eye. "Why did they need singers?"

"You'll see." I leaned forward. "As the nation marched to the place where the battle would start, the choir began to sing."

Give thanks to the Lord. His love endures forever.

The army walked behind them, their song going before them. *Give thanks to the Lord. His love endures forever.*

But in front of the song was God. I imagined him moving ahead of them, arms splayed, so big and so wide and so tall that nothing created could ever get past him to hurt his children.

Give thanks to the Lord. His love endures forever.

With each step, with each singing of the phrase—*Give thanks to the Lord. His love endures forever*—the children of God would hope more, fear less, wonder at the goodness of their Father.

"They sang the whole way," I said, surprised at the tears in my eyes. "And God heard them. He was pleased with their song."

"He likes it when we sing to him, doesn't he?"

"Oh yes. I believe it's his favorite thing to hear." My heart beat a little faster, my smile grew a little wider. "He heard them and protected them because he cared for them."

"Then what happened?" Hugo asked.

"When the army of Judah got to the battlefield, do you know what they saw?" I asked.

"Is it scary?"

"I don't think so." I took his hand between both of mine. "When they looked down at the field, they saw that the battle was already over. God set the three nations against themselves and they fought each other instead of the people of Judah."

"Who won?"

"No one," I said. But then, thinking it over again, "God won."

"The end?"

"Yes." I leaned over and kissed Hugo's cheek. "Now, fall back to sleep fast if you can. You have school in the morning."

"Aunt Betty?" he said just as I stood up. "Do you think they were scared?"

I nodded. "I do."

"Even when they were singing?"

"Yes, even then," I answered. "But they kept singing anyway."

I left his room, pulling the door half closed behind me. When I got to the middle stair, I paused and listened. Hugo was singing.

fifty-five

Clara and I sat side by side at a table in the dayroom. I'd brought the family photo album along on my visit, hoping it might cheer her up a little bit. Even with all of the noise around us from the other visiting families and the scraping of chair legs being moved across the floor, we were able to keep our focus on the pictures pasted onto the black pages.

"Was this Dad's?" she asked, starting from the very first page.

"Yes," I answered. "It was in a box in my basement. I hadn't looked at it in years."

"Well, I know that this is Mother." She touched a square in the middle of one page.

Her words slurred, her voice thick and sounding so different from normal. She even moved slower. When I'd asked if she was all right, she'd looked at me as if she had no idea what I was talking about.

"Do I look like her?" she asked, still touching the picture of our mother.

I nodded. "And I think that's her sister. The girl next to her."

"Aunt Thelma?"

"Yes."

"Is she still alive?" she asked.

"Oh, I don't know." I smoothed my skirt over my knees. "I haven't seen that side of the family since Mother died."

"And Dad's side?"

"They've all passed on," I said. "I think we're all that's left."

"Huh." She held the back of her neck, rubbing it with her right hand.

I watched as she turned the page and then another.

"Why wouldn't Dad talk about her?" Clara asked after a minute of gazing at a photo of our parents standing under a tree, holding hands but not smiling into the camera.

"It was too hard for him, I think," I answered.

"I don't have very good memories of him." She dropped her hands into her lap.

"He wasn't the friendliest father."

"But she was kind, wasn't she?" Clara asked. "That's how I remember her at least."

I nodded. "Most of the time."

"And so pretty." Clara touched the picture.

"Mama was a beautiful woman," I said, nearly choking for the grief of calling her not Mother but Mama. "Even at the end she was beautiful. There was a certain light in her eyes."

"What else?"

"She was so special." I pulled my lips between my teeth, biting down and hoping it would keep me from sobbing. "She was an artist and a storyteller and a singer. When she was well, her imagination had no boundaries, and she loved to play make-believe with us. A sunrise was never ordinary to her, she couldn't walk past a flower without taking notice."

Clara's lips parted just slightly, the way they always had when she was paying very close attention, and her eyes softened, tears moistening them.

"Do you remember when she tied an apron around her neck backward for a cape and put an old Christmas wreath on her head as a crown and paraded around the apartment to play Queen of England?" I asked.

"And we wore canning rings on our wrists as bracelets."

"You remember," I said.

"What else?" Clara asked.

"Oh, goodness." I shut my eyes, trying to think of something. "Mama wasn't afraid of anything."

I smiled at a memory of my mother luring a mangy, skinny mutt into the tenement with the heel of a stale loaf of bread, convinced that all it needed was a good meal and a thorough grooming. I laughed as I told my sister about how the already balding dog lost even more of its fur in Mother's hairbrush.

Clara's eyes widened, making her look a good ten years younger.

"When Dad came home, she hid that dog in the closet." I shook my head. "Dad screamed when he went to hang up his jacket and found that beast. He thought it was a rat."

She covered her mouth with a bony hand and laughed, her eyes squinting like they had when she was small and something had amused her.

On and on I went, filling our hour together with every memory of our mother—our mama—that I could think of. As I told them, I could see the light get brighter in Clara's eyes. It made me dig through my mind for more stories to tell her. More stories to draw Clara back home.

But our time was nearly up. I couldn't think of a time when I'd resented a clock so much.

"I wish we could have had her longer," Clara said.

"Me too."

She turned the page to find a picture of our tall and stunningly beautiful mother standing between us, her arms around our shoulders. Us girls looked into the camera, shy smiles on our faces. Mama, though, had her face turned toward Clara and a toothy smile on her face.

"You'd just said something funny," I said. "You might not realize this, but you were quite a funny child."

My sister took my hand, squeezing it once before letting go.

"Did she love me?" she asked.

"Oh, Clara," I said. "You were the sun to her. She loved you so much it was almost unbelievable."

When we reached the last page of the photo album, I ran my fingertips along the black paper around a picture of Clara and me taken not long after we'd moved to LaFontaine. We stood at the bottom of the steps to our apartment over the bakery, her arm slung around my neck. I smiled in the photo, but she held her face as straight and serious as could be. "You were so angry with Dad when he took this picture."

"Birdie, I want to tell you something."

I lifted my head and realized that my mouth was hanging wide open.

"What is it?" I asked.

"I'm afraid that Hugo's going to forget me," she said. "Like I'm forgetting Mother."

"He won't."

"But what if he does?"

"I'll do my best to remind him." I smiled.

"Do you think he'll be glad when I get out?" she asked.

"Gladder than any boy ever was."

A stab of jealousy throbbed in my gut.

I gritted my teeth and denied it.

CHAPTER

fifty-six

During the years of the Depression, no one had any money for tickets to the symphony. Our family, in particular, never could have afforded such an extravagance. Even if we could have, Dad wouldn't have allowed it.

To him, music was a waste of time, not to mention money.

Every once in a while, though, a ragtag group of musicians would set up folding chairs and music stands in the park. They'd rest violins on their collarbones or cellos and basses between their knees. Then the most enchanting music emerged, beckoning everyone to come near, to listen.

Granted, they may not have been the best musicians in the world. It didn't matter, though. They brought beauty to a dark time.

One day my sister dragged me to the park, her long legs moving faster than my short ones ever could have. Even at two years younger, she had already outgrown me. Still holding my hand, she pushed her way to the front of the crowd, not apologizing for shoving or stepping on toes.

I said "sorry" for her.

I'd been ten or eleven by then. Old enough to be mortified by the way she acted.

She didn't move an inch through the first few songs the tiny orchestra played, her hand still holding mine tight. Even when everyone else clapped, she stood still.

"Do you know Dvorak?" she called out to them after they finished a rousing foot stomper. "New World?"

I squinted at her. "How do *you* know that?"

"The radio," she answered, dropping my hand.

One of the men—a cellist, I remembered, with a neatly groomed mustache—nodded and lifted his bow.

"Let me sing," Clara said. "'Goin' Home.'"

He nodded again, and she stepped out from the crowd and turned to face us.

A few of the people behind me muttered, and I knew that I was blushing. Embarrassed, I thought about turning and running back home.

Instead, I stayed and watched my too-thin beanpole of a sister in her sun-faded housedress fidget, rubbing her thumbs across the tips of her fingers, her arms hanging stiff at her sides. I'd thought that if my father had seen her there, he would have put an arm around her, leading her away and telling her that she had no business doing such a thing.

I'd bitten at the inside of my mouth, steadying myself to be completely humiliated.

But as soon as the cellist played the first note of the song, I watched Clara's shoulders relax, her fingers still, her face ease into beauty I couldn't ever remembering seeing before.

She opened her mouth and sang.

The sweet ribbon of her voice hadn't surprised me. I'd heard her sing more times than I could have counted. But it was the way her sound wove together with the cello. How the violin joined in after a few measures. The way the rest of the crowd stilled themselves so they could hear her.

By no means had my sister possessed the most beautiful voice I'd ever heard. But what she lacked in talent she made up for with passion.

Even at just nine years old, she knew enough to make her voice vibrate at the very end of a held-out note and to let it rise and fall in volume. Standing in the park, watching her, I knew that she felt every tone, every word, every rhythm.

When she'd finished, the crowd offered their applause generously, and Clara took her spot beside me once again. The musicians played two or three more songs before packing their instruments into ratty cases and carrying them away. The audience dispersed, and Clara and I stood alone, grass tickling my foot through the hole in my shoe.

"You sounded beautiful," I forced myself to say through the lump of envy stuck in my throat.

"You think so?" she'd asked, once again taking my hand.

We walked around the perimeter of the park, not saying much of anything to each other.

The jealousy faded, and I allowed wonder to replace it.

My sister sang how I imagined an angel sounded like.

Sitting in the third row from the front, listening to Albert's LaFontaine Symphony Orchestra debut, I couldn't help but think of that magical moment of my little sister in the park.

Of course, they didn't perform Dvorak that evening, and there were no vocalists in the performance. Still, I thought of Clara.

How motionless she would have stayed throughout the movements, how she would have cried, unabashedly, the entire time.

And I thought of how she might have called out a request and taken the stage, gracing us all with a surprise song.

Giving us a gift we hadn't even known to ask for.

After the performance, the Sweets stood in the lobby of the concert hall, waiting for Albert. Pop beamed from where he stood, leaning back against the wall and with cane in hand, making sure to let everyone who passed by know that his son was one of the cellists. Nick squirmed, pulling at his necktie, and Dick kept his nose in the program, reading the names of every orchestra member. Stan and Marvel were off to the side, chatting with someone who lived in their neighborhood.

As for me, I watched Hugo where he stood waiting for all of the musicians to exit the doors that led backstage. He held out his program to each of them and an ink pen I'd dug out of my handbag, asking them for their autographs. They all obliged, smiling down at him.

When Albie emerged, I nearly didn't recognize him.

I'd known him for over twenty-five years but had never seen him stand so tall or walk with such an easy stride.

Oh, how that made me feel proud for him. All the way to my toes.

The moment Hugo saw him, he ran at him, arms wide. He gave him a hug with such force that I was surprised when Albert didn't fall over backward. Still holding on to his cello case, Albert leaned over, putting his hand on Hugo's back, patting it a few times.

"Did you like it?" Albie asked.

Hugo let him go and looked up at him, nodding so hard I worried that he'd give himself a sore neck.

"Maybe next time I'll get you better seats."

"But we were in the front," Hugo said.

"Yes, well, the best seats are in the back."

"But I liked where we sat." Hugo tilted his head. "Can you sign my paper?"

"Of course I can."

He took the program and the pen, resting it on the top of his hard case and signing with a flourish. When he lifted his head, he met my eyes and gave a shy smile.

I couldn't be sure, but I thought I saw a little pride behind it.

fifty-seven

The fourth week of September, the most eventful thing that happened was an elephant rampaging through Lansing after escaping from the circus. She ran wild through the streets, chased by thousands of people, only making her more afraid and dangerous.

I knew the story had ended badly by the *State Journal* headline alone.

Police Kill Berserk Elephant.

I was careful to throw that copy of the paper out before Hugo could get his hands on it, holding my breath with the hopes that no one would tell him about it at school.

As far as I knew, nobody had.

I'd gone to visit Clara that Friday and ended up sitting next to someone I scarcely recognized. Her cheeks had gone sunken and her skin sallow. When I'd asked a nurse if there had been any change, she'd just told me that it was typical for a patient to go through highs and lows.

"Fall can be hard on some of them," she'd said before turning and walking away from me down the hall, her shoes squeaking on the hard floor.

Before I knew it, September passed and October began. The leaves were changing, and Hugo was asking after costumes for Halloween.

At the beginning of summer I never would have believed that I'd be planning out how to construct a giraffe costume for a five-year-old. I would have told whoever suggested such a thing that they were out of their minds.

Most nights Hugo still wanted a story and I was happy to give him one.

It was a Wednesday in the middle of the month and unseasonably warm. The mercury had risen above eighty, and I regretted having put away all of my summer clothes for the year. Hugo had all of the covers off his bed and had worn only PJ bottoms to sleep in.

Flannery sat on the sill of Hugo's wide-open window, looking out into the night as if she was expecting visitors.

"Aunt Betty," Hugo said. "Will you tell me a story?"

"I would love to." I fanned myself with my hand. "But I might need a little help to tell it."

"Once there was . . ." he started then lifted his eyebrows toward me. "Your turn."

"A canary named Willa who lived in the forest." I wiped my brow. "She wasn't like all of the other birds of the forest; the robins and sparrows and blue jays."

"Because she was yellow," Hugo offered.

"Yes. But also because she was the only canary and the only one who knew the special song she was born with."

"What did it sound like?"

"Now, that's the trouble," I said. "I can't even sing her song.

At first, Willa liked being different from everyone else. She liked that she was the only spark of yellow to fly between the tree branches and that her song was different, higher than the other birds."

"She was unique," Hugo said.

"That's a very good word," I said. "Yes, Willa was special. But after a while, being different began to make her feel lonely."

"That's too bad."

"Since she felt so sad, she stopped singing her song."

Hugo rolled over on his side, facing me.

"The chickadee missed Willa's song and so did the starling who tried to mimic it, but it couldn't come close." I tightened my arm around his shoulders. "They decided that they needed to find a friend for Willa. A friend who was like her."

I told of how they searched all over the forest, trying to find another bird just like Willa. They found a goldfinch. It had bright yellow plumage like Willa's, but instead of singing, it let out squeaking cheeps. They found a warbler who could sing. The trouble was, it was a song Willa had never heard before. Next they tried a duckling, but that baby couldn't fit in a nest.

"The two friends gave up hope of finding Willa someone like her," I said. "They came to her tree and sat on the branches nearest her nest and told her they were sorry for failing."

"At least they tried," Hugo said. "Doesn't that count?"

"It did," I said. "The starling and chickadee hung their heads, but because they'd cared so much for Willa, she started to sing. It was a song like nothing they'd ever heard before. Long and high and clear, Willa's notes were beautiful and filled the entire forest with music."

"Because friends can make us feel better when we're sad?"

"Yes."

"The end?"

"For now." I kissed the top of his curly-haired head.

"Is Willa like my mommy?"

"What's that?" I asked.

"Because she's special like Mommy is?"

"Yes," I answered. "Your mommy is so special, isn't she?"

"So are you." He rolled so he was flat on his back with his arms out at his sides. "I love you, Aunt Betty."

"I love you, Hugo."

Oh, how my heart melted.

And not from the heat of the evening.

fifty-eight

I stood just inches from the mirror in my bathroom, the lights on either side lit up. Turning my face from side to side, I noticed every fine line that my cold cream was supposed to keep from forming.

Between my brows and at the corners of my eyes and around my mouth. Tugging with my fingers at my hairline, I tried to smooth the lines on my brow. But that only made me aware of a few wild grays sprouting up from my scalp.

Pulling them, I wondered how long before plucking all of my old lady hairs would leave me completely bald. Not long enough, I suspected. Not nearly long enough.

"You're getting old," I said to my reflection.

My reflection got its revenge by showing me the billy goat hairs growing long and coarse out of the point of my chin.

Tweezing those, I sighed.

In the morning, I would be forty-one years old and I was not ready for it.

Turning forty hadn't been so bad, at least I hadn't thought so. Of course, I didn't offer the number to anyone, but I did consider it a badge of honor. Living into my forties and feeling more self-assured than ever before.

But between the Octobers of my birthdays, something had shifted. On the eve of forty-one, I could no longer feel assured of anything about my life.

Well, there was one thing.

I was getting old. Not only that. I was starting to look old. In a world of Jackie Kennedys, I was on my way to becoming an Aunt Bee.

"Now, you just stop it, Betty Sweet," I whispered to myself, clicking off the lights on either side of the mirror. "You are going to start being nicer to yourself."

I straightened my neck, holding my chin higher, and looked my reflection in the eye.

My mother had never aged. Never had a wrinkle or a gray hair or the pull of gravity on her body. Not that I remembered, at least. She would, in my mind, always be in her early thirties.

Still meeting my own eyes, I smiled, and reminded myself to be grateful.

It was a privilege to have another year.

Albert knocked on the door at quarter past eight, and when I answered, he told me to hold the door for him, he had something for me.

He called from his car for me to shut my eyes.

"It's a surprise," he said. "For your birthday."

"But that isn't until tomorrow," I protested, albeit weakly. It was no secret that I liked being surprised.

"Well, then this is early." He put his hands on his hips. "Please close your eyes. For my sake if nothing else."

"Oh, all right." I pushed my lids shut. "But if this is another cat, I'm not taking it."

"I promise, it's not alive."

I heard him shut the car door then felt him walk past me and into the house, his footsteps getting farther away from me, and then the light thud of something being lowered to a wood surface.

"Can I open them?" I asked.

"Not yet."

I felt his hand on my elbow. He pulled me forward.

"So help me, if you make me stub my toe," I said.

"Don't worry," he said. "I'll be careful with you."

Careful. I thought that was a good word for Albert Sweet.

He led me to the other side of the room, to the corner that housed the record player and my writing desk.

"Okay," he said.

I took that as his permission to open my eyes.

When I did, I had to hold on to the back of the straight-backed chair I had tucked up under the desk.

"What's this?" I asked.

"It's a typewriter," Albert supplied.

"Yes, I see that."

"For your stories." He grinned and shrugged.

"How thoughtful," I said.

"Would you like to try it?" He pointed at it. "It works."

"Oh, but I don't have the right paper."

"Ah."

He rushed across the living room and out the front door, presumably to get some paper from his car.

I pulled out the chair and sat down, putting my fingers on the keys. They were white with black letters painted on them. I took my fingers off them and touched my palms to the sides of the machine.

It was pink. What Norman had always called "Betty Sweet pink." Somewhere between salmon and bubble gum. Half standing, I looked down at it then shifted and looked at it sideways.

I'd never seen such a beautiful typewriter before.

Albert came back in and showed me how to roll the paper in, what to do when I got to the end of a line, and everything else I might need to know.

"This is such a nice gift, Albie," I said. "How did you ever afford it?"

"Oh." He blushed. "It's not from me."

"I don't understand." I turned to face him.

He sat on the arm of Norm's easychair, legs stretched out in front of him and arms crossed.

"It's been in my apartment for months," he said. "It's where Norm was hiding it from you."

"I'm sorry?" My fingertips tingled and my heart felt like it weighed a hundred pounds in my chest. My stomach flip-flopped, and I thought I might faint for how light my head became.

"Back in May, Norm found this at some shop in Lansing," Albie started. "He had me hold on to it because you would have found it at Marvel's, and Pop isn't good at keeping secrets."

"Oh, Albert," I said.

"I nearly forgot." He pulled a folded-up paper from his back pocket. "This was rolled into it. I took it out because I was afraid you'd think I wrote it."

He handed it to me.

"Happy birthday, Betty," he said and then turned and left, shutting the door behind him.

I waited until he was gone to unfold the paper, smoothing it on the desk to the side of the typewriter.

There were only four words on the paper, but I knew it would soon become one of my most treasured possessions.

I LOVE BETTY SWEET!

"I love you too, Norm Sweet," I whispered, knowing he could no longer hear me. Knowing that those days were gone.

But loving him just the same.

fifty-nine

I was late getting to the dayroom, and I worried that Clara would think I'd forgotten about our visit. Her doctor had stopped me in the entryway, wanting to give me an update on her progress. While his news was good and his smile kind, I found him to be long-winded.

By the time he shook my hand and bid me a good day, I was more than a little anxious to get to my sister.

When I made it to the hallway, I noticed all the nurses on the ward gathered around the door, and my heart sank. All sorts of scenarios played through my head of what could have happened inside to draw such attention.

But then I heard music, rich as chocolate and smooth as cream.

Slowing, I took my time getting to the entrance, the music calming me, settling me down.

"What's going on?" I asked.

"Someone's brought a cello," one of the nurses said.

"Albert," I whispered. "Excuse me, can I go in?"

The nurses parted for me, and I made it into the dayroom.

On an ordinary day, the lighting was stark against the dingy white walls. But that day, the sun shone in just right, a cheery yellow tone filling the room. Usually the patients chattered or moaned or shuffled across the floor. But in that moment, they were quiet and listening.

Albert sat on a metal folding chair in the far corner of the room, head bent over his cello and making the bow go back and forth across the strings, filling everything around him with beauty. I had no idea what song he played, but it little mattered. In my mind it was nothing short of a masterpiece.

Clara, too, sat on a chair, right on the edge of it. She held her hands together under her chin, and her full attention was on Albie's face. She hadn't smiled so radiantly in a very long time.

I stood, frozen where I was, knowing that what I was watching was my sister falling in love, and it was more hope than I could have asked for.

At the end of the song, Albert held the final note, not moving for a moment before looking up. Clara stood slowly, taking the two steps that separated them. Leaning down, she kissed the top of his head.

I thought the blush from his cheeks could have warmed that whole room for the rest of the month.

"You're telling me that Albert Sweet played his cello, by himself, for a room full of people?" Marvel asked, pouring hot water into a cup before handing it to me. "My brother?"

"Yes. I was just as amazed as you." I grabbed the string and bobbed the tea bag up and down in the water. "And she kissed him."

"She did what?" Marvel put the kettle down on the stove harder than I thought she'd intended to.

"Well, on his head."

"Still." She rushed across the room and sat down. "Honey, I think that was his first kiss."

She grabbed a stack of papers on the table, tapping them against the surface to make them even.

"And, equally good news," I said, sitting at the table with her, taking half of the pile when she handed it to me. "The doctor said that Clara should be able to come home by Christmas."

"What a good day." Marvel beamed. "What do you think Hugo will say?"

"I thought I wouldn't tell him." I rested my hands on top of the papers. "Just in case."

"Good idea." She nodded. "Better to be surprised than disappointed."

We got to work folding the paper in half, fliers advertising that Sweet Family was taking orders for Thanksgiving pies.

MOM SWEET'S SECRET RECIPES! AVAILABLE FOR THE FIRST TIME EVER!

Pumpkin and apple and mincemeat and pecan and French silk.

Stan had made sure the advertisement read "Limit Two Per Order," claiming it would make people more interested.

From the handful of orders we'd gotten the day before from the sign in the front window, I thought his scheme just might work.

When Mrs. Brown had asked if we were strict about the two pie limit, I'd told her we would fudge it just for her.

She'd placed an order for half a dozen.

"That other place won't take orders for anything," she'd said. "Talk about lazy."

Marvel and I chatted away as we worked, getting the fliers ready for the twins to deliver door-to-door that afternoon, and I thought of the pie I would order just for Clara to eat at Christmas. French silk. Her very favorite.

Home by Christmas.

What a good day that would be.

sixty

The Friday before Thanksgiving, I spent the entire day at Marvel's house cutting, gutting, roasting, and pureeing pumpkins for the men to bake into pies the next week. At noon, Albert dropped Hugo off from school.

The poor boy still got absolutely worn out from his mornings in kindergarten, especially that day. It was all I could do to make sure he got half his lunch in him before he fell asleep on his plate.

Once he was wrapped in a blanket and fast asleep on the couch, I went back to work with Marvel in the kitchen.

By midday we'd hardly made a dent in all we'd need to do, but we took a break right around one thirty to eat a little lunch and put our feet up.

"When I was little, Mom used to make me scrape out the innards of the pumpkins," Marvel said, spreading a dollop of mayonnaise on her ham sandwich. "Of course, then we were only making pies for family, so we had far less to do."

"Not 124 of them?" I said, resting my head against the back of my chair.

"Not even close." She slapped the bread on top and cut the sandwich in half with the knife. "She told me to take the gunk from the pumpkins outside to the burn barrel, so I gathered it all in an old newspaper and lugged it out there. But I tripped when I stepped out onto the porch, falling face-first into the pile of goo."

"Oh no," I said, shaking my head.

"Do you want to know what I tripped on?" she asked. "Normie's football helmet."

"He always did like to leave things lying around, didn't he?"

"So I picked up every last bit of the pumpkin guts and dropped them into the helmet." She laughed. "My biggest regret was that I wasn't there to see him put it on."

She took a big bite of sandwich.

But then we heard the sound of the front door opening and closing.

"Who's that?" she asked, getting up and going to the door between the kitchen and the living room. "Boys?"

Marvel stood, her back to me, with hands on hips. The boys, in front of her, both looked confused.

"What are you two doing home already?" she asked. "It's not even two o'clock."

"I don't know," Nick answered.

"Did you get in trouble again?" She raised an eyebrow. "What am I going to do with you boys?"

"No, Mom. We didn't," Dick said. "Teacher sent everybody home."

"She said we should ask our mothers why," Nick added.

Marvel shook her head. "I don't believe that for a minute."

"Honest to goodness," Nick said.

The telephone rang, and Marvel put a finger up next to her face. "That is probably your teacher. So help me, if you boys got suspended again . . . don't you move an inch."

She stormed over to the phone and answered it, making her voice sound friendly, a jarring sound after her fire and vinegar from a moment earlier.

"DeYoung residence," she said, her back to me. "What, Stan?"

"Is something wrong?" I asked.

"Turn on the television," she said, hanging up the phone.

The four of us rushed to the living room and waited for the television to warm up before we could see what was going on.

Walter Cronkite at a desk covered with papers and telephones and what looked like an apple. He turned toward the camera.

"There's been an attempt on the life of the president," he said.

"Oh gosh," Marvel said, dropping into the easy chair.

I folded my legs and sat on the floor, Nick and Dick on either side of me.

"What's going on . . ." one of the twins started, but stopped when Marvel shushed him.

". . . condition as of yet unknown," Cronkite went on.

"He'll be fine," Marvel said. "They'll have the best doctors in the world . . ."

I leaned back against the easy chair behind me, not wanting to get up, not wanting to move until Mr. Cronkite told us that President Kennedy was going to be all right. Praying that he would.

We huddled together, the twins and I, watching with eyes wide and mouths silent. Every moment I expected to hear that all would be fine. Every moment I feared the opposite would be true.

" . . . a bullet wound in the head . . ."

Lifting a hand, I covered my mouth, hoping that I hadn't gasped without realizing it.

Rumors that the president was dead, Cronkite reassuring that it was unconfirmed. Still my heart sank. Marvel moved to the floor to sit with us. Nick or Dick put his head on his mother's shoulder and cried quietly.

The television showed images of a large room in Dallas where the president had been meant to deliver a speech. Hundreds of people wandered about in their finest clothes.

The front door opened, letting Stan, Albert, and Pop in. All three of them with white and drawn faces.

"Is he . . ." Stan started.

"We don't know yet," Marvel said. "Not for certain."

Albert put a hand across his mouth, and Pop shook his head.

"It is official. The president has been assassinated in Dallas, Texas . . ."

"Have mercy," Pop said.

"What does that mean?" Nick asked.

"He died, honey," Marvel whispered.

"What's going to happen now?" Dick asked.

No one had an answer.

sixty-one

We stayed in front of the TV all day watching updates and news bulletins, not eating or talking or blinking unless we really needed to. Hugo had gotten up from his nap and sat on my legs until evening when he fell asleep again.

"I should get him home," I whispered.

"Let me help," Albert said, reaching under Hugo's shoulders and knees, lifting him as if he weighed nothing. "We can take my car."

Albie had me get in the front seat before handing the boy to me and shutting the door as quietly as he could.

I held Hugo draped over me all the way to my house, where Albert again lifted him, carrying him inside.

"We'll just let him sleep in his clothes," I whispered, leading Albert up the stairs and into Hugo's room, pulling the covers down.

Getting out of the way, I watched him lower the boy to the bed, being careful to hold his head steady. I couldn't remember ever having seen a man so gentle with a child before, so tender.

With an ache in my chest, I thought of what good fathers both he and Norman would have made.

What a good father Albert might be. One of these days, at least.

He pulled the blanket up and tiptoed out of the room. I followed and pulled the door closed.

"Thank you," I whispered. "You didn't have to do all of that."

He waited to respond until he was at the foot of the steps. "It was no trouble at all."

The telephone rang and I checked my watch. After ten o'clock.

"It's probably Marvel," I said. "Maybe there's something new?"

I took the call in the kitchen, Albert leaning against the doorway behind me.

"Hello?" I said.

"Mrs. Sweet?" The voice on the other line sounded thin, hesitant.

"Yes." A fluttering filled my chest unlike anything I'd ever experienced. "And who is this?"

"I'm Nurse Rita," she answered. "Calling from the State Mental Hospital."

"All right." I put my hand on the counter, holding on, bracing myself for the worst kind of news.

"I'm sorry to be calling so late," the nurse said. "We've been trying all day."

"I wasn't home."

"The phone lines have been backed up for hours." She cleared her throat. "Because of the president."

I thought I heard her voice crack, and I wanted to tell her to get on with it, to give me the horrible news already. The anticipation of what was to come made me want to scream.

"Is Clara all right?" I asked.

She hesitated before answering me.

"Mrs. Sweet, Clara will be discharged first thing in the morning," she said. "I thought you'd want to come get her so she wouldn't have to take a bus."

My knees buckled, and I felt Albert's hands steady me.

"Is everything okay?" he asked, his eyes wide behind his glasses.

"Yes," I said into the phone and to him at the same time. "Someone will be there in the morning. Thank you. Thank you so much for calling."

I hung up the receiver and told Albert the news.

Never in all the years I'd known him had I seen him smile so big.

sixty–two

On the day Norman came home from the war, I got us locked out of our apartment.

All afternoon and into the evening we'd been busy with a parade and picnic and celebration, all in Norm's honor. La-Fontaine's favorite war hero received an apt welcome home.

By the time it was all over and we'd gotten to the door of our place, I knew that Norm was antsy to get inside with me. It had, after all, been a very long time since we'd been alone together. He kissed me long and deep while rummaging in his pockets.

When he found only loose change and a jackknife, he asked where my keys were.

My eyes widened when I realized that I'd left my handbag on Mom and Pop's kitchen counter, my keys safely tucked into the inside pocket.

I felt awful.

Norman groaned at the realization.

I cried.

We sat on the concrete slab, our backs leaning against the door, our shoulders touching.

"What should we do?" I'd asked.

"No idea," he answered.

"Maybe we could walk to your folks' house." I turned my head to look at him.

"If you don't mind, I think I'd rather just stay here with you."

"I don't mind at all."

At first we didn't talk. I put my head on his shoulder and he rested his hand on my thigh. When I shivered, he gave me the jacket of his uniform. When he yawned, I told him I wished I could make him a cup of coffee.

"I thought of when I'd get to see you again every day I was over there," he said. "It got me through some awful things."

"And here I've locked us out of our home." I leaned my head back against the door. "I feel horrible."

"It's not all that bad." He turned his body so he could face me. "Someday we'll look back on this and laugh."

"Oh, I don't know that I'll ever think it's funny."

He drew in a long breath, holding it as he shut his eyes.

"What are you doing?" I'd asked.

Opening one eye just a crack, he shushed me.

"Norman . . ."

"Quiet."

I pinched my lips together and tried to stifle a laugh.

"Okay. I think I got it." He opened his eyes and leaned over to kiss me. "I want to remember this moment for the rest of my life."

"Why? It's frustrating and disappointing. Why remember this?"

"Because it's another scene in our story."

I lifted a hand and touched his face.

"You are such a good man," I said.

"We'll see if you still feel that way after I break into our apartment." He winked before getting up.

We'd had to pay the landlord for the broken glass in the window. It was worth every penny.

Clara would come home from the sanitarium to a quiet house. There would be no parade or confetti or banner to welcome her. I'd asked Marvel in the nicest way I could to let us have a day to ourselves. She'd agreed.

I didn't think she had it in her to celebrate. No one did, really.

If I knew her, she'd spend the day watching the news so as not to miss a single update about Kennedy's assassination. I only hoped Stan would remind her to eat something.

As for me, I couldn't have the television on. It was too much and I dreaded seeing Mrs. Kennedy, a new widow just like me. A woman who lost her husband far too soon.

Hugo came down for breakfast, still wearing his clothes from the day before, and I was glad I'd agreed to let Albert pick up Clara. I needed to talk to the boy. I needed to have a little bit of time with him, just us.

"Hi," I said.

"Hi." He rubbed his eyes.

"Are you hungry? I made oatmeal."

He nodded. "Can I have brown sugar, please?"

"Of course."

I fixed a bowl for him, pouring just a little cream into it, swirling it together with a spoon.

"Did you sleep okay?" I asked, setting the oatmeal in front of him.

He told me he had. "I'm still sad, though."

I knew he meant about the president. It seemed impossible to explain something so difficult, so ugly to a boy of five and a half. Especially since I didn't fully understand it myself.

All I could think to say was that I was sad too.

"Why would someone want to hurt him?" His eyes, big and round and watery, met mine.

"I don't know."

Hugo dipped his spoon into the oatmeal but didn't scoop any to eat.

"Would you like to hear some good news?" I asked.

He nodded.

"Your mommy is coming home today." I touched his cheek. "What do you think about that?"

"Is she better?"

"I think so."

"Then why are you crying?" he asked.

"Because I'm happy."

He slid off his chair and climbed into my lap, his arms wrapped around my neck. I rested my cheek on his head, his hair tickling my skin.

"We'll have to take care of her," I said. "She'll need rest and good food and lots of snuggles."

"Will she be as tired as she was before?"

"I hope not."

"Can we take her for adventures?" he asked.

"I think we can." I held him closer. "Maybe we can all go see Santa Claus together."

"Santa isn't real."

"Who says?" I asked.

"Nick and Dick."

"They were just pulling your leg." I smoothed his hair with the palm of my hand. "In fact, I have a story about Santa. Would you like to hear it?"

He nodded.

In all the months I'd known him, Hugo had never said no to a story.

I hoped he never would.

We stood at the living room window, waiting for Albert to bring Clara home. Hugo nibbled his thumbnail and I kept my arms wrapped around my middle, holding myself together.

I wondered if I'd be able to do for her all she would need. The doubt settled like a lump of raw dough in my stomach.

Flannery slinked in, hopping onto the stool between us, and I thought how if anyone looked in from the street they'd think us an odd trio.

It had turned out to be a gloomy, gray, drizzly kind of morning, and before long, we were fogging up the glass with our breath. I used my fingertip to draw a heart.

"Mommy says we shouldn't do that," Hugo said. "It just makes the window dirty."

"Well, who is it around here that cleans the windows?" I asked. "I'll give you a hint. It's me. And I say we can draw pictures on the glass just this time."

He got a little sparkle in his eye and huffed air onto the window before tracing the shape of a star. I made a heart and he made a squiggly line.

"What's that?" I asked.

"A snake," he answered.

After a few minutes his space on the window was covered, finger drawings fading away little by little. I picked him up, even if he'd gotten quite a bit heavier over the past few months, and held him higher so he could fill the area at my eye level.

That was when we saw a pair of headlights slicing through the gloom, cutting all the way until they stopped in my driveway.

"Is that her?" Hugo asked, his voice just a whisper.

"I think so."

I let him down and he ran across the living room, swinging the front door open and leaping off the porch. I didn't try to stop him and I didn't warn him of how soaked to the bone he would get out in that rain.

Albert got out of the car first, opening an umbrella over his head and rushing around to the passenger's side to let Clara out. He offered her his hand and she took it, rising up out of the car.

Hugo launched himself at her and I worried that he would knock her over. She didn't fall, though, and she didn't stumble. She caught him, letting him wrap his legs around her waist.

I hadn't been that happy in far too long.

EPILOGUE

SPRING, 1964

On Friday nights we let Hugo stay up a little bit later than during the week. He'd sit between Clara and Albert on the couch, eating popcorn and watching *Route 66*.

I let them have those evenings to the three of them. I'd shut myself up in my bedroom to read or write. Sometimes I'd go to bed. Getting up before dawn to work at Sweet Family certainly did wear me out. Since Lazy Morning closed up shop at the beginning of March, we'd been busier than ever at the bakery.

That night, though, I decided that I wanted to be outside. The winter had been a mild one, but long—as Michigan winters often were. It was nice to be in the dying light of an early spring day.

I kicked off my shoes and let my toes wiggle in the grass.

The lawn needed a good mowing, something I was more than happy to pay Nick or Dick to do. When I sat down in the middle of the yard, though, I was glad for how soft it was under my behind.

I shut my eyes, thinking of the last time I'd allowed myself the luxury of sitting in the grass. I remembered the last kiss Norm had given me and the way his voice had sounded when he told me he loved me for the very last time.

While I was at it, I let my mind meander over other moments we'd shared. Those memories, the story we lived together, made me miss him. But it was the missing that made him feel closer to my heart somehow.

How I'd loved Norman Sweet.

How I loved him still.

The back door opened and closed, I heard it squeak on its hinges. I didn't jump to my feet or open my eyes even. I kept them shut until I smelled the apple and wood aroma of chamomile tea.

Clara handed me the steaming cup before sitting beside me.

"Is Hugo down?" I asked, turning to see that the light was on in his room.

"He's getting into his pajamas," Clara answered, blowing into her cup. "He wanted a story."

"I can tell him one." I wrapped both hands around my mug. "Did Albert leave?"

"Just a few minutes ago. He needs to be at the bakery bright and early." A smile on her face, she nodded toward the back corner of the yard. "Did you forget to bring in the laundry?"

Sure enough, I'd forgotten the sheets and towels I'd hung out to dry earlier in the day. Some things simply did not change.

"I'll bring them in," she said, getting to her feet. "You go tell Hugo his story."

"Are you sure?"

"Yeah." She offered me her hand, helping up. "But I'm not folding the fitted sheets."

"That's okay. I never do."

She put her cup on the porch and made her way across the grass where I already had a basket waiting.

I didn't hurry inside. Instead, I watched her, my brave and noble sister. Clara the conqueror.

Somewhere—not too far away—I heard a bird calling out. A robin, I knew, from the trilling, singsong of its voice. Clara had heard it too and turned back. I could see her smile even in the fading light.

I went inside, not wanting to keep Hugo waiting. But as I climbed the stairs I imagined the bird perched in a nearby tree, not willing to be scared off by anything.

As the night got darker, the bird would stay right where she was, singing even as the sun went down.

AUTHOR'S NOTE
and ACKNOWLEDGMENTS

*I*n August of 2018 my family and I went on a trip to Detroit to see a Tigers game and enjoy the city. I was at the end of a summer that had been full of false starts in my writing life and I was absolutely certain I'd never have a good story idea again.

But then I stepped into the aquarium on Belle Isle and looked up at the jade-colored tile of the ceiling, and Betty's story popped into my head. It was magical and surprising and something that has never happened to me before.

I have no illusions that it will ever happen again, either.

I readied myself for a novel that would be easy to write.

Boy, was I wrong.

Writing Betty's story touched on deep wounds in my heart—watching a loved one struggle through a mental health crisis. It also made me mindful of my worst fear—losing my husband.

Needless to say, I depended on a whole bunch of wonderful

369

people to love me through the writing of this book. I can't possibly name every single one, but I'll do my best.

My agent Tim Beals, who never wavered in his belief that this story mattered. Thanks, Tim, for being such a calming force in my life and career.

My editor Kelsey Bowen, who offered grace, kind encouragement, and gentle critiques which all added up to making this book what it is. It's such an honor to build stories with you.

To Kristin Kornoelje for assuring me that I'm not the worst comma abuser in the world and for prodding me to strengthen the foundations of this novel. You make me a better writer.

To the ladies who I like to think of as the Revell Book Pushers, Michele Misiak and Karen Steele; thank you for the emails declaring your confidence in my abilities. Thanks also for putting this story into the hands of readers.

I'll forever be grateful for friends who pray. Specifically Karee, Shelly, Ash, Amelia, and Alexis. You girls are the Marvel to my Betty and I will always love you for it.

Judy and Sarah, thank you for sharing your lives with me. You made Clara's story so real in my heart.

Big thanks to Erin Bartels for our conversations about story in Cleveland. I hope you know how you lit a fire under my behind when you said, "You know how this story ends. Just write it."

All the hugs and high fives to Catie Cordero for reminding me how much I loved writing when I was plumb out of steam.

Ginger, Sam, and Betsy, I am thankful for the stories you inflicted on me during our shared childhood. I couldn't have asked for a better crew to be my siblings. I love you guys.

Dad, thanks for making up some of the most outlandish stories to tell us when we were kids. I'm still trying to figure out which ones were true.

Mom, thank you for reading books to us and creating great voices for the characters. And thanks for making sure there were always books around for us to read.

Thank you, Jocelyn Green, for listening to my self-doubt and reminding me to be as kind to myself as I am to my friends.

My eternal and deepest gratitude to Sonny Huisman for blowing up my phone with Scripture that spoke of God's love for his children. You kept me floating with your care for me. Thank you.

To my kids, who I love more than chocolate, coffee, and a good long book. You three know what a big deal that is.

And to my own true love, Jeff. I never would have made it through this novel without your willingness to lend me your courage, your steadiness, and your confidence. I love living this story with you.

Every speck of glory to God.

Susie Finkbeiner is the CBA bestselling author of *All Manner of Things*, which was selected as a 2020 Michigan Notable Book, as well as *A Cup of Dust*, *A Trail of Crumbs*, and *A Song of Home*. She serves on the Fiction Readers Summit planning committee, volunteers her time at Ada Bible Church in Grand Rapids, Michigan, and speaks at retreats and women's events across the country. Susie and her husband have three children and live in West Michigan.

Meet Susie

SusieFinkbeiner.com

"*All Manner of Things* should be at the top of everyone's reading stacks. Beautiful. Honest. Artfully written. A winning novel."

—**Elizabeth Byler Younts,** author of *The Solace of Water*

After Annie Jacobson's older brother is deployed to Vietnam during the war, tragedy at home brings their estranged father home without welcome. As tensions heighten, Annie and her family must find a way to move forward as they try to hold both hope and grief in the same hand.

ℛ Revell
a division of Baker Publishing Group
www.RevellBooks.com

 RevellBooks

Available wherever books and ebooks are sold.

Printed in the United States
By Bookmasters